SAMARA KALZ

Book cover, sprayed edges, end pages background and art (Mia and Xavier under the stars) by Nate Eidenberger @a.peculiar.artist

Mia and Xavier in the cave, Hyda's portrait art by Victor Manthyreas @koijix

Character art (Mia and Xavier) on end pages by Asha Nyr

Headers By Samara Kalz Canva pro.

Editor Vicky S.

E-Book ASIN: B0FSLMCXNZ
Paperback **ISBN:** 979-8-9937207-0-8
Hardback **ISBN:** 979-8-9937207-1-5

First edition 2026

Author's Note

D ear reader,

This is a work of fiction. All names, characters, places, creatures, and events are products of the author's imagination or are used fictitiously. Any resemblance to actual persons living or dead, events, or locations is purely coincidental.

Dedication

To every woman who's been told she's too late, too old, too far behind, you are none of those things. You are still becoming. The world may try to measure your worth by timelines or titles, but your strength cannot be charted. Your dreams are not expired, they are waiting, patiently, fiercely for you to believe in them again. Keep going. You are more powerful than anyone has dared to imagine. Keep believing and dreaming because dreams do come true.

Prologue

Freya

20 Years ago in Eterna

Flashes of fire light up the sky, followed by a loud explosion that echoes into the night. It startles my quiet night of nursing, even though I know this is a distraction to take over, to make the change our land strives for. Change is long overdue for Eterna. I slowly put my babies in their bassinet. Looking at their cute, tiny faces in deep sleep, I can't help but wonder what the future holds for them. I tiptoe to the window to look out into the distance. The dark night sky is smokey red from all the explosions, acrid smoke polluting the air. I send a prayer for everyone to stay safe as I rush to grab the window and clasp it shut. I'm glad my babies are sleeping through this chaos.

Eterna was once peaceful and quiet. I keep reminding myself this needs to happen because there is no other way. I walk back to my bed, the cool tiles soothing my sore feet as I stretch my aching body in hopes of easing the postpartum pain.

"General Hyda! Hyda, where are you?"

Silas's voice resounds in the halls of the house.

Neglecting to put my white robe on top of my sleeveless silk night-gown, I rush out of the room to see why my husband is shouting for our general.

When he finally comes into view, he's running through the dimly lit hall. "Honey, what's the matter?" I ask breathlessly. I meet his dark brown eyes full of fear, expecting the worst possible answer. I tremble, not wanting to hear the bad news he's about to deliver. I can't compre-hend what he's saying as he rushes to hold me. His rough, masculine hands brush against my exposed skin. I inhale the musky smell of his body, mixed with smoke and sweat. His touch and scent soothe me, making me feel safe, knowing he's here with me. He abruptly shakes me and says, "Freya, honey, I need you to focus. We need to leave in a few minutes. They are coming for us. Our plan was discovered." I shake my head, refusing to believe what I'm hearing.

Our eyes meet again as tears fall down my cheeks. So many thoughts cross my mind, and I'm unsure of what to do. We were supposed to be prepared for this. Our plan didn't have the option of failing.

Releasing me, he takes me by the hand and guides me back to our room. I rush to the bed and gaze at the infants I birthed three days ago. My legs give out and I collapse to my knees. My hands are shaking, chest tight, throat dry like I've swallowed dust. I grip the floor, trying to hold myself together. *I never thought it'd come to this, having to stay behind. We'd been waiting to have these babies, and now I have to let them go. I choke back a sob, reaching out to touch them. For their safety and the future of Eterna. I'm overwhelmed, terrified of the future. Silas promised we wouldn't have to do this unless it was necessary. Now it's essential to let them go. I'm crumbling to pieces. A million knives are stabbing me in the heart, having to let go of my babies.*

Silas rushes to my side. I lay there in his arms, unable to grapple with the reality of what I have to do next. I'm only brought back to the present when Hyda comes rushing through the door. My best friend is dressed in her formal black clothes with the gold badges of her rank stitched on her shoulder. Her garb, once so pristine, is now full of dust, as if she has been rolling in the dirt. Blood covers her hands and new cuts have appeared on her face. Her blue eyes are wide with horror.

"Hyda?" I say as my heart crumbles.

"Silas. Freya." She pauses for a second, letting out a heavy sigh. "We have lost a lot of our own soldiers and people. I commanded everyone to retreat and go into hiding. I was trying to find my beloved Mateo, but he got lost in the chaos of the explosion. I... I... couldn't find him."

Her voice breaks off; she's holding back for my sake. Silas crosses the room in a couple of steps, reaching for her in an embrace, patting her on the back, doing his best to ease her pain, even though none of us want to admit this is really happening.

"Your husband is a brave man. He'll find us." I can see how unsure Silas is, panic in his eyes. I know my husband too well and so does Hyda. Her armor cracks, allowing her tears to plummet. "Hyda, we must stick to the plan. Take the kids to safety. They are our salvation," Silas whispers to her.

He then rushes to the small brown cabinet next to his side of the bed, where he keeps all important items locked. He places his ring, which serves as a key, in the lock and opens the wooden door to bring out a sealed box of vials containing portal keys.

I gasp. I never thought it would come to this. No one has ever used these portal keys. Elder Otto entrusted us with them before his death. He told us to use them in case of an emergency. They will open a door outside of

Eterna, but we don't know what is on the other side. It's terrifying to know Hyda will have to take our kids and hide for a couple of days there until it's safe to return. Silas and I made the decision to be the last two standing and not abandon the rebellion no matter what.

"Silas, please, not yet. I need more time!" I beg.

"Freya, we're running out of time," my husband answers with an apologetic voice.

Ignoring my plea, he walks towards the babies, picking them up and gently carrying them as he brings them to me. I tightly embrace them. We stand there for a few minutes, savoring these last moments as a family. My tears flow uncontrollably, falling onto my babies' tiny hands. Smelling their sweet baby smell with a hint of lavender, wanting it to be carved into my memory. I hand my babies to an inconsolable Hyda.

I plead with her, hot tears burning my face. "Please keep them safe. I trust you and love you. Please tell them I love them in case anything happens to us." Another explosion interrupts our hasty goodbye, this one near the front of our house. Silas grabs Hyda with the kids in her arms, secures a satchel with the portal keys box to her back, and leads her down the secret passageway in our bedroom to safety. Just as he manages to close it behind them and turns to me with sad eyes, the bedroom door swings open and soldiers rush in. Everything moves at an unnatural speed. Soldiers appear in every corner of my bedroom. Silas says something I can't make out as one soldier lunges at me. I try to dodge and kick him, but I feel a strong pulse of pain and my vision starts to blur as another soldier lands a strong hit to the back of my head. The next moment, I'm lying on the ground. The last thing I see is a soldier standing over me before my vision goes pitch black.

Chapter 1

Mia

Present time / Brookstone

M *ia! Mia! Mia!*
My eyes open in a haze, and the whisper of someone calling my name rings in my ears. My surroundings are blurry, and I feel as if I've been hit on the head. My birthmark is stinging again. I lay in my bed and stare at the ceiling, waiting for my vision to clear. I remove some stray strands of hair that seem to be clinging to my face and neck as I sit up, drenched in sweat. I look around the room; the shadows are lurking in every corner. I reach for my nightstand lamp and switch it on to illuminate the darkness. I'm not someone who fears the dark but, feeling this disoriented, I need to make sure I'm safe and at home.

Everything is where it should be—or at least, the way I left it, from what I recall—but I can't shake the feeling that something is wrong. I keep trying to remember what happened last night, but it's no use. I can't seem to remember anything. *Did I drink last night? I never overdrink, no matter what the occasion is.* I decide to get up. I need to wash my face and collect my thoughts. I put my feet down and land in my purple, fluffy slippers with sparkles. I smile, remembering when my mom and I got matching ones as a joke since I always wanted a pair as a child, but they only had them stocked in adult sizes. I soak in the feeling of the fuzzy material and walk to my bathroom. *Why can't I remember last night?*

Switching on the light, I lean toward the sink and roll up my sleeves. My bronze skin prickles with goosebumps at the loss of my warm nightshirt. I search my reflection for cuts, bruises, or any trace of the confusion twisting in my stomach. But there's nothing different about me. I open my big hazel eyes in the mirror and watch them catch the light. My mother once told me they shift like weather, brown in shadows, gold in sunlight. I blink and tug at my shirt collar, my fingers grazing the burning birthmark on my shoulder. A hiss escapes me, and I squint. I turn around to check if something's wrong, but everything looks the same. It's the same strange birthmark I've always had. Sometimes, I try to see shapes in it, like people do with clouds, but no matter how hard I look, it always just resembles a bush with sharp edges. I trace it again with my fingertips, hoping it might tell me something. It doesn't.

I jump in the shower to wash the sweat off me. Turning the faucet on, I step in and let the hot water soothe my skin as it slides down my body. I stay a little longer than I usually do, lathering my hair and soaking in the smell of fresh coconut from my shampoo. I rinse my hair and body. Before stepping out, I reach out and grab my towel. The steam follows me like a protective ghost as I walk towards my closet to choose my clothes. I decide to wear my black jeans with my favorite blue sweater. After wringing out the remaining water with the towel, I comb and detangle my long, wavy brown hair, and throw it into a ponytail. I look around my cozy apartment, smiling at the space I share with my best friend Natalie. We've lived here for almost three years now, since we turned eighteen. We went apartment hunting together despite our families' arguments about not wanting us to move out. They wanted us to stay with them, safe at home, until we convinced them that we would be living together and not alone. We have so much history together. Calling us best friends feels too small, too ordinary. She's woven into my life, more like a sister than anything else. These days, she's rarely home, spending most nights at the hospital. I'm always happy to be with her when she's home.

I head to the tiny kitchen, glancing at Natalie's dark room. I open the fridge to find nothing to eat other than two pizza slices of questionable freshness, to say the least. *So that's a pass on breakfast,* I think to myself. I go back to my room to find my phone and keys on the floor and pick them up. I choose to go to my parents house to find answers, because not remembering a single thing from last night? That's not like me. It doesn't make sense. I remember waking up in the morning, getting ready to go to my parents house, maybe even making tea... but after that, it's just blank. The more I try to recall, the more it slips through my thoughts. Like my own mind is keeping something from me. I wasn't tired enough to just black out. Something's off, and I need answers.

As soon as I step outside my apartment, the cold January air hits my face. It's so refreshing to breathe in. I look around for my car. It's not in its usual parking spot but on the other side of the street. I've never parked there before. I try to shove down the strange feeling in the pit of my stomach. The air feels heavier, as if it's holding its breath. Crossing the street, my skin prickles and I can't help but look behind me, expecting to find someone but there is no one. No sound, no movement, yet I don't feel alone. I rush to get inside my car and quickly lock the doors. I glance around, checking my surroundings one more time, a thin layer of ice coats the pavement in the parking lot. Leafless trees line the street, their bare branches rattling in the wind. Somewhere near, a bus rumbles past, but the neighborhood feels still and quiet in that particular way that only winter makes you feel. I let out a breath of relief. I turn the ignition on and head to my parents' house as fast as I can. As I drive, the road is familiar, it's the same route I've taken a hundred times. Somewhere along the way everything starts to blur, not the scenery but my sense of time. I drift in and out, thoughts slipping like sand. One moment blends into the next, and I'm suddenly parked in the driveway of my parents' house. *How the hell did I get here?*

I pull down the overhead mirror and rub my eyes, staring at myself. My phone rings, and I practically jump out of my seat. *Ugh, what's wrong with me?* I've never been the type of person who gets spooked this easily. Glancing at my phone, I see it's Natalie but I decide to let it go to voicemail until I finish speaking with my parents.

As I make my way over to the house, a strange pressure builds behind my eyes, like the world around me is shifting just slightly out of sync. The street tilts beneath my feet, and I blink hard, trying to steady my focus. *God, there must be something seriously wrong with me.* I ring the bell and wait a minute before my dad opens the door. He has the biggest smile on his face.

"Mia! How good to see you," he says excitedly. "Come on in and give me a hug, baby girl."

I always cringe when he calls me that.

"Dad, I'm not a baby girl anymore," I grumble to him while leaning into his comforting arms. I've always felt safe when he's with me. My dad is a surgeon and pays extra attention to details, so of course, he can usually detect when there's something wrong with me. Hell, they both do. My parents are always very attentive and overprotective.

"Come on," he says and leads me to the kitchen, where, of course, my mom is fixing something for brunch, since they wake up so early.

Rounding the corner from the hallway to the kitchen, she stands in her usual blue scrubs. Her black hair is in a bun. Growing up, they had to manage their time so one of them would always be available in case I needed them. They are great, loving parents. I'll always remember one of them rushing to school to get me when I was sick or in trouble, as if there wasn't anything more important than my well-being. When I was ten years old at summer camp, I started having nightmares and anxiety after a week, and even though my dad had been in surgery all day and my mom had a full schedule, the moment I called, she dropped everything. She drove an hour to pick me up, left her work behind and held me close in bed until I felt safe and calm again.

When she sees me, she comes rushing to hug me. Then she steps back and looks at me. Her beautiful, white, freckled face turns to worry.

"Sit down, honey. What's the matter? You don't look so good," she says with concern. I hate to worry her.

"I'm fine, just tired and feeling a bit strange," I answer with the best steady voice I can conjure.

"Did you have anything to eat?" she asks, trying to make me feel better.

I shake my head. She walks back to the kitchen to prepare something quick, while Dad is questioning me like I'm one of his patients. I hate it, but I know this is the way he shows his love. I tell him I don't remember what I did last night, nor how I got home. I mention that my birthmark is stinging again, like it does every now and then. He makes a spinning gesture with his hand, requesting I turn around and show him my shoulder.

I promptly turn to show him, and as I do, I swear I see him and Mom share a strange look, but they both school their features before I can read too much into it. I get this weird feeling that there's something amiss here, but the feeling gets lost as his cold hand grazes my skin and my body is covered in goosebumps. A shiver crawls up my spine like an electric current.

"Dad. Cold hands," I complain.

He lets out a hearty laugh, remembering how much I hate cold hands on my skin.

"Sorry," he adds quickly, peeking at my birthmark. He examines the skin and surrounding flesh. "Everything looks normal, nothing is wrong with your birthmark. Mia, darling, maybe you're just tired and had too much fun last night with your friends. Did you ask Natalie what you guys did last night?" He asks with a face that betrays no emotion.

"No, not yet. I'll call her later today to ask," I answer with a bit of frustration in my voice.

My mom appears with a plate of salty crackers and cheese in one hand and a glass of orange juice in the other. Handing them over to me, she says, "Honey, why don't you go into the living room? Eat this snack and rest while I finish preparing brunch for us."

Taking the food from my mom and heading to the living room, I glance back at my parents. They're communicating silently again. It always bothers me when they don't speak their minds, as if I'm still a child and they have to be guarded around me. I brush it off and walk into the living room to see leftover decorations: half deflated balloons hanging around the window, some streamers still clinging to the wall and ceiling, a banner that says, "Happy Birthday Dear Mia."

I'm confused. Realizing I have no recollection of coming here and celebrating with them, the uncertainty overwhelms me. *I know I made plans to celebrate with them, but why can't I remember coming here last night?*

I set the plate and glass on the coffee table, and sit on the gray couch that I've fallen asleep on a million times throughout my life, always snuggling with a blanket and watching movies with my parents. I've always been happy growing up here.

"Was I here last night?" I speak loud enough for them to hear me in the kitchen.

My dad peeks his head from the doorway, surprised at my question, looking at me with curious eyes, "You don't remember being here last night?"

I shake my head. He raises his eyebrows in confusion and ducks back to the kitchen to continue his conversation with my mother.

I'm halfway through finishing my snack when my attention is brought back to my parents whispering in the next room. I try to concentrate on what they are saying, but I can't make out the words, even as their whispers seem to grow louder. I feel silly about trying to listen in on them, so I go to the kitchen and interrupt them.

"What are you two whispering about?"

They are both startled at first, before exchanging a look. Dad lowers his eyes and shakes his head. Mom steps forward and puts her hand in mine, then looks into my eyes. She guides me softly towards the kitchen table.

"Honey, we have something to tell you. Why don't we all sit down?"

It takes me a second to drag myself into a chair across from my parents. My hands are sweaty as I brace myself for what they are about to say. My dad puts his hand on top of mine.

"There was never a good time to tell you this," He shifts in his seat, as if trying to get comfortable and failing. He seems at a loss for words. I can tell he's struggling. My body tenses. Whatever he has to say can't be good.

"This has happened before, Mia. You were too young to remember. You have been forgetting days from your life at different times and ages all throughout your childhood." He pauses.

I can see the intensity in his eyes as he struggles to continue.

"But then again, maybe you're just tired or stressed about your art," he backtracks, hesitation clear on his face. He opens his mouth, draws in a breath, and closes it. He squeezes my hand tighter and forces a smile on his face. He stays quiet for a minute.

"What your dad is trying to say is..." My mom picks up the subject. "...twenty-one years ago, we had been married for just a year. One night, we were out on a date and we were on a walk in the park. We heard crying, and that's when we came across a baby wrapped in a blanket on the grass. Our hearts jumped at the sight! We looked around everywhere, but there was no one else around. That baby was you, honey." She grabs my hand as she delivers the news.

The room feels like a vacuum. I can't breathe. My throat is tight, my cheeks are heated, and my eyes burn with unshed tears. I look at both my parents to see if they are making a cruel joke, but their faces are the most apologetic and concerned faces I've ever seen. My dad squeezes my hand even tighter, holding me as if he's afraid I'll disappear if he lets go. In reality, he's grounding me in place.

He clears his throat. I see the pain in his eyes. He's collecting the right words to say. I'm simply shocked and lost as to what I'm hearing. This is not a subject to be kept quiet this long. I look up at him as he continues,

"Honey, we love you. We asked around everywhere; we took you to the hospital and ran all the possible tests and data to see if someone had reported any missing newborns. When social services came to take you, we couldn't let you go. Looking at those beautiful hazel eyes and your smiling little face, we fell in love with you from the moment we saw you. Right there and then, your mom and I felt you were meant for us. So we brought you home and proceeded with the adoption." He wipes his face with his hand, then continues. "When you started to grow up, every now and then, you wouldn't remember what happened the day before. At first, we didn't think anything of it because you were just a kid. It's very common in the early ages that kids don't remember what they did, but as you grew, those forgotten days started happening more often. That's when we started investigating to see if it was a medical concern, but you were healthy. We hit a dead end every time. The last time it happened was when you were fourteen. So we eventually thought you had outgrown the memory loss episodes."

"How could I not remember all of this happening to me?" I ask, my voice shaking, not believing what they are saying.

My mom continues explaining what they remember happening to me throughout my childhood years, "You always seem to recover the next day as if it never happened. You forget the day as if you never lived it. Since medicine couldn't explain it and you hadn't had any in a while, we thought it was over."

With a sigh, my dad continues, voicing his frustration at not being able to link those forgotten days of my life to anything he can explain, "I wish we had some family history so we could see if it was anything hereditary. Darling, this doesn't change a thing. You are and will always be our daughter, and we'll help you figure this out. No matter what it takes." My dad's voice is barely a whisper now as he continues, "Your mom thought it was time for you to know all this."

I stand up, feeling suffocated, I let go of my dad's hands, unable to draw enough air into my lungs as they both look at me, horrified, worried about my next move. I start moving towards the door when I hear my mom say, "Mia, honey, please stay! Let's discuss how you feel and take it one step at a time.'

Her eyes look at me with unshed tears, and I lift my hand to stop her from talking.

"I need air. I'll call you guys later. Please give me space to process. I can't believe you kept this from me. I'm twenty-one years old! I should have known earlier. I deserved the truth!" Everything is so overwhelming right now. I look at both my parents one last time, shaking my head. My mom opens her mouth to say something, but I cut her off. "I can't." With that, I storm out of the house.

Outside, I breathe in the cold air that makes me feel numb. Compared to the chilly winter air, my body feels like an inferno on the verge of exploding. I've never felt such anger. Tears threaten to spill out, but I refuse to cry and crumble. I don't want to break down. I'm not weak. I walk back to my car and take a couple of breaths to try and calm myself. I need to think. I need to process all of this. For now, I settle on calling Natalie in hopes that she might shed light on what happened last night. Maybe it'll help me remember. I tap Natalie's name and wait for her to pick up.

"Hey, girl!" Her voice is loud and cheerful. "How are you?"

I try my very best to collect myself before answering. "I'm fine. Sorry I couldn't answer you earlier. I'm at my parents' house."

There's a pause, then Natalie says, "Is everything okay with them? Weren't you there just last night celebrating?"

I contemplate telling her what I just learned. She's my best friend, and I always tell her everything—but I'm not ready to talk about this. Not yet.

"Yes, everything is fine," I lie. "So what did we do last night, by the way?"

She laughs, a little confused. "What do you mean, what did we do? Don't you remember?"

"Natalie, if I remembered, I wouldn't have asked!" My voice comes out sharper than I intend. I'm flustered, trying to get a hold of myself. My emotions are all over the place, and I just need more information before I can make sense of what's happening to me.

"Okay, okay, down, girl," she says with a scoff. "I'll tell you. You don't have to be so pissy."

I totally deserve that.

"Sorry," I mumble. "I'm on edge. I'll fill you in later when you come home. I'm just... trying to figure out something. Could you please just tell me everything?"

She doesn't push back. She never does when I sound like this.

"I wanted to take you out dancing and maybe meet some cute guys at that new club, remember? But you said you'd celebrate with your parents and meet me later at home. You wanted this birthday to be just us girls—pizza, cupcakes, and a movie. So that's what we did. Then I left before midnight for my shift at the hospital. You walked me to my car, and I watched you head back to our apartment."

I process her words, then ask the question I dread.

"Did I have too much to drink?"

"No, actually. You said you weren't in the mood."

That stuns me more than I expect. I go quiet. I'm trying to piece it all together, but nothing fits. Nothing feels right.

"Mia?" Natalie's voice is soft now, cautious. "Are you sure you're okay? Do you need me to come home now? You're scaring me. You sound... lost. I've never heard you like this. I don't want to push you, but you know I'm always here for you, no matter what it is."

I close my eyes. I hate making her worry, but I can't let her in. Not yet.

"Relax," I say. "I'm okay. Don't worry too much. I'll talk to you later."

"Mia..."

"I'll tell you everything later. I promise."

Before she can protest again, I hang up. I grip the steering wheel, stare through the windshield, and drive back home.

Chapter 2

Mia

Brookstone

I set my car in park and let my hands drop in my lap for a minute, not realizing how hard I was holding the steering wheel. Looking at my reflection in the rearview mirror, my eyes welling up with tears I'm holding back, I feel a little sorry for myself. I wipe my eyes, not wanting to cry. Convincing myself that I'm angry more than sad, I let out a breath. I pull the keys from the ignition, grab my things, and exit the car.

Once I'm inside, I head to my favorite spot in the apartment. A corner in the living room where I keep all my painting supplies. All my precious brushes, in different shapes and sizes, are lined up neatly along the back wall. There's something comforting about the way their fine, silky tips glide beneath my fingers. They tickle my palm in a way that gives me butterflies in my stomach. Looking at all the paint in round buckets—acrylic, oil, and water colors of all shades—lifts my spirit somehow.

My inspiration corner is right beside the window, where the city lights illuminate the skies, painting them into a mural of dreams. I remember the first time we saw this apartment. Natalie didn't love this part of town as much, but I was sold the moment I gazed out this window. I remember seeing all the buildings on the horizon and the long line of trees on each side of the street, but the most beautiful thing was the river in the far distance that merges with the sky, making the sun look like it's bathing in its center. That is the sight that I fell in love with from the moment we moved in. So I made this my corner.

Today, I'll paint until my fingers are numb, my body is weary, and I no longer feel the dread of the day weighing down on me. Maybe, just maybe, I'll be able to produce something that is worthy of the art gallery I'll be exhibiting in at the end of the year. I have just a few pieces done and I need to get to work. Exhibiting in an art gallery with accomplished artists is one of my top dreams. This is what I want to do for the rest of my life. I was finally called after submitting my portfolio to so many places that I stopped counting. This is a shot that I can't lose. I've dedicated all of my time for this opportunity. The savings from my old art assistant job are running out, and if I don't get my big break at this show, I'll have to start job hunting again and fast. The last thing I want is to ask my parents for money, and I can't expect Natalie to cover the apartment on her own. I need this to work out.

I try to focus and stop my thoughts from wandering off to dark corners of my mind. I don't want to think the worst of my biological parents. I just need to understand why I was left at the park all those years ago. Where did I come from? Most importantly, why am I having these bouts of memory loss? I pick up my paint and brush. Then, I set the canvas on the easel. I take a deep breath, trying to clear my mind and just let my hands work. I make navy blue strokes all over the white surface until half of it is fully painted. Then I pick up some orange, yellow, and white and keep striking my brush one stroke after the other until I'm not sure what I'm painting.

I lose sense of time. Lifting my gaze to the window, I'm shocked to see it's already dark outside. I've made many paintings now piled up in the corner, none of them to my satisfaction.

I drop my paintbrush to the side and step backwards, putting some distance between myself and the canvas. I stare back at the final painting. A dark night with a single star in a sky that is surrounded by green, bushy forests. In the distance, a tiny golden flame glows; the only sign of hope among the shadows. Feeling satisfied at expressing the darkness I feel within my soul, I pick up all my supplies and bring them to the sink. I run the brushes under the water and watch as the paint starts swirling down the drain. It's a therapeutic and calming feeling to see all the colors come down from the brushes and mix in a brownish color as it rushes down the drain. I finally set them to the side of the kitchen sink to dry. I remember Natalie has work all day and won't be home till later. My stomach growls. I only ate what my mom gave me at their house.

I need to go to the store down the street to get some essentials for the week. I get my purse and phone, shrug on my jacket, and go out for a walk. *It will clear my head*. It's a cold night, but not too cold for a January winter. Some days, it becomes so cold I wouldn't dare step outside. The gust of wind would freeze anything in an instant. One day, Natalie and I wanted some ice for drinks. All we needed to do was set some water out for ten minutes on the balcony to have it frozen.

I walk a couple of minutes, taking in all the people on the buzzing street. It's always so crowded, but I love it. Seeing different people all rushing to do whatever needs to be done. Some days I'll sit on a bench and just watch people come and go about their business. Other days, I just watch random artists sketching chalk art on the sidewalk or listen to musicians play on the street. Tonight is fairly quiet. Just people hurriedly getting back to their homes. I look across the street at a construction site, and a small flash of light catches my eye. It glints from a pile of concrete, almost as if it's pulsing. Everything around it is ordinary, but this light has a clarity, a cool shimmer that feels deliberate, like it's trying to be noticed. I blink, and it's gone. I glance around, wondering about its source but come up with nothing. I quickly dismiss it, chalking it up to the exhaustion I feel, and continue on my way.

I stop by the store and go through the usual motions. I pick up a few essentials and check out. Nothing out of the ordinary. As I leave and start walking again, that strange feeling creeps back in, the sensation of being watched, just like this morning. I glance over my shoulder, scanning the street, but nothing seems out of place.

Then I see it, that same flash of bright light, still pulsing in the distance, just in a different spot across the street. I know I should keep walking. There's no reason, no *sane* reason, for me to get closer to a glow leaking out of rubble. But something in me pulls before my feet begin to move, like a thread hooked behind my ribs is tugging, gentle but firm. It's absurd. I'm not the type to chase strange lights like a moth to a flame. I'm adventurous, but rational. None of that matters now. My body's already moving, curiosity blooming into something I can't name. It's not fear. Not yet. Just this aching pull, like whatever is down there already knows me, and is waiting.

My heart skips. I hurry across the street to where I think the light came from, hoping to catch it again, to finally understand what it is. But when I get there, there's nothing. Just the usual noise of the city. I stand still, at the edge of a dark, dusty construction site staring at the empty space of rubble where the light had been, frustration building. I've seen it more than once now. Whatever it is, it's real, and I need to know what it means.

Chapter 3

Mia

Brookstone

The next morning, as I get ready to go out for a run, I stand in front of the mirror. I pull back my hair into my regular ponytail, but something is off. The strands slip through my fingers at chin length, soft and unfamiliar. My waves are gone. I tug a strand forward to examine it more closely, and the color stops me cold—cherry red. I freeze in shock. I squint at my reflection to see if I'm imagining things. Before my mind can even begin to process it, my eyes catch movement. A tall figure. A man, standing right behind me.

Alarm bells go off in my head, and my heart is pounding in my ears. My first instinct is to scream and call for help, but the sound catches in my throat, stuck between fear and disbelief. My body is trembling, barely able to stay upright. I compose myself long enough to turn around, attempting to run, and I'm stunned to find no one there. I glance around my room, searching for the man, but come up empty. I turn back to the mirror. He's there again.

He's nothing but a shadow drowned in smoke, a silhouette hovering just beyond the glass. I try to make out his face, but wisps of smoke and darkness obscure it. Then I hear a voice, distant and echoing, like whispers bouncing off the walls of my mind. It is calling a name, but not mine, barely audible and difficult to understand. The figure lifts a hand, reaching toward me, not in threat, but as if urging me to act. I'm mesmerized, caught in the moment as if under a spell. My hand lifts on its own, drawn toward his as though pulled by an invisible force. Something deep inside me knows I shouldn't, but I can't stop.

As his hands touch my skin, a shiver runs up my spine, as if an electric current is taking over my body. A loud scream attempts to escape my lungs, but no noise comes out. *I can't breathe.* I can't breathe. I close my eyes and try to draw a breath. When I open my eyes again, I'm lying in my bed, drenched in sweat. *It was a dream, just a dream.* Relief washes over me. I slowly start to catch my breath and steady my heartbeat.

Needing to escape the torturous feeling that this dream put me in, with shaky hands, I tear the sheets off my sticky skin and get up to take a shower. I walk to the bathroom and shower quickly. I'm in no hurry, but I just feel mentally exhausted from thinking too much. I've always had vivid dreams. I used to wake up in the middle of the night, screaming in fear at whatever my mind had shown me. My parents would comfort me and help me fall back asleep. As I get older, the dreams only grow more intense. Now they feel painfully real. I can't shake the sense that I'm being pulled into them, lured into some other realm where I'm meant to solve something. I just don't know what.

Stepping out of the shower, my thoughts drift back to that figure, the man. There's something familiar about him, and whatever he was trying to tell me is tugging at the edges of my mind, like a message half remembered. Could this be connected to the memories I've lost? Am I starting to remember something? Something that slipped away while I'm living here with Natalie? I can't brush this off anymore. I need to take action. I need to figure out what is happening to me. For now, I settle for small steps, starting with talking to Natalie.

Her door is closed. I try not to make too much noise as I make my way to the kitchen. I turn the electric tea kettle on while in search of breakfast. By the time I finish spreading the cream cheese on my bagel, the hot water is ready. The aroma of tea hits my nose, and it's the best smell to inhale in the morning. Most people feel that way about coffee, but I've never been a coffee person. I attempt to work in my journal while I eat breakfast, but my mind is still on that dream. Feeling completely unmotivated, I toss the journal aside with a huff, deciding to wake Natalie up to talk about what's been going on. I need someone to bounce ideas off of. I haven't seen her the past couple of days. Her schedule is so full with work. She doesn't come home some days and just ends up sleeping at the hospital. But it's time I fill her in on the new mess that is my life.

I get up and start walking towards her room. As my hand brushes the doorknob, the doorbell rings. I'm not expecting anyone, especially at eight in the morning. Intrigued, I make my way to the door and look through the peephole. My mom is standing outside, carrying something in her arms. I pull back for a second. I'm not ready to talk yet. I'm no longer as angry as I was with her two days ago, but I still feel so confused and betrayed by her and Dad. I mean, they dropped that truth bomb on me, and I'm still barely recovering.

"Sweetheart, I know you're in there. I can hear you shuffling behind the door. Please let me in. I have something to show you." My mother's muffled voice carries through the door. I take a step back, taking a deep breath before opening it.

"Hi, Mom," I whisper, so low I wonder if she even hears me. I motion for her to come in. She hesitates before stepping through the door, looking into my eyes, assessing my feelings before she walks inside.

"I know you're lost and not ready to listen to any more explanations, but I really wanted you to see what I have in here." She nods towards the box she's holding. She slowly sets the small box on the table and looks my way. I haven't moved from my spot by the door. I just stare back at her, unsure of what to say. This just feels so strange to me. Mom and I have always been like friends—talking to her has always been effortless—yet here I stand, not having a word to say. I walk silently and take a seat next to her. She reaches her hand under the tiny table and squeezes my knee, trying to comfort me.

She looks at me and gives me a sad smile as she starts to explain, her eyes not leaving my face.

"Okay, let me show you what I have in here for you." She lifts the box onto her lap and opens it carefully, as if the contents are too precious to rush. One by one, she takes out the pieces of my childhood, placing them on the table in front of us. First, a pair of tiny white shoes.

"These were the first shoes I ever got you," she says, cradling them in her palms before setting them down. Next, a pale dress and a floppy little hat. Then more—a toy, a faded ribbon, a bracelet made of string and beads. She places each item with reverence, her fingers lingering just a little longer than necessary.

As she lays them out, she tells me the story of each one. Her voice drifts into the past, soft and full of light, and I can see it in her eyes, how clearly she remembers. Her face glows as if the years have folded in on themselves, letting her relive those small, quiet moments that meant everything.

She has placed over a dozen items on the table when she says, "And the most important thing I want to show you is this!' She reaches in and pulls out an old white cloth that looks like a blanket of some sort. It looks delicate and beautiful. It has designs around the edges stitched in silver and gold. At the center, the letter C is embroidered. I reach out and run my fingers over the stitching, tracing it over and over again as my mother explains.

"This is the only thing you were wrapped in when your father and I found you. I kept it for you, but there was never the right time to show you or tell you about it. We were so scared. We both know you're strong, but no one is ever ready to go through something like this. You are and will always be our daughter. Nothing on this earth will change that. We are here for you."

I nod and say nothing. Feeling overwhelmed with emotions of love, anger, and confusion.

"We can do a search again if that's what you choose, honey," she continues.

I still have nothing to say. I just continue to hold the blanket in my hand, absentmindedly tracing the letter C on it.

"But this is all we have, and it's not much of a lead," she says, pointing to the blanket in my hand. I want to answer her, but I'm choking with unshed tears and at a loss for words.

My mother leaves her seat and kneels in front of me, placing both her hands on my knees.

"Mia, please say something," she whispers, urging a response from me.

Feeling defeated, I see her searching my eyes, waiting for me to say something. Anything. I try to find the right words, any words to comfort her, but I come up empty. She lets out a sigh and gets up to walk away, giving me space.

My inner self doesn't want to let my mom feel like that. She's a wonderful mother and I'd never want to cause her sadness. It just seems that we are stuck in this place, an awkward silence, simply because I can't find anything. *What is a person in my place supposed to say though?*

It's all so much. I don't know what to think, say, or do. I look back at all the items placed carefully around the table, and the one thing I'm certain about is how much my mother loves me. I stand up, reaching out to hug her, still holding the blanket tightly in my hand.

"Thank you, Mom. This means so much," I say against her shoulder.

I pull back and see that her eyes have welled up with tears. I take her hand and guide her back to our seats.

"I'm not upset with you. I just feel lost and confused. I didn't mean to hurt you or Dad the other day, but this is something that you guys should have told me about earlier," I explain.

She nods and says, "I know, my love, I know. And we are both very sorry. We'll always be here whenever you need us." She kisses me on the head and leaves.

Chapter 4

Mia

Brookstone

It's been half an hour since Mom left. I'm still sitting at my kitchen table, lost in my thoughts. Different scenarios where all this turns out to be a bad dream or a cruel joke run through my mind. Fiddling with the edge of the blanket in my lap, I bring it close to my face and inhale the scent, hoping it will trigger something inside me, but nothing other than the smell of old clothes rushes through my nostrils. My chest is tight, eyes stinging with unshed tears. I feel sad, but if I cry, I don't think I'll ever be able to close the floodgates. I've been filled with dread since my parents told me I'm not their biological child. Maybe I should just consider myself lucky that at least I have a family that loves me, and they've done everything in their power to make me feel loved all my life. Still, I can't shake off the feeling that I won't rest until I find out where I came from and who my biological parents are. Do I have brothers or sisters out there? Are my parents alive? Was my birth mother a single mother? A drug addict?

I shake my head and rustle my feet. Finally, I get up and walk to Natalie's room.

I twist the door knob and let myself in. It's pitch dark in here. I can barely make out where her bed is, even with the dim light from the hallway. She has some of those blackout curtains where no light can filter in the room. I don't want to scare her, so I whisper, "Natalie... Natalie, wake up."

I hear nothing. I make my way to her nightstand and flick the light on. I squint my eyes as the light assaults them. A pile of clothes is on her bed, but she's not there. Maybe she had a late-night shift again. I sit on her bed, disappointed about not finding her. I need to vent to her. I grab my phone from my pocket and tap on her name. Her phone rings once, twice, before she picks up with a cheerful voice.

"Hello, bestie."

"Hey, can we meet up? I could really use some girl time. I need to tell you something you'll never believe, and you haven't been home in a couple of days."

"Sure, you know I'm always up for girl time. And yes, I'm so sorry. It's been such a busy week. I'm so tired and ready to come home for a shower and a good meal," she says excitedly.

"Okay, do you have time to slip out for lunch? I can meet you at our favorite pizzeria in an hour."

"Yes, I think I can manage that. One of the girls owes me a favor, and I can ask her to cover for me for a couple of hours."

"See you soon then."

As we hang up, I move to pick up the box and things my mother left for me, storing them in the closet for safe keeping. I pick up the blanket and stuff it in my bag. There's something important about this blanket. I can feel it in my gut. When I hold it, it gives me a strange sense of comfort.

I glance toward the living room window as I pass, admiring the sun peeking through the drapes. Something draws me toward opening the blinds to let the natural light into the apartment. As I open them, I'm blinded by just how bright it really is outside. I squint, letting my eyes adjust. Instead, I feel as if I've been struck by something. The blinding light leaves a stab of pain through my head, and I lose my balance, falling to the floor.

Without warning I'm no longer in the room. I see two tall men talking, discussing something I can't understand. Their voices are so unclear and muffled like they are in a deep tunnel. I strain to listen, to understand what they are saying, but it's no use. Then a girl approaches close to them. *Wait, what?* That's me! I'm a passenger in my own mind, watching the scene unfold like a movie.

I try to focus. That's my face; that's me. I hear a strong buzzing sound, then I open my eyes. I'm again drenched in sweat and lying on the floor. My phone is buzzing and ringing. *I think I passed out and had another dream?* More questions, more strange dreams of things and people I can't make sense of. Confusion and dread fills me. I need answers and I don't know where to start looking. All these things happening to me can't be normal. I manage to grab my phone that is still on the floor a few feet away from me.

"Natalie?" I manage to say.

"Where are you? I was starting to worry. You're never late. You said an hour!" she yells.

I pull the phone away from my ear. Her voice is too loud in my confused state. I try to calm my breathing and wait for the ringing in my ear to subside. *Has it been an hour?*

"I'm sorry. I'll explain everything. Wait for me. I'll be right there I promise."

I lift myself from the floor, pick up my bag, and head out the door. Dragging my feet on the sidewalk, my head is rushing with the events of the past few days, thinking about how I'll tell Natalie. In the haze of it all, I'm surprised to find myself in front of the pizzeria, panting and trying to catch my breath. I see my reflection on the glass door, and I look like crap. Completely lost and drained of energy. The door chimes as I open it, and the hostess greets me with a smile. The smell of fresh baked pizza hits me, and my stomach growls. I look around the small couches and round tables that surround this cute, cozy place that we love so much in search of Natalie.

As I walk towards the table where Natalie is waiting, she's still in her ceil blue scrubs. She looks slimmer too, which makes me think she hasn't had a good meal in a couple of weeks. Her honey blond hair is in a high bun, making her high cheekbones and pointed chin stand out. Freckles are scattered on her small nose and cheeks. Her skin is paler than usual, and dark circles under her light hazel eyes show the lack of sleep. I need to remind her that she needs to get some rest.

I approach the table where her eyes are fixed on me. She rushes to me and pulls me into a strong embrace that I didn't know I needed until I feel my body relax into her. I pull back and she looks deep into my eyes.

"Well, you look like someone who came back from the dead."

"Oh Natalie, you have no idea," I respond while throwing myself on the couch across from her. I feel myself sink into it. I set my hands in my lap as I look down at them. I start picking at my chipped black nail polish, realizing I don't remember the last time I got my nails done. I lift my face to meet Natalie's eyes. She's still observing me with raised eyebrows, waiting for me to start talking.

"Spill it. You're scaring me. What's going on?"

"Okay," I whisper, gathering the courage to tell my best friend everything that's weighing me down. I'm afraid once I say it out loud, it'll be real and I can't take it back. "You know how I called you the other day asking about what we did on my birthday?"

She nods.

"Well, it seems that I don't remember a thing. I started freaking out, so I went to my parents house to kinda... I don't know..."

"Get answers?" Natalie answers.

"Umm, yes. But then they told me that I've been like this all my life, and I never knew or realized." I sigh and continue. "Not just that. I'm also adopted." Natalie's eyes tear up, and she looks as shocked as I am.

She gets up from her seat and comes to sit next to me, giving me another hug. Her voice is muffled in my shoulder as she says,

"Why didn't you tell me right away? I'm always here for you." She sits back and squeezes my hands in hers. "What do you need? What else do you know? You know we can figure things out together."

I look at my friend and see all the concern and worry in her face, as if it's a reflection of my own.

"I don't know, Natalie. Where do I start? I need more answers. I didn't want to worry you. I needed space to collect myself and see what I could find out." Looking away and not wanting to make eye contact or unload any more of my burdens on her, I choose to keep details about my nightmares to myself for now.

"Also, to be completely honest, I felt once I said it to you, it would all feel so real."

"Mia, I understand it's all a shock, and God knows how I'd feel if I were you. Let's look at the silver lining, even though you're adopted, you have amazing parents that have kept you happy all your life. Plus, you'll always have me."

"I guess you're right. You remember when we were younger? I've always told you that I felt as if something was missing despite all the care I got from my parents? Now I can't help but feel that this is all connected." I put both hands on my face, not knowing what to do. Something is stirring in me, something pushing at me from the inside. I feel like I'm swimming against the current. I'm feeling uneasy about the whole situation.

"Mia, you have always been my best friend, and I feel your pain, but what is bothering you the most? Is it that you're adopted or that you don't remember what's going on? Talk to me. Let's try to solve this together."

"I don't know... I don't know what to think or do. I'm just so damned lost," I snap back at her, frustrated, and it just makes me feel guilty. She's trying to help and knows I'm so angry that she doesn't say anything back.

We stay sitting here in comfortable silence until our food and drinks are placed on the table in front of us. I lift my head, half expecting to see anger or judgment, but all I see is a friend who is waiting patiently and giving me space by just sitting there.

She smiles. "While I was waiting for you, I ordered our favorite."

I give her a half-hearted smile. "Pineapple pizza with extra cheese."

We eat in silence. Natalie leans in, putting her hand out for me to hold. I take it, and she squeezes my hand tightly, telling me,

"Everything will be okay. You're the toughest person I know. You will get through it all. I know we'll find answers in time."

Chapter 5

Mia

Brookstone

Natalie and I walk side by side. The street is getting quieter as it's no longer rush hour. We reach the end of the road where we have to go to different parts of town, me back home and her to the hospital. Natalie offers to walk me back, but I assure her that I'll be fine and will see her when she gets home later. We hug and say our goodbyes as we go our separate ways.

As I walk towards the apartment, I hear a shuffling noise behind me. I turn around, thinking it might be Natalie following me, but I don't see anyone there. I continue with faster steps, but then I get that feeling of being watched again. Without stopping to look around, I pick up my pace. I catch something to my left out of the corner of my eye, and I freeze in place. Slowly turning toward what caught my eye, I see what appears to be someone lurking in the shadows of the alley. My heart rate picks up as I feel an unsettling feeling in the pit of my stomach. Ignoring my trembling body, I squint and see a person with a hooded, long, black cloak. I yell without thinking,

"I see you. Why are you following me?" The hooded figure turns the other way and starts walking fast. I contemplate what to do, my body moves before my mind can argue. Fear claws at me, warning me to turn back, but something stronger, adrenaline or maybe desperation, drives me after them. I quicken my steps, wanting to catch up, but the shadow maneuvers, trying to lose me, then disappears inside a store at the end of the street.

I walk closer to the store, guided by a single dim light illuminating the street, casting shadows at every corner. Rubbish and dust cover the ground, and the stale smell of sewage fills the air. I lift my shirt over my nose to prevent myself from heaving. This is a side of town I usually avoid on my walk back home. As I get closer to the store, I glance to the side, a dirty window to that building the hooded person disappeared into. Wanting to get a closer look, I come face-to-face with the foggy glass. I try to see what's inside, but not much is visible. From what I can see, there are cluttered shelves with things I can't quite make out from my vantage point. I look up, an old, half-shattered sign on top of the door that reads *Auracle* with the E dangling sideways from the wall. I dare to inch closer to the door, deciding I'll go in and see what's inside. I reach for the doorknob and twist slowly, trying to be as quiet as I can in hopes I don't run into a trap.

The door squeaks. I cringe at the sound as I push forward. I get a whiff of lavender, jasmine, and vanilla. A mix of candles and maybe essential oils. This place seems so old. It's very quiet with no sign of anyone. In the far corner, sits a single dim lap that barely lights the place. There are different sized tables with scattered candles on them, some burned out and some new. There are some books on the shelves in different corners of the space, covered in spiderwebs and dust. *Maybe it's some kind of abandoned bookstore.* One of the shelves carries jars that have various items, sticks and dried herbs; some have feathers and bones. *Not a bookstore. What the hell is this place?*

Goosebumps scatter on my skin as I feel I'm being watched again. I turn around, but nothing is there. Against my better judgment, I decide to go deeper into the store, squinting to see what's at the end of the room. *What was I thinking coming in here alone?*

I find a big table where an old rusted register machine sits. That's when I hear the wood floor creak behind me. I turn to the side, something moves. I get spooked for just a minute, but then the adrenaline of this odd night kicks in. I'm ready for a fight. I'm not much of a fighter, but I can hold my own if it comes down to it. I got pepper spray, decent aim, and just enough fear to make me dangerous. I move towards whatever was there to find myself facing a long, black curtain. *How on earth can I fight something I can't see?*

Extending my hand slowly, my fingers almost graze the fabric to peek at what's behind it, when suddenly, the curtain slides open. I freeze. I'm standing face-to-face with someone who is dimmed by the darkness and shadows of this place, as if in protection. Jumping back, I let out a scream of surprise. Then I hear an old woman's voice that is deep and calm.

"Now, now, child, there is no need to scream." When she extends her hand to her side, I step back, ready to bolt in case she has a weapon, but then realize she's reached for a matchbox. It is now sitting in her palm.

She walks past me, so slowly, as if her steps are calculated, knowing every inch of this place, even if she can't see in this darkness. She takes the match and lights several candles around the table in the center of the room. I'm anchored in place, looking at the hooded woman. The adrenaline is wearing off and I'm anticipating her next move, regretting putting myself in this scary situation. When the candle light shines on her face, she's an old woman wearing a black hooded cape, wrinkles around her eyes and mouth haggard with age, black and silver hair that make a halo around her face and thin pressed lips look back at me. I'm so captivated by her big, dark blue eyes. It feels as if she's looking through my soul.

I gather the courage and find my voice just to snap, "Were you the one following me? And why?"

"The time has come. It's the beginning." She shuffles around, looking at some papers on the table in the corner. "The full moon of the twenty-first year." She's not looking at me now but at the window, as if she's examining the moon.

"I asked you a question. Why aren't you answering?"

"The answers are within your reach, if only you seek them."

"I don't understand what is it that you want from me? Stop watching me."

She turns fast, yanking me by the arm, taking me by surprise.

"I've watched you all your life. Now, go! I have much work to do. You're wasting my time."

She dismisses me with her final words, ignoring me as if I'm no longer standing here with her, but I'm not ready to give up.

"I'm not leaving before you tell me what is going on. Why on earth would you watch me and refuse to give me answers? Who sent you? What's the purpose of all this vagueness?"

Instead of answering me, she pulls me by the hand and drags me all the way to the door, opens it, and shoves me outside, slamming the door.

I snap back to reality once I hear the lock click in place. I let out a loud breath and put both hands on my face, trying to figure out all the weird things that are happening to me. *Who was that lady? How can she think she can behave like that and get away with it? What does she mean she has watched me all my life? Is she a stalker? I should call the police. I reach for my phone ready to dial. What would I tell them? I have no evidence of any wrong doing. No, I have to take matters into my own hands.*

I return my phone to my pocket and pound on the door again, demanding the woman to open it. The opposite building's windows open, and someone starts screaming at me for being too loud and to stop that fucking pounding, which I choose to ignore. After what feels like hours, my arms give out and feel numb. I put my back to the door and slide to the ground, my feelings rushing out all at once and the wave of tears consumes me. I break down into a million pieces. All the feelings and insecurities I was holding in my heart and mind flash in front of me, and I keep wiping tears that don't want to stop sliding down my cheeks. The wind starts to pick up, and I realize I'm shaking, but I don't know if it's from being cold or from exhaustion. I stand up, look around, and make sure I know this place well enough to come back to it at a later time, and make my way back home.

I toss and turn, those blue eyes haunting me and a million questions unanswered before sleep overtakes me.

Total destruction. Dead cattle everywhere, the air heavy with the smell of decomposing corpses. I'm walking in a field that is half green, half yellow and dried. I look at my feet as I walk, a dead bird is on the ground. Something else catches my attention. It is not a bird I'm accustomed to seeing. This bird has a different plumage, long with different shades of royal blue. I lean down to brush my fingers on the soft feathers. That's when the bird opens its eyes and looks at me. I'm relieved to realize it's not dead. Maybe it is sick or really tired. Its eyes follow my fingers as I stroke its feathers.

"What is wrong with you, sweet thing?"

I get a sudden feeling that pushes me to reach in my pocket. I find a golden yellow seed. I hold it out to examine what it is. The bird's eyes follow my movement.

"Do you want this seed?"

I lower the seed into the bird's mouth. I smile as I see the bird eat the seed whole. Suddenly, a cloud of dust surrounds me. I close my eyes to avoid the dried grass particles flying around me. When I open them, the bird has transformed to a larger form, bigger than a horse, with a massive beak and wings. The shades of blue collide with the sky and the sun. It's beautiful. This magical creature is a sight that steals my breath away. The bird starts to approach me, and I take a step back.

As I lean backward to look at it, I get the feeling that I'm no longer alone. I turn around and see big blue eyes. A scream escapes me...

Jolted awake, I put my hand on my chest, feeling my erratic heartbeat as I try to calm my ragged breathing. *Am I losing my mind?* I need to calm down and take deep breaths. I really need to stop waking up like this.

Chapter 6

Xavier

Eterna

The smell of liquor and sweat clings to the walls of this bar. It's always so crowded here. It's themed like those vintage, old-time saloons from the Wild West. The whole place has wooden walls and floors. Dim, candle-like lights glow in every corner, giving it a cozy atmosphere. I don't know why Cerene loves this place so much. It is always filled to well beyond its capacity so that you have to brush up against people to get to your table. I agreed to meet her wherever she wanted today, especially since Gideon wasn't able to come out with us. Now, I sit alone at the crammed bar, nursing a beer while Cerene stands on the stage singing karaoke. I smile as I watch her sway from side to side as she sings. She seems happy, and for that I'm grateful. Seeing the pure joy on her face reminds me of all the good times we've had over the years. It feels as if it was yesterday, us hand-in-hand running through the green fields, catching butterflies and finding food. Some days we slept with full bellies, while other days we weren't so lucky. Yes, our life has been hard, but along the way, we've made some good memories.

I'm knocked back into reality as I hear her call my name through the microphone. I lift my head to look at her with wide eyes. She's motioning for me to come up on stage with her. I laugh and shake my head, mouthing, "You're crazy."

She shrugs and speaks into the mic again. "Come on, now. We don't have all day." Her laughter seems to echo through the whole place. The whole bar goes quiet as I approach the stage. All I hear is the sound of my boots on the wooden floor.

Once I'm on stage, Cerene grabs a guitar from the band's gear at the edge of the stage and hands it to me.

"Will you play my favorite song while I sing it?"

I know what song she means. I nod and smile back at her. I take a couple of minutes to tune the guitar as she speaks to the crowd.

"Today, I'm celebrating my birthday. This man behind me sang me this song when I was a teen and started rebelling. But, being the wonderful brother that he is and my very best friend in the world, he made me see how important it is to stick together." She glances my way as I strum the first note. With that, her beautiful voice sings *Grow As We Go*" by Ben Platt.

As I play the guitar, a rush of memories flash through my mind. The day Cerene had her heart broken for the very first time by the next door neighbor, Keith. He just up and left her with no note and no goodbye. She just wanted to leave and start someplace new. She cried all night as I held her. I sang this song for her. I don't remember why, but I found it so fitting for our situation. I didn't like to see her sad. I was terrified of the day that she'd decide she didn't need me anymore. I didn't want her to leave. She was the only family I had. We simply survived better together. Having her close was the only way to keep her safe. Memories keep running through my mind—the time I taught her how to fight, how to be ruthless. The way I kept pushing her, and challenging her. I got my ass kicked more than once—and I was fine with it. I wanted her to be fearless and strong. I'll always be proud of the person she grew up to be.

Someone shouts from the crowd, loud enough to cut through the music, but not clear enough to understand. I stiffen anyway. Yelling like that usually means trouble. Shaking my head from the memories, I look at the man's face as he gives Cerene a look I'm not comfortable with. A look of hatred and envy. People know what we do for a living. Before I get the chance to tell him off, Cerene jumps down from the stage and punches the man in the face. All hell breaks loose in the crowd. I let the guitar drop with a sharp clatter and shove into the crowd, trying to reach her. Voices rise, chairs scrape, and half the room surges toward the exit. The other half just stands there, too drunk or too stunned to react. I push through bodies, elbows, shoulders, the stink of alcohol and sweat thick in the air. By the time I reach her, she's straddling the man, who is slumped against the floorboards, completely unconscious. She shakes out her hand, her knuckles red from the hit. I try to help her stand, but she protests. I want to grab her and leave, but before I can say a word, the police have arrived and are pulling her away from me. All these damn bars have those magic alarms that detect when a fight happens to ensure Eterna stays safe. Being left behind, I have no choice but to follow the police to the station.

I pace in the police station, waiting for Cerene to be released. It took hours for the police officers to do their thing. They finally agreed to let her out, I'm not sure how she managed that but I'm not asking questions. Now, she's standing across the hall, getting her personal items back from the officer. From this angle, I see her tucking her chin length hair behind her ear. As she moves, the light catches on her cherry red highlights peeking out of her dark brown hair. I can't make out what she's saying, but as I watch, the officer raises his eyebrow. I know she's using her relentless sarcasm to get under his skin.

"Cerene!" I call out before she gets herself in another situation.

She turns to me with a smirk on her face.

"Xavier, there you are!" she says sweetly with a fake smile as she walks towards me. I run my hands down my face and sigh in frustration.

"We were supposed to be going out to have a good time, for God's sake! But you can't help yourself, can you? You must get in trouble every single time. I always have to come get you. One day, they're going to lock you up for good." I'm almost yelling at her once we are outside the station. It comes out harsher than I intended it to, but she really tests me some days.

"Relax, will you? That man had it coming. What did you want me to do? Just stay quiet and not say anything about all that bullshit he was saying about us being thieves?" she says, unfazed by my tone.

"You could have just let it slide this time. People don't always understand what we do. It's your twenty-first birthday, after all."

"Oh wow, such an accomplishment. Twenty-one shitty, glorious years on this planet!" she snaps back at me.

"Come on, you know I don't give a crap about my birthday." She crosses her arms, bumps my shoulder and walks in front of me.

I stay quiet, not wanting to argue any longer. I stand in place for a minute. She looks over her shoulder at me and grumbles,

"Let's go home. I'm tired."

I catch up to her and link my arms with hers.

"Let's go home," I repeat. "Before you end up in trouble again. Then I'll be really pissed off."

She stops for a minute and turns to look at me with the sincerity she rarely allows people to see.

"You know, you don't have to protect me, Xavier. I can look after myself."

I look back at her, taken aback by her sudden vulnerability.

"As you're well aware, I'm officially twenty-one years old!" she shouts to the skies, mask back in full force.

I tug her by the arm and pull her forward.

"Oh, Cerene, don't you already know by now I don't care how old you are? You will always need me!"

She laughs, but she squeezes my arm tighter.

We walk the long way home, passing the same streets we always do in South Eterna. It's early morning now, and we look like last night's leftovers, definitely doing the walk of shame. Cerene is wearing those leather black pants and a sparkly black shirt with chains across her back.

When I look at her, sometimes I still can see that small little girl I grew up with. She was so curious, but always scared, and followed me around in the orphanage as if she knew I was her only hope in life. When we were captured at the edge of Eterna as children, we were declared as orphans and dropped into the nearest orphanage without anyone doing any background check on us or bothering to listen to our story. No one knew we weren't orphans at all.

I still remember it clear as day. When my mom grabbed me from our home, we ran so fast, I didn't understand what was going on, though I knew something was wrong. There was a lot of smoke in the streets that day. All I understood was that we needed to hide. I was standing with a baby in my arms and dust had covered both of us from head to toe.

I was only five years old when my mom left her with me, hiding behind a tree, handing me her hourglass necklace and telling me to look at the sand in the hourglass and that she'd come before it ran out. She emphasized not making a sound until she returned for us. She hadn't returned when soldiers discovered us. The memory still haunts me to this day. My mother's face has started to fade with time.

I'm not sure I remember what she looks like anymore. The authorities assumed Cerene and I were siblings, and I let them believe it, too. That was the only way they would agree not to separate us. I needed to keep her safe with me. This was what my mom wanted, and I promised her I would. She placed that little baby in my arms and said, "This is baby Cerene, guard her and stay hidden. I have to cross to the other side and make sure we can all go safely."

When Cerene turned ten years old, I told her the truth. I told her everything I knew. We were running from something—something I was too young to understand. My mom was supposed to keep us safe, but somehow she wasn't able to get back to us in time. That was when we made a promise to never leave each other, no matter what happened. We had to stick together. We both had hopes that my mom would make her way back to us someday, but we never said anything out loud to one another. That day never came.

When I turned seventeen, the orphanage kicked me out, and I took Cerene with me. With time, life became cruel and hard. We gave up on childish hopes. We grew tougher, and Cerene grew bitter as she slowly stopped caring much about anything.

I couldn't blame her. Life has been hell for both of us while on the streets and fending for ourselves. At first, I'd trick her into playing hide and seek because she was too young, and I was afraid she might get hurt. I'd wait for her to hide, then pretend to search while slipping away to convince a merchant to give me a piece of fruit, or whatever small thing I could find for her to eat. As she grew older, I began training her to defend herself. I'll always be grateful to our trainer in the orphanage for taking the time to give me extra lessons. He was the closest thing to a mentor I ever had.

I'm jolted back to the present when Cerene opens the iron door that leads up to our apartment building. We take the three stories up in silence. The moment we step inside our apartment, Gideon looks up from where he's sitting at our small kitchen table.

"You guys didn't come home last night! I was worried. What happened?"

Cerene answers him with a question. "Why are you up so early?"

Gideon looks at me for answers. "We were at the station. You know the drill."

He gives me a knowing look, then looks back at Cerene, careful not to say anything to piss her off.

"What's going on with you? It's early," I ask, changing the subject.

"Haven't you heard? It's happening again all over Eterna—well, at least all through the south as far as we know. The land is becoming barren. More crops and cattle dying." he sighs.

I run my fingers through my hair.

"I don't get it. Why is magic growing weaker, and why aren't the Elders doing anything about it up north?"

Gideon shrugs and shakes his head as I take a seat next to him, worry clear on my face. Cerene looks at us both and rolls her eyes.

"Oh, come on, guys! Who cares? You know everything dies. Even you beautiful men will eventually kick the bucket!" She then disappears to the back of the apartment, probably to wash away the stench from the police station.

"Did she just call us beautiful? That's an upgrade?" Gideon asks, amusement filling his eyes.

I laugh under my breath and turn my attention to all the maps Gideon has spread out all over the table, "So all these places circled in red are where we are seeing magic fade?" I ask.

Gideon leans back in his chair and answers with a sad nod of his head.

My eyes roam the map one more time. Magic has never faded for as long as I've lived. Eterna has always glowed with it. Our history books taught us how the Elders preserved this part of Earth. We've been tucked away from the world simply because we have magic. Being kept away from others kept us protected. Our lives depend on magic. Our streets are magically lit and cleaned. Our crops magically grow. Our transport system depends on the magnificent Zarkas. Those small magical birds transform into beautiful beasts big enough to carry us where we need to go. Eterna completely operates on magic. If that is faltering, then our land will crumble. Not to mention, we would be exposed. Whatever power the Elders use to shield us from the rest of the world will fall apart, too.

"What are we missing?"

I look up at Gideon who has his hands behind his head while rocking back and forth on his chair.

"Don't ask me," he says. "I've been up all night studying these, and I've come up with nothing."

I notice how tired he looks. His usual glowing brown complexion is dulled by lack of sleep. His dark brown eyes are rimmed with red from straining so much over these maps. His natural curly hair is untamed and seems to stand up at odd angles along the ends.

"We need to spread out and find out more, focus on what's changed and why, we need to find out what will happen to Cerene's magic," I say, looking back at him.

Chapter 7

Mia

Brookstone

I try to clear my mind by going for my usual morning run, but I keep thinking of all the events that have transpired over the past couple of days. I woke up today determined to piece everything together. I have to dig deeper and find out more about my birth parents. I think about the woman with the blue eyes in the shop. She said that she was watching me all my life. That thought alone terrifies me. She didn't give me a chance to ask more questions, not that she answered the ones I was able to ask in the first place. I take a turn onto the street I was on last night, it doesn't look as eerie as it did in the shadows and the dim light. I come to a stop right in front of it. Locals are leaving their apartments to go about their business. The shop is no longer dark and has a sign on the door that says *Open*. I take a minute to catch my breath before deciding to go in again.

As I push the door open, a chime sounds, one I didn't notice last night. Inside, the store feels quiet, too quiet, like a place few ever visit. The air is still, undisturbed by footsteps or voices. Dust settles on shelves and objects, untouched and forgotten. The dim light flickers faintly, adding to the sense that time moves slowly here. The whole vibe of the store has me on edge. My curiosity pushes me forward. No one seems to be in the store. Walking through it again, I notice that it has a psychic reading section where the dark curtain was hanging last night. *So it's not a bookstore, but maybe a magical oddity store of some sort.*

"Hello?" I wait for someone to answer me, but it is too quiet for my comfort. "Hello, is anyone here? I need some help."

A few seconds pass before I hear shuffling in the back of the store. A door behind the register, painted the same color as the wall, opens, and I'm again greeted by the same dark blue eyes that haunted me all night.

"Hello, child," she answers with pressed lips as if I'm here to annoy her.

"Hi, my name is Mia. I was here last night, and I..."

She raises her eyebrows and stares at me before I can finish my sentence. "Child, I know who you are."

"Listen, lady, I don't know who you are, and can you stop calling me child? My name is Mia," I scoff back at her.

She lets out a sinister laugh and says, "I'm Hyda, protector and general of our order."

What order? Does she think she's in some kind of movie? I step closer to her and say,

"Listen, Hyda, with all due respect, I don't know what you're talking about, but I'm here to ask you again—why were you watching me last night? You said you have been watching me all my life, and I'm here for answers."

She smiles, this time with less intensity on her face.

"All in due time. You will know all and more."

"I need answers now," I press, balling my hands into fists. I shuffle my feet trying to ground myself because this woman is making my blood boil with rage. She just looks at me and turns around to scramble through some papers again.

As I'm about to scream at her, she suddenly turns.

"Go now, child. Meet me again when the full moon rises in three days' time. I'll have answers for you then. For now, I have much more important work." She turns and disappears behind that hidden door in the back before I get the chance to ask her anything else. What is it with this woman leaving me twice now with more questions than I started with?

I turn to leave, regretting coming back here, when something draped on a chair beside the register catches my eye. I move closer to inspect it. I can't believe what I'm seeing. It's a replica of the baby blanket that my mother gave me, but it has a different letter on it. I feel a pull toward it. I reach out my hand to grasp it when the sound of the door chimes. Distracted, I turn to see other people come into the shop. I put my hands in my jacket pockets as I rush out of the damned place.

My brain is a storm of thoughts. *Is this woman my actual mother? Does she know anything about my past?* Now I'm certain that she knows some information and is holding back on me. She's very vague and seems guarded, but I have to make her talk. I'm certain she knows something. Maybe she'll solve part of the puzzle and help me figure out why I'm losing my memories. She's definitely a link, and I'm determined to get to the bottom of this in order to be able to go on with my life. I make a mental note to bring my blanket and show it to her next time I see her.

I barely make it through my day-to-day for the next three days. I'm half convinced that I'm losing my mind while waiting for the full moon to return to the blue-eyed lady. I tried painting to distract myself, but that didn't do much. Half of my paintings appear dark and somber. They won't work for the art gallery unless they decide that they want something gloomy. I always paint bold and unique, thrilling abstract pieces, but now my canvas is full of blue eyes and the shape of a man with no face.

Natalie came home a couple of times and was made aware of everything going on. She advised me against going to the shop again, telling me, "You can't trust everyone." She's probably right. My parents would agree, too. Despite what everyone thinks, I know deep in my bones I'll go because the more I think about it, the more I feel she's a piece to my puzzle. Part of me thinks this is a dangerous territory. I'm putting hope in a complete stranger who, for all I know, may be leading me down a path of lies and deceit, but I'm going to have to give her the benefit of the doubt.

For what feels like the hundredth time today, I double check to make sure it's going to be a full moon tonight. Hyda didn't specify a time. She just said come in three days' time when the moon is full. It has been so difficult to keep my emotions and anxiety in check. I'm just waiting for the day to slip by so I can get the answers I need. I'm pacing in my apartment and looking at the clock that feels like it hasn't moved. It's still noon, and I need to occupy myself with something because I'm driving myself crazy. I look around at all the paintings I made this week. Most of them are inspired by my racing thoughts and the restless dreams that plague my sleep.

I break my pacing when my attention is drawn toward the apartment door opening. I stop and turn to see Natalie. I furrow my eyebrows.

"What brings you home at this hour?"

She laughs her usual contagious laugh.

"What kind of friend would I be if I didn't come with you on your questionable quest? Did you really think I'd let you go alone after everything you told me about that woman?"

I wave her over to sit on the couch.

"What if she sees you and refuses to answer anything?"

"Then we'll deal with it. I'm not letting you go alone. End of story."

I let out a sigh, lips lifting slightly in a smile.

"Fine." I know she's not going to change her mind.

We order take out, and we eat while sitting together on the couch, looking out the window in silence, waiting for the time to pass. Natalie nudges my leg.

"Have you met any cute guys lately?"

I burst out laughing and she joins me.

"If I did, you'd hear about it," I say while still laughing.

Natalie has always had a habit of using humor to get out of awkward silence. I remember when we were in school, the teacher asked a question she didn't know the answer to. Instead of just saying she didn't know, she ran out of the class and screamed "Fire! Fire!" The whole class was in tears.

"If you count that mystery guy from my dreams, then maybe."

"What guy? Why haven't I heard about this dream of yours?"

I lean back on the couch, throwing my head onto the plush pillow, getting more comfortable. I gesture toward my art that's sitting in the corner.

"There he is. He's always haunting my dreams, or maybe I should call them nightmares. I can never see his face. But I know he's tall and muscular, as you can see. There is something about him that pulls me in, yet terrifies me."

She stands and moves closer to my paintings to get a better look.

"I thought these were for the gallery. Are all of them from your dreams?'

"Unfortunately, yes. None will work for the gallery. They are too dark. They won't take them. I didn't even ask if they would."

"Mia, why not? These are really good."

She brushes her fingers over the dark figure in the painting, around his shoulders.

"Mmm... he's gorgeous even without a face. When did you start having all these dreams of him?"

"You know I've always had vivid dreams, but after my birthday they seem different, persistent" I answer.

She nods but has a distant look on her face as she ponders my answer.

"Anyway, let's focus. Do we need a plan for today?" I continue, changing the subject. I don't want to talk any longer about my dreams or this man that is haunting me. I have so much on my mind and don't want to linger on a dream that most likely means nothing.

During the next few hours, Natalie and I go though what we'll ask Hyda and decide to play things by ear. There's no use planning something we can't control. The whole idea of going back to meet this lady again seems reckless, but Natalie always has a way of calming me down and making things feel doable.

Chapter 8

Mia

Brookstone

Natalie and I are standing in the alley in front of the Auracle. Natalie is glancing in all directions. Looking at her, you wouldn't know it, but I know her well enough to know she's on edge and is trying not to show it because she wants to be brave for me. That's Natalie—cool, collected, and funny—a girl who wanted to have fun without ever getting in trouble. She's the opposite to my awkward and chaotic nature. The yin to my yang. Mischief has always been my thing. Ever since I was a child, I remember loving breaking the rules in any game because it added more fun and excitement. I crave chaos and adventure, whereas Natalie likes order and predictability. This is how I know she's way out of her element by coming with me tonight. I grab her hand to put her at ease when she asks,

"Shall we?"

I look at her. "I'm ready whenever you are."

She nods, and we both face forward as I push the door open.

I'm surprised at how the store looks. It's not the same as it was three days ago. Tables have been shifted to the sides of the room, and the shelves are obviously cleaner than they were previously. Candles light the place. Metal candelabras cover the walls and creep up the corners like vines. *Who still uses candles for lighting?* The smell of lavender and sage is so potent it burns my nose, making me want to sneeze. The secret door in the back is half open and I can see Hyda with her back to me, fussing in the back room. Her hair is messier than it was when I saw her last. This woman gets more peculiar-looking every time I lay eyes on her. I could swear she senses my presence. She stops suddenly and turns, as if awakened from a haze. She starts walking towards me with intention. That's when she spots Natalie and looks from her to me and back. I see her wanting to say something, but she presses her lips tightly together as if she's thinking about her next words before voicing them.

I break the silence. "Hello, Hyda. I hope you finished whatever important work you kept mentioning and you're ready to give me answers."

She raises her brows "Who do we have here?" She lifts her arms and gestures toward Natalie. I start to open my mouth, but stop as she says with an all knowing tone, "Natalie Baker, how are you doing, sweet girl?"

Natalie and I freeze, shocked that this stranger knows her name. *What the hell? Who is this woman?* I can see Natalie's calculating gaze and know that she's freaking out at the realization that Hyda wasn't only following me, but she knows my friends, too. But how? And why?

Hyda speaks again. "Oh child, don't be so surprised. I told you, I've been watching you all your life. Heaven knows you two have been stuck like glue."

"Velcro friends, as my mother called us," I mumble to myself.

Natalie clears her throat. "Hmm... this doesn't explain how you know me and why you were watching Mia."

Hyda gestures to a table. "Come, both of you, sit. This old woman's legs are not as strong as they used to be, and I've been on my feet all day."

We look at each other as we walk to the table and take a seat. At this point, I'm not only anxious to know, I also want to grab Hyda by the neck and rip the truth out of her. She's taking her time, and I can't determine if this woman's intentions are good or not.

Hyda sits last, bringing with her a small envelope. She sets it on the table. She rests her hand on top of it. My eyes snap to hers the moment she starts to speak.

"I assumed you weren't going to come alone. Best friends are so important, and I haven't had one in a long time. You have so much of her, my dear child."

I look her in the eyes, pleading for answers I seek badly. "So much of who? Who is her?"

She continues without answering me. "The beginning is here, and I see the struggles in your eyes, my child. If you haven't felt them, you wouldn't have felt me in the shadows. You haven't noticed me in twenty years. They have warned me to look for the signs, and I've been waiting. I thought the day would never come and I'd wither and die without anyone seeing me." She pauses, as if lost in the memory of something or someone. "There is so much to do. You have to be prepared. You have to be trained."

She starts shuffling in her seat and talking fast, repeating the same sentence again and again like a person in a frenzy.

"The beginning is here, the beginning is here, the beginning is here," She stands and pushes away from her chair, then starts to pace in place, talking to herself as if Natalie and I are no longer in the room with her. "What if you can't survive it, the truth, your destiny?"

I look at Natalie. Her face looks so pale. She's looking straight ahead at Hyda, her eyes shifting side to side as she follows Hyda moving left to right, trying to process all of this.

I slap my hand on the table and Hyda stops and looks at me. I stand up and raise my voice a bit. Natalie flinches next to me.

"Look, Hyda, or whoever you are. You're not making any sense. You promised me answers, and you're not delivering. You're confusing me with all your rambling, and I have no idea what you're talking about. Let's try this again. Start at the beginning."

She stops her pacing and turns to me. She smiles a different smile—a kind smile—one of a proud mother who is seeing her child take their first steps. She seems to snap out of her frenzy for a few moments.

"There is the fire that burns in you. Your words and demands are spoken like a leader." She reaches over the table as if reaching for my face. I shrug back, and she retreats.

I'm startled by her clapping her hands together as she turns back around to get something from behind the counter.

"Alright, you said you want answers?"

"Yes!" I say exasperated. I open my purse, pull out my blanket and set it on the table. "Are you my biological mother?"

Her head turns unnaturally fast to look at me, and I feel my heart beating at full speed while her blue eyes look into my soul. Her answer comes quick and sharp. "No."

"Then, explain the blanket. You have one just like it over there." I point to the one that is still draped on the chair. Her eyes widen in surprise as she turns to see what I'm pointing at... and walks over to the chair, then picks up the blanket with ease like it's something precious. As she walks back to us, I take the time to look at her, noticing the hunch of her back and her slow steps. She hugs the blanket and sniffs it.

"I can still smell my child on it." She laughs. "Or maybe it's just my memory. This blanket looks like yours because the person who made it had one made for my own child."

I swallow hard and let out the breath I didn't know I was holding. I turn to Natalie to check that she's still okay. I lower myself onto the chair one more time and ask Hyda with a kinder voice, "Please Hyda, tell me the whole story. I need to understand. I've been lost for days, and I need to go on with my life. How can you help me?"

I see a flicker of sympathy on her face. She closes her eyes and nods. She then leans forward to pat my hand that's on the table in assurance. "I'll explain everything, my dear." She slides the old yellowed envelope toward me but doesn't say anything else.

Natalie reaches to hold my other hand in assurance. She doesn't say anything either, but looking into her eyes, she's no longer afraid or anxious. She's just as determined as I'm to get to the bottom of this. We sit there in silence for a few minutes until Hyda starts talking.

"I'll tell you the whole story, but you'll have to keep an open mind."

Natalie and I both nod at that and wait for her to continue.

"Long ago, there was a land called Eterna. It is preserved from the rest of the world because it operates on magic. Eterna is a land so beautiful, prosperous, and green. We all lived in peace and harmony, it was the safest place on Earth. There were the royals who were the native people of that land, people who possessed magic. Then there were the commoners, people that were born in Eterna, but didn't possess magic of any kind. And of course, there were the Elders, the leaders, who possessed high power. Among them lived seers who prophesied the future. They were a group of people that made sure everything was as it should be—a government of a sort. They kept the order and balance of our world. They were kind, fair, and just. With time, those Elders passed the leadership from one generation to the next. As the world changed, the people did, too. The younger generation of Elders got high on power and turned greedy. They started to become corrupt and things weren't as just as they once had been.

"The people of Eterna are strong and brave. They wouldn't stand for this. They started speaking up against inequality. We took a vote, we rallied and signed a petition for change, but nothing happened. The Elders had the final say and ruled above all. We lost the possibility of change. A group of royals decided to work in hiding—to support everyone who was being suppressed—and provided food and shelter to those in need. The word got out, and people started getting hurt or abducted. The rebellion was falling apart. One of the biggest and oldest royal families was entrusted with a message, a prophecy, handed to them in secret from the last Elder seer in Eterna. That prophecy foretold that a time will come when there will be one salvation. The rebellion should never give up. You and I, my child, are from that land. We are from Eterna."

I stare at her wide-eyed, not knowing if I should believe anything coming out of her mouth. Then her words from earlier replay in my head. *You will have to keep an open mind.*

I clear my throat. "I don't understand what all of this has to do with me, and if I'm from wherever you're saying, how did I end up here?"

"Patience, child. The story is far from over. People didn't really think anything of the prophecy. They weren't sure it was true, as it was handed down from one generation to the next. We believed the prophecy would never come to fruition... until you were born."

She takes a breath, reclines in her chair, and with closed eyes recites,

"Ignite and flow, ignite and flow.
Under the full moon of a winter starless night.
Two souls will be born to the royal blood.
Marked by the goddess of eternal magic.
Granted the power of salvation.
Blood will be spilled.
On their twenty-first year their magic will call.
Eterna will die an eternal death without their power.
Fire and water will collide.
Lightning will follow.
The loss will be great.
Sacrifices will be made.
Heed the prophecy or face the doom.
Time will be ticking."

She gestures toward the envelope.

"This is all I could remember of the prophecy. I wrote it down so I wouldn't forget."

I rub my hands on my face in frustration because I feel more puzzled and frustrated than when I stepped foot in this store. I'm seeking answers and I get more mysterious events the deeper I dig. So I decide to change my approach once again. "Hyda, who are my parents, and are they alive?"

"Your parents are of royal blood, and I'm not sure if they are still alive."

I swallow hard, trying to take away the lump that is stuck in my throat. *My parents may be dead, before I even get the chance to meet them. That would be a miserable, sad ending to my search.*

"What do you mean you don't know if they are still alive?"

"I haven't seen them in twenty-one years, my child. I was sworn to protect you, no matter the cost. I had to leave everything behind."

"Is that why you were watching me?"

"Yes."

"Okay, Hyda, I'm losing my patience here. What is my connection to everything and your so-called prophecy?"

Hyda gets up from her chair and walks to the back room, disappearing for a minute only to reappear with something in her hand. It's a vial containing a crimson liquid. Alarm bells ring in my head and my eyes snap to Natalie. Worry in her eyes too, and as if in sync, we both stand up so fast we send the wooden chairs tumbling behind us. Hyda lifts one of her hands in the air to indicate she's not going to harm us.

"Relax, I need to show you something." She pops open the vial, pours some of the liquid in her hands and indicates for me to come closer. "I need your hands, my child. This is just a magic activator."

I hesitate. *This is wild. What magic?* A power I can't control seems to take over me and pushes me towards her, forcing me to extend both of my hands in front of me. She rubs the crimson liquid on my hands, then puts her hands under mine. I can hear Natalie protesting behind me, but I'm too caught up in this strange feeling to look back. It feels sticky and warm, but it doesn't seem to have any odor. I look up to see Hyda looking into my eyes. "Repeat after me, my child. Ignite."

As if possessed by another being, I repeat the words. The moment I say the word "ignite," I watch in horror as a flame blooms into my palms. I'm suddenly sobered by the sight of flames bursting from my hands. I pull my hands away and start screaming. I shake my hands and it's gone, as if I imagined the whole thing, I turn my hands over and... nothing. All of a sudden, my throat feels dry. I was on fire. *What's happening to me?*

Heat is coursing through my body. My blood is boiling inside me. What did this woman do to me? What have I done? I let out a scream, my body is trembling, then everything goes dark.

The wind is so strong, it makes me sway. I try to keep my balance, not wanting to fall. It's very dark. I can't see anything here. *Where am I?* Then I see a flash of light. I look in the direction I saw the flash, and there it is again, the same light I keep seeing. I follow it until I'm standing again in the middle of a deadened yellow field. I hear something, but I don't see anything nor anyone. The wind is so chilled against my exposed arms. When I look at myself. I'm wearing black leather pants and have a dagger at my side. I run my hand over it, and it feels so familiar, like I was born accustomed to having it at my side.

I hear voices again. I concentrate until I hear two distinct, muffled female voices screaming at each other about something urgent. I try to focus my eyes on them, but everything is blurry. I realize it's Natalie's voice.

"What did you do to her? Explain yourself or I'm calling the police."

"Calm down. She's fine. I didn't do anything to her. She'll be fine."

I move my hands and feel a soft cool linen under me. *Am I in bed?* My eyes feel heavy, and I struggle to open them.

Once I do, I see Hyda and Natalie both looking at me, and the moment they realize I'm awake, Natalie rushes to hug me.

"Oh my god, Mia, are you okay? I was terrified." She grabs me by the shoulders and starts to drag me up the bed. A bed in a part of the store that I don't recall seeing before.

"That's it, I'm taking you home."

Chapter 9

Mia

Brookstone

Natalie is supporting my weight, helping me walk to the street with Hyda on our tail, begging for us to stay so she can explain what comes next and something about the awakening of my magic. I'm too tired to focus. Too much has transpired during the night. To my surprise, when we step outside, we're hit by the morning crisp air. And I realise that I've been unconscious or asleep all night. I try to focus, but I'm assaulted by the argument going on between Natalie and Hyda.

"Natalie, she's going to be okay. She needs to adjust to this new sensation of her power. It's been dormant, waiting to be awakened," Hyda yells behind us.

"We are done here. Leave us alone."

"I can't. I'm her protector and the only person who knows what is going on."

"What's wrong with you? Don't you understand? I'm taking Mia home."

When Natalie hails a cab, the car screeches to a stop. I'm still leaning on her for support when she opens the door and eases me inside. I scooch on the worn-out leather back seat so Natalie can sit next to me. Everything is hazy in my mind. I hear Natalie give the driver the address. The car starts moving, and I notice from the window that Hyda is still standing outside looking at me, begging silently for me to stay.

I turn my face away and close my eyes. The feel of the leather underneath me is so sticky, and the smell of the cab—a mix of cigarettes, leather, and the winter air—is enough to make my stomach turn. The driver looks at us in his mirror and shakes his head in disapproval, assuming we were out partying too hard. After a few agonizing minutes, the cab comes to a stop, and I feel Natalie open the door and lean down to try to pull me out. I manage to get out of the car while leaning my weight against her. I've never felt this weak before, not even on my worst sick days. *What did Hyda do to me? What was that liquid she put on my hands? That's when I started to feel the sensation of something stirring within my blood and body.*

"Can you walk up the stairs?" Natalie asks, trying to get me to move. I nod. My head is spinning as I grip the cold iron railing of the stairs. It's a welcome feeling that cools whatever fire is still burning within me. By the time we reach our doorstep, I'm completely out of breath, and sweat is covering my brow and forehead.

"Come on, let's get you in the shower. You're burning up."

"What's happening to me?"

"I hope to God it's nothing, or I'm going back to kill that woman."

A small laugh escapes me as I look at my best friend and see the worry in her eyes.

"Sorry, it's not funny. I know. I love you, Natalie."

Once we are back safe in our cozy apartment, she starts drawing me a bath and helps me out of my clothes. Wincing from the cold, I put my legs in the bathtub one after the other and lower myself slowly as my body adjusts to the water. Natalie steps out, leaving me to soak for a bit. My mind wanders off, thinking about my dreams and the flashes I keep seeing around me. Concluding Hyda does know a lot about me and my parents, I'll need to go back to her. What she did with that liquid and the fire is something I still can't fathom. *Was it magic? But whose? Mine or hers?* I'm determined to find out more, and I'm definitely not dropping this subject. I must uncover the truth.

Natalie walks in holding my bathrobe. "I prepared something for both of us to eat whenever you're ready to leave the tub," she says as she lays my robe next to the bathtub.

"Thank you. I'll be right out."

"Do you want me to call your parents?"

"No," I snap. I take a deep breath and look back at her. "Sorry, didn't mean to be rude. Can we please leave my parents out of this for now? I know you mean well."

With a nod of understanding, she walks out, closing the door behind her.

Chapter 10

Hyda

Brookstone

I rummage through all the shelves that are lit with candles. I haven't been able to sleep after the girls walked out of my shop, filled with dread. *Did I scare her off? Will she come back?* It would be a big problem if she doesn't. I'll have to find a way to get her back. I have the feeling that things are getting bad back home. I knew the time was coming, but I would have been more prepared if I had seen the signs earlier. It's only been a week since things shifted. I could feel something was off. It's that low, nagging feeling in the back of my mind, like something's out of place, just slightly wrong, but I can't put my finger on it. I have to come up with a plan to get her back. Lord knows there is so much at stake, and so much more she doesn't know.

For now, I just need to make sure the portal keys are still good so they are ready when we are. After managing to put all the books and candles away from the shelf, I run my fingers along the back edge to the old latch that I hid twenty years ago. I brush my finger over it. I hear a clicking sound that indicates my hiding place is open. I bend down and move some of the boxes on the floor under the shelf. One of the tiles that I hid so well is now shifted to the side. I smile at the memory of how I built this thing with my own hands using all the knowledge I still had from being a clever general. God... it sure feels like ages ago. I reach into the cubby and bring out the small box—once so shiny, now full of dust and cobwebs. I wipe it clean with the hem of my shirt, then slowly lift the lid and inspect the last three portal keys. I remember using three of them while trying to find a way to bring the kids back. That old feeling of dread creeps in, but I shake it off. Now is the time, and I can't help the hope rising in my chest. *I thought the time would never come to use it and go home again.* If she's not coming back, I'll have to go to her.

Chapter 11

Xavier

Eterna

Cerene must've slept because she never came out of her room. Gideon is passed out on the couch, while I've spent the past two hours studying all these maps. We started this hunt the day we realized Cerene's magic was off. People usually hire us to find missing things, and others want to obtain rare magical objects undercover. We typically do the dirty work for a hefty sum, and we never fail. The three of us have become the perfect people to do this job. We are skilled and make a great team. Gideon is a bookworm who does an amazing job researching and gathering information. Cerene, on the other hand, is relentless in getting the job done and is not shy with her magic. She controls water and has learned to do tricks with it over the years. She can conjure water from thin air, and she can practically make you drown as you stand there. As for me, I'm the mastermind of all plans. I'm a strategic thinker who looks into every possible scenario for our mission to ensure our success.

We keep looking for clues about what is making the magic in Eterna falter, but until now, we have had no leads. At first, the change in Eterna seemed very insignificant, but as the days have gone by, we started finding things that no one has been able to explain—a whole swathe of land dead or animals dying for no reason. The problem is, no one is addressing it. I scribble a note for Cerene and Gideon to gear up and meet me before sunset near the Elder's district. With that, I go out to do my own research in town.

Once I'm downstairs and out the door, the streets are loud and buzzing with people. It's late afternoon and everyone is occupied. Merchants are piling up more goods while buyers are looking at items to purchase. As I walk the streets of downtown Eterna, I hear whispers between merchants and people, gossiping about magic and other everyday topics. Some are trying to gain potential customers' attention to sell their goods. I have many eyes and ears around town, people who owe me favors for saving their lives or getting them out of trouble when they needed it. Being on the streets can teach a person a thing or two, and everything comes in handy at some point. My first stop is to see Jake, the magical crop merchant.

As I approach his shop, I'm surprised to see his place is quiet. Usually, it's busy and buzzing with customers at this time of day. If I didn't know better, I'd think his shop is closed. I slide the old brown straw curtain he has at his entrance to the side and duck my head down to enter. At six and a half feet tall, every shop entrance is too low for me. Once I'm inside, I find Jake slumped onto his chair in the corner, behind all the sacks of seeds and grain. He seems to be lost in thought and hasn't noticed my entrance.

"Jake!"

Startled by my voice, he drops something on the floor that makes a loud *clang* as he sits up. "Oh man, you scared me."

I furrow my brows in confusion as to why Jake would be scared. "What's going on?" I ask, concern filling me.

"I went to the supply farms early in the morning like I always do. When I got there, the Elders were there before me. It struck me as odd. I've never seen an Elder there. They have purchased all the Bazer from the farm." Jake puts his hand on his face, clearly distraught and almost in tears as he continues. "They have left none for the common people."

I move closer to him and put my hand on his shoulder, squeezing it lightly in hopes of giving him some comfort. "Don't you have anything saved?"

He uncovers his face and looks at me, then gestures for me to follow him to the back of the store. As we approach a dead end, I'm puzzled. There is nothing around us other than walls. He crouches to the floor and lifts the side of the brown-yellow carpet we are standing on to expose a small tile. He wiggles the sides of the tile to lift it, exposing a wooden box with a silver lock under it. I wait silently for him to tell me what's going on. He hands me the box to hold while he places the tile and carpet back in place. He then starts unbuttoning his shirt to get out a small silver key hanging around his neck. As he retrieves the box back from me, he tells me,

"This is the only stash of Bazer I've saved for emergencies. When magic started to fade, I thought maybe one day we would lose the Bazer, too. But I wasn't able to save enough. Since we have none to sell, this will be only for very important things now."

"Jake, this business with the Elders is all so unusual, and if I'm being honest, very concerning. What do they know that we don't?"

I explain to him that I came to get some Bazer and one of his famous Klinxer potions that I always purchase when we go on a mission. Jake has many potions for different purposes, but this potion, if consumed, gives anyone without magic temporary magical abilities, like to communicate with people telepathically. The Elders made sure we weren't able to get our hands on it, no matter how hard we tried, but Jake here is one of the few people who is able to make it, and I'm lucky to have discovered that.

"I do have some potion left, but you have to be very careful in using it. I don't know when I'll be able to make more. I can sure share some of the Bazer with you, but tell no one else that I have any. I trust you, brother."

"You know me better than that, Jake. My lips are always sealed." I'd never give anyone the pleasure of knowing where I buy my goods. Especially when it comes to magical things.

He nods in understanding. We walk together to the front of the store. I look around and keep my eyes on the windows, making sure no one else walks in and sees me purchasing the items from Jake. After a few minutes, Jake hands me a small velvet pouch containing the Bazer and six small vials of potion. As I hand him the money, he tells me,

"Use them wisely, and pray we get more supplies. Good luck in whatever your mission is."

I thank him, hide the items inside a secret pocket in my jacket, and exit the shop.

I take a shortcut from Jake's shop to the Elder's district. Throughout my walk, my mind keeps going over what Jake told me, and I don't know what to make of it. As I round the corner at the end of the street, I see Cerene and Gideon talking and laughing. Gideon looks very annoyed as always. Cerene must have found a way to get under his skin. These two are always bickering and teasing each other, as if they were little kids. I swear, sometimes I look at Cerene as the bratty little girl I once knew, who thinks she can outtalk anyone about anything. Gideon is always so logical and critical. Some days, it is so entertaining and funny, but other days, they are just purely annoying. I instinctively reach for my necklace and fidget with it to keep my composure as I approach them.

"I'm glad I got here before you two started killing each other."

Gideon shrugs and Cerene just scoffs as she asks me, "So, do we get the pleasure of knowing why we were summoned by Your Highness? We are all geared up. What are we doing this time?"

I narrow my eyes at her as I bring out the potion and sack of Bazer from my jacket and dangle them in front of them. They both watch me with wide eyes.

I clear my throat and start telling them that these are going to be very rare to obtain. I fill them in on what Jake told me. I can see the horror on both of their faces because this may be the beginning of the end of our world, and our source of income. We are only able to survive from the money we get from these missions. If we don't have them, then what?

Our conversation is cut short when we see a group of armed guards coming and going through the street, then realize that there is unusual movement near the main Elder's villa. It's a place no longer occupied by anyone. It's there for their major meetings, or when there is some important event. We know better than to just stand around in this part of town. All it takes nowadays is one wrong look and you could get locked up. We decide to take higher ground on top of one of the buildings not too far away to see what's going on. It's absolutely useless. We can't seem to see anything from here. All the Elders that gathered make a quick dash into the main villa without wasting any time.

While crouching low, we come up with a plan to go inside and observe the situation. I'll infiltrate while Cerene and Gideon keep watch. I bring one of the potions out of my jacket, making sure I have the correct one before taking a sip from it, handing it to Cerene and then Gideon to do the same. With that, I give each of them one piece of Bazer—these precious little almond shaped golden seeds—for emergencies only. I ask them not to use it unless it is absolutely necessary.

We stay on top of the building, trying our best not to be spotted by the guards in front of the villa. The Elders haven't had a meeting in more than six months, yet this one seems to be a big gathering. We can see them coming in large groups; hundreds of them are going into the building. We haven't seen this in many years. This must be because of the loss of magic in the land. With the potion in each of our systems, we are able to mindlink with each other. We must find out what this meeting is about.

"I think we are onto something," I say into both of their minds. Mindlinking is exactly as it sounds. If I think about something, it will echo the same thought in others' minds. It takes practice to be able to do it correctly. People can take advantage of this power and use it to get into others' minds and alter their thoughts. If used with ill intent, one has the ability to drive a person into madness simply by trespassing on their inner thoughts again and again, altering minor things one brick at a time. We only use it for its more basic purpose—to talk into each other's mind without actually physically talking to each other. We use it often enough that we have learned to separate our innermost thoughts from the thoughts we want to project.

That's when Cerene's voice comes into our heads. "Boys! It looks like everyone is here."

Gideon and I hum in agreement.

"Cerene, please stick to the plan. Don't make a move. We are just scouting," I tell her as I hear her inhaling a deep breath. I can practically see her rolling her eyes at me. She was never a person who listened to anyone. She always channels all her anger at these missions, which sometimes means she strays from the original plan. It's always for a good reason, but is almost always reckless. We need to lay low. It isn't the time to stir shit up. We need to find out what they are hiding from our people.

I look at Gideon, then say, "Both of you stay put. I'm going in."
I give Gideon a look he knows too well, and he knows if I'm caught for any reason, he needs to get Cerene and leave.

I crawl slowly until I get to the other edge of the building, where there is a fire escape. I slowly lower myself to the side by shifting my legs, my body flush with the ladder. I start going down slowly, making sure there are no guards at the end of this street. I know Gideon and Cerene are both watching me and keeping an eye for anything that might come my way. Once my feet hit the ground, I start walking cautiously, looking in all directions while ducking behind the columns around the walls of the villa. I hold my necklace for good luck.

Relieved no one is on this street, I start moving fast alongside the wall. Once I'm at the end of the alley, Gideon and Cerene give me a signal through the mindlink that it's all clear for me to make a run for it to the opposite wall of the villa. I manage to scale the wall effortlessly, placing my foot between the bricks as I climb. I work out and train, because you never know when it'll come in handy. I've always stuck to my routine. I wake up early, work out, then go train. Most days, both Gideon and Cerene join me too.

Once I'm on the other side of the wall, I tell the others through our mindlink,

"Guys, I'm in." I make sure that my clothes are not dusty from the wall and walk normally. I try my best to blend in. I'm wearing the same black pants and black button down shirt all the guards are wearing and pretend I know where I'm going. I've been in this villa before. I've memorized its blueprints. I have a vivid memory as a child of walking the halls of this place. There is a big garden on both sides, a walkway with a shade on top of it, with wild blue and purple flowers flowing down the walkway as if it were a castle from a fairytale. It's like I'm walking under a waterfall of endless bloom with the sun peeking through the small spaces between them, giving the hallways a shimmering, colorful light. *Eterna is such a magical place.*

I concentrate on my mission and walk under the blossoming path to the end of the walkway. I find two doors, but I'm unsure which one to go through. I need to keep acting natural. As I come closer to the door on my left, I hear muffled sounds. Someone is in there talking. I look around to make sure there aren't any guards coming this way, then I rest my ear at the door and listen in.

There are lots of voices all talking at once. I'm sure I don't recognize any. The Elders and I don't exactly run in the same circles. It seems that the Elders are arguing. That's when one voice becomes louder than all of them, calling for silence. Everyone stops talking.

The voice continues. "We are here to find a solution. Stop your nonsensical debates about who is right and wrong."

A feminine voice rises. "You have one of the Vegas in your ranks. Why don't you get answers from him? he's one of the oldest bloodlines in Eterna. Ask him about the prophecy. You need to find out what we need to do, or we are all exposed."

Chaos erupts as the chatter in the room once again grows loud, and they begin complaining about not having their magic at full force and about their land dying.

All of a sudden, I hear Gideon's panicked voice. "Cerene, no." I huff. Typical Cerene. I wonder what she's up to now.

I move away from the door and start to turn around when I hear the sound of guards screaming something at each other. I start walking towards the chaos. "Gideon, what's going on?" His voice comes in and out. He seems like he's running. Then, he answers me between breaths.

"One minute she was right beside me on top of the building, and the next, she was jumping over the wall."

I know she's getting into trouble. She can never sit still for long, and that's something I can't stand about her. It was cute when she was younger, but now it's just annoying. I start running as a guard comes toward me, screaming orders to take my assigned place. He continues to tell me there is an intruder. I nod as if I'm one of them, then run back through the walkway, taking a left towards the wall I came from, looking for Cerene. Suddenly, someone clamps my shoulder, and I turn around ready to attack, when Cerene's face, with a mischievous smile, appears in front of me.

"Fuck! Why did you follow me?" I say angrily.

She raises her eyebrows at me and shrugs her shoulders. "Didn't want to miss the fun. What can I say? I needed a walk."

I quickly pull her behind one of the columns so we can't be seen and say, "Scale the damn wall. Guards are coming our way."

"Fine... fine, relax. I can handle the guards." She huffs back at me, but thankfully, I watch her as she starts to move up the wall, climbing as fast as she can.

I see her left foot slip as she loses balance, and out of nowhere, she falls hard to the ground next to me. I look at her with horror. *Did someone strike her with magic from above without me seeing?*

I hear the guards come closer to us. I let out a horrified scream through the link. "Gideon! We are in trouble. Where are you, brother?" It takes him a moment to respond to me.

"Above you." Before I can look up, with a loud *thud*, Gideon manages to land with a Zarka and scoop us from the ground. Carrying Cerene and holding her as tight as I can, we go airborne on the Zarka's back.

Flying away from the villa, Gideon turns his head to look at us.

"What the hell happened down there? Is she hurt?"

I take a deep breath, "I don't know, man. I don't think she's hurt, but she may be a little banged up from the fall. One minute she was scaling the wall, and the next, she was on the ground beside me. I think she's just unconscious." I try to calm myself, but I don't think I've ever been this scared for her safety. I tighten my thighs around the bird's body to keep myself balanced. Doing so while holding Cerene in my lap is not so easy. I've been there every time she has bitten off more than she can chew. We have been through many close calls on missions, from getting stuck in caves with no way out to being chased by guards, the list goes on. And with Cerene, it's a long list. But this... seeing her fall in front of my eyes is a whole new feeling. I've seen her climb thousands of walls with ease. You'd think she was born to do this. Losing her footing and falling doesn't make sense.

In the back of my head, I know something is not right with her. I take a deep breath as I try to ground myself. I attempt to speak with her through our mindlink, but I wait for a response that doesn't come. I draw my gaze away from Cerene for a moment, focusing on Gideon. "Gideon, please take us somewhere safe to check on her."

Chapter 12

Mia

Brookstone

I can almost feel my muscles expanding under the warmth of the water in the tub. I submerge my head to help quiet everything inside me until I feel pressure building in my lungs, threatening to suffocate me. I come up for air with a gasp. I get out, grab my robe, put it on slowly, and snuggle in the plush fabric. I'm still not feeling like myself, but the water did soothe my muscles. I close my eyes and inhale the soft lavender lingering in the air. Flashes of fire spring to my mind. I shake my head and look at my reflection in the mirror. I should be more concerned about what happened last night with the fire, but for some odd reason, I'm not. It almost feels like coming down from a high, the same feeling as getting off a rollercoaster—scared while you're on the ride, then the adrenaline kicks in, and when it's over, you miss it.

I step out of the bathroom, Natalie is sitting on my bed with a tray full of fresh fruits. On a plate lay a couple of triangular cheese sandwiches that she clearly just made. What beckons me is the steaming cups of tea. I smile and hustle to sit next to her. I immediately pick up the tea cup and smell the aroma I love so much.

"I adore that you know exactly what I need to calm down," I say with a slight smile.

She chuckles. "That's exactly why we are best friends."

We sit in silence for a few minutes, eating fruit and glancing at each other between bites. Natalie clears her throat.

"Are we going to address the elephant in the room?"

I burst out with a laugh. "If that elephant is the fire that came out of nowhere into my hands and didn't burn me, then sure let's address it."

"Mia, I'm serious. What happened last night was very wild. You were unconscious all night. I'm still trying to wrap my head around everything and can't come up with a logical explanation. That lady is deranged. It could be some kind of an illusion... and sh—"

I cut her off before she finishes her sentence.

"Natalie, that was no fucking illusion. I can still feel the fire. It's inside me, in my blood. I don't know how to explain it, but it is there."

She looks at me, realizing we can't just pretend this didn't happen, and that I'm not going to let this go. She lets out a loud sigh and leans in closer to hold my hand. I could almost swear I could see her brain fighting to make a logical explanation out of this.

"I take it you will go back to that place then?"

I nod as she squeezes my hand in understanding.

She presses her thin lips together before saying, "I'll call in sick and go with you." She pauses for a second and continues, as if surprising herself. "But I'm not happy about this. I'm terrified of what might happen moving forward. But you know I'll always support your decisions, no matter how wild they are. And I know, Mia. I know how hard it's been for you. We have been friends since we both can remember. I've seen you struggle. I know you have always wanted more. Since we were kids, you have been curious about everything, and it almost feels like life keeps disappointing you. It's like you have been searching for a grander part of this ordinary life."

I nod again and thank her, not bothering to argue. A tear pricks at the corner of my eye as gratitude swells in my chest for the person sitting across from me. Glancing at Natalie, my emotions are reflected in her face.

"I take it that asking you to stay behind is not an option?" I giggle through my tears.

"Not even if you beg," she answers as she leans over to give me a hug. With that, she stands from the bed, and picks up the tray.

"We should both get some sleep." She says as she walks out of my room and closes the door after herself.

I'm tossing and turning in my bed, trying to rest, but I'm unable to cool down enough to fall asleep. Slowly, my skin is warming up. I kick off my covers, feeling too sticky to bear them touching my skin any longer. My room is pitch dark, yet I see small sparks of light flying in the air, and I can't make out what they are. They look like small fireflies dancing in the night. I know there is no way there are fireflies in my room. They disappear and reappear with every blink of my eyes. I do that several times and it helps me relax; something about these tiny sparks comforts me. They dance in little patterns almost, as if they are communicating with something deep inside of me, and a sense of calm washes over me. I close my eyes and let sleep take over me.

I'm standing in a beautiful green garden that has a clearly defined brick walkway. The bricks on the archway are white and seem to be very old, like architecture from the Roman times. It is so stunning and it takes my breath away. A beautiful waterfall of flowers flowing down on each side of the archway. In the distance, I hear a feminine voice, a sweet melody, singing a tune that is so familiar, yet I can't recall where I've heard it before. Feeling the lush soft grass under my feet, that's when I realize I'm barefoot. Looking down at myself, I'm wearing my pajamas. The realization hits me that I'm in one of my dreams, so aware of my surroundings, feeling flustered, and with that, I suddenly wake up.

"Okay, this is new!"

Any hope of me falling back asleep is gone after that dream. Instead, I get up and work on another painting. I try to recreate the view from my dreams. I use what I can draw up from the memory to translate to my canvas. By the time I set my brush down, I hear Natalie yawning behind me.

"I hope you got some sleep before we go and face that woman." She laughs under her breath.

I turn to her. "That woman has answers I need. She can be different and all, but I must seek her out and try my best to understand what I need to know about my heritage."

She hums in agreement as she sniffs her cup of coffee. "Okay, I'll go change and get ready for the day."

I watch her disappear into her room, then glance back at my artwork. *It feels so familiar, yet I know for a fact I've never seen this place in my life.* With that thought in mind, I retreat to my room to get ready.

Chapter 13

Xavier

Eterna

The Zarka lands with a *thud* in a clearing close to the city, forming a cloud of dust around us. Gideon dismounts quickly and helps me with Cerene, who is still unconscious. I cradle her tight to my chest as I walk fast behind Gideon. He rushes ahead of me into the Healing House, shouting for someone to hurry. Moments later, he returns with a short, older man who I assume is the healer. I follow them inside, and a young woman guides me to an examination room. In the dimly lit space, I lay Cerene down on a narrow bed with crisp, clean white sheets.

I step back and look at her, and if you didn't know any better, you'd think she's just sleeping. Time seems to slow down, and my anxiety builds as I wait. I can't help but notice my hands are shaking. I tuck them behind me just as Gideon and the healer walk into the examination room, having finished the registration paperwork.

The healer looks at me and I nod in greeting. Observing his white, long beard, tanned skin and bright green eyes. His white coat makes him look like an angel.

"What happened here?"

Gideon and I answer in unison. "We don't really know."

I clear my throat. "One minute she was standing; the next, she fell to the ground."

He places his hand on her wrist, then brings the stethoscope to her chest and listens to her heart. He turns to his table of supplies and grabs a cotton pad, then adds a bit of smelling salts to it. He brings it close to her face. She starts to stir and slowly opens her eyes. The healer smiles.

"Hello, young lady. Are you okay? It seems that you just fainted. How are you feeling?"

She blinks. "Who are you?"

"My name is Noah and I'm a healer."

I step close to the bed. "Cerene, you scared the hell out of me. What happened?"

"I'm fine, don't worry. It's nothing." She looks at me and shrugs.

"It's not nothing!" I snap at her, then close my eyes and take a deep breath in frustration. I don't want to raise my voice at her, but I just wish she'd for once understand the seriousness of the situation.

Noah asks her, "Has this happened before? Can you explain what you're feeling?"

I keep assessing her, looking for injuries. I see her bite her lower lip and try to look anywhere but at me. I know that she's hiding something. I know her too well. Cerene is amazing at many things, but lying isn't one of them. She has the most obvious tells. like avoiding eye contact and biting her lips. Classic Cerene.

She answers Noah. "No. It never has, and I feel fine."

Her answer fuels my anger, and I look toward Gideon to see him watching the interaction between her and the healer with disbelief. Noah asks her a couple more questions about her breathing, her eating habits, and daily routine. He tells her to come back if she feels bad again and asks her to rest for a couple of days and eat well.

We leave the Healing House, and I'm fuming. Cerene is hiding something from me, and I don't know why. Does she not trust me anymore? Did she suddenly turn twenty-one and think she's too old to talk to her older brother? All three of us make our way back from the healer's place on foot. We walk in silence. I only occasionally turn and check if Cerene is okay while she rolls her eyes and huffs at me, until Gideon wraps his arm around her.

"You scared us back there. I thought you were going to kick the bucket before us." They both start laughing like it's a joke. I stop in front of them, looking at them until they can see the rage in my eyes.

"I just want you to answer one question. Why were you lying back there? This has happened before, hasn't it?"

She starts to bite her lip, and I cut her off. "No. No, Cerene. We are not doing that. Your shitty lying skills worked on the healer, but not on me!"

She opens her mouth and closes it again and mumbles, "Yes, it happened. It's nothing."

I chuckle in disbelief. "Nothing? That wasn't nothing!"

I slightly lower myself so that my face is close to hers and lock eyes with her, invading her personal space.

"You're my little sister. It is a fact that you seem to have forgotten over the last couple of weeks. Everything that happens to you, you brush off as nothing. First, your magic is fading, and now, God knows what you're keeping from me. I'll say this now, and I hope you don't forget it. It's not nothing and it matters! So start explaining."

She lifts her face in defiance and looks at me with her beautiful, big brown eyes.

"Look, so I fainted once before this after my birthday. I was coming out of the shower and I fell in my room. It's no big deal. I feel fine. I probably just need more sleep." With that, she places her hands on my chest and shoves me away.

"Let me be. If at any point I feel unwell, you will know about it. I want to go home."

"Come on, guys," Gideon starts, trying to defuse the situation. I know he's going to try to ask us to go out and do something fun. He's playing his role as the peacemaker, which he's usually successful at, but I snap at him.

"Can't you see she's being childish?"

Cerene lets out a bitter laugh. "Childish, huh? I'm not childish. You're just an overprotective, annoying dick at times. Stop suffocating me. I know you love me. I know I'm your sister. But even brothers let their sisters live their lives. When I need you, I'll tell you. We went on a mission and I fainted. Big deal. Please get over yourself. We have more pressing matters at hand." She's practically screaming the words at me now. She throws her hands up in the air and turns around, heading to our apartment.

I feel Gideon's hand clasp my shoulder. "Let's go home, brother. People are looking at us."

I look around and realize he's right. We are at the edge of the market, and passersby are looking at us with speculating eyes as they make their way to their shopping. I know he's right, but I'm too worked up to care. I back down and remove Gideon's hand from my shoulder. I leave him standing alone as I head in the direction of our apartment using a shortcut. I need to be alone for a little bit.

I arrive home before them and head straight to my room. I grab my guitar from the corner where I always keep it, then let my body fall on the bed, trying to think back on the day's events. I strum the strings. *She made me lose my temper.* This woman has a way of bringing out the ugly side of me. She doesn't ever seem to understand how much I worry about her. Regardless of everything that happens in our lives, we always manage to be honest with each other. When did she start hiding things from me? It's not the time to fight.

All the things I heard on our mission are stressing me out. If the Elders are trying to seek help from a Vega, then it must be serious. I haven't heard of that family in a long time—well, at least for the past twenty years. I was too young to remember, but from what I know, there isn't anyone still alive from that family line. If this is true, then they would be the only ones who hold answers. They were the oldest family that ever lived in Eterna; they were royalty. There were stories about a prophecy. My thoughts are interrupted by the sound of a soft knocking on my door.

I turn towards the door, Cerene has already let herself in and is standing there against the now closed door with her arms on her hips, looking at me.

"Uh-oh. Not the guitar! Someone is stressed."

I raise my brows. "How can this overprotective dick assist you?" I ask, throwing her words from earlier back at her as I put the guitar on the floor next to the bed. She takes a couple of steps, then I feel the bed dip next to me as she comes to lay beside me.

We are side by side now, looking at the old ceiling. I start to fidget with the necklace around my neck.

"Does this infuriating man know how much I love him?" Cerene asks as I feel her eyes lock on my necklace. "Because some days, he just acts like an idiot and forgets that I'm an adult and no longer a little girl."

I chuckle. "Fair point."

"You know, some days I envy you that you have a piece of your mother with you. I wish I had something. Anything to tie me back to a family." She says the words like a whisper, almost as if she regrets saying them. I revert the conversation back to today, because I feel guilty that she doesn't have something like this necklace. It's something that I often think about, and as much as I love having something that ties me back to my mother, it sometimes feels like a betrayal to Cerene that I can't answer any questions about her family. I don't want to have this conversation with her now, at the risk of pushing her even further away from me.

"You know I worry all the time. Seeing you like that was sobering, to say the least. I haven't forgotten that you have grown into an adult. On the contrary, Cerene. I'm so beyond proud to see you grow into the woman that you are today. You've always been so strong-willed and stubborn, but that only assured me that you can take care of yourself. You being unconscious today actually just reminded me of how mortal we can be. And I won't lie, that scared the shit out of me. So maybe cut this man some slack?"

Her eyes soften. "Slack has been cut." she says and continues, asking, "So... what did you find out on the mission, and what did I miss?"

I turn my head to face her, her eyes lighten with mischief as she anticipates my words. "We will need a way to get to the Elders to find out more about the Vega family."

She sits up abruptly, looking at me in horror. "I thought they were all dead."

"So did I."

Chapter 14

Mia

Brookstone

Natalie and I lock our door and start descending the stairs. As soon as our feet hit the pavement, we freeze. Across the street, standing perfectly still, is Hyda. She's already watching us. The sounds around us fall silent, even the wind seems to fade. Everything narrows to her. Her cloak shifts slightly in the breeze, the hem brushing the ground like it's meant to be silent. Her eyes lock onto us, unreadable but sharp, like she's been waiting. Natalie turns to me and mumbles,

"What the hell?"

I lock eyes with Hyda. I know she came to explain. I cross the street and Natalie follows, until we're face-to-face with her. She looks tired. The dark circles under her eyes indicate that she didn't sleep. I open my mouth to ask her what she's doing here, but before I can say a word, she starts to explain.

"My dear child, I'm sorry I frightened you girls the other night. That was never my intention. I need to explain. I'm here to protect you. Nothing more, nothing less. I mean you no harm. My duty is to you, and I pledged my life to your family's service long before you were born. Please let me explain and teach you all I know."

She stands there in front of me, pleading with her eyes as she waits for me to answer. I can't help seeing the sincerity in her words. Now, in the light of day, I see the truth in her eyes. She isn't someone to fear. Sure, she's definitely odd in the way she dresses and how she carries herself. At first glance, she looks like she's wearing clothes similar to the ones people wear at the renaissance fair, but studying her more, she's wearing black pants and a wide black blouse, and a leather corset that has some daggers strapped to her sides. It's all hidden under a black, hooded cloak. I see now why she looked so much like a shadow in the dark. Yet, there's elegance and confidence in her stance.

"Okay." That's all I can muster to say.

Natalie is standing next to me, questioning my answer with a look, but I don't pay her any attention.

Hyda nods. "It would be my honor, my child. Come to my shop when you're ready."

She starts to walk away but stops in her tracks as I say, "I'm ready now." I can see the surprise on her face.

"Very well then."

I turn to Natalie. "I need to do this, but I understand if this is all too much for you. You can walk away now and I'll still love you all the same. You don't have to come with me."

"But I want to," she answers with a certainty that lets me know there was never a chance she'd do otherwise.

I nod and then we both follow Hyda back to her shop.

The minute we enter the shop, Hyda takes us to the back of the store to an area I didn't see before. In the shadows of the night, it was invisible to the naked eye.

Hyda pushes the door open, and it makes the squeaky sound of old hinges that need to be oiled. She switches the light on as she enters the room. Once inside, I find it's a big, well-lit room. On one side, there are cabinets with glass doors housing different sized daggers and a few grenades made of glass with blue glowing liquid in them. What catches my eye is one medium-sized dagger that is purposely placed alone on display on the top shelf. Its silver shines, as if it is polished every day. It has designs of the phases of the moon on the hilt. The top of the hilt is a beautiful ruby that looks like a cherry on top. I can't help but feel how familiar it looks, but I don't recall where I've seen it. Shaking the thought away, I turn to the other side of the room to see it has a small wooden bench and a small table.

I turn around and see Hyda assessing me. "What is this place?" I ask her.

"It's where I used to do my training every morning, but I haven't been in this room for quite some time now." She gestures to the corner where the table is. "Would you like to sit? I need to tell you the rest of the story."

I find Natalie next to me, and I grab her hand as we make our way to the bench. We sit together, listening to Hyda as she continues her story.

"You won't believe me until you see it," she says quietly, eyes distant. "Eterna is a place of wonder. The danger of losing it is catastrophic. It's a land that glows with vibrant energy. You will see colors of bloom and stars like you have never seen before. The land itself is made of magic as I explained to you before. I want you to know that you come from a great line of royal blood. Your presence is crucial to save it all. Your duty is to embrace your power and own it. I must teach you how to control it. That's the only way I can help. I'll answer anything you need. You have to believe me, I'm not here to misguide you."

If I'm honest with myself, I've always wanted my life to be a little more than ordinary. I've felt it simmering under my skin, but I still couldn't have imagined what she told us. Me, a child born to a royal family in a magical place, holding the power to make the balance right and save a land I've never been to and the people who live there. I don't fully understand the depth of the whole story just yet. Hyda is my guardian and was unable to go back to Eterna without me. My birth parents might not be alive because she hasn't seen them since the night they gave me to her. And now, it's up to me to go back. To save our land, like she said. If it wasn't for Natalie sitting next to me, I'd think I was hallucinating.

"You might've been feeling a bit strange, your magic will keep pushing your body to its limit till you start wielding it." she presses her lips and continues, "or the alternative, which is not good. Someone might be trying to draw your magic away and steal it. Only people from Eterna can try to do that."

I stare at her in disbelief. *My magic.* How crazy is that? It's been dormant, and I had no idea I possessed it. This already has me feeling defensive and terrified. Who would want to do that? *How can I feel scared to lose something I didn't know I had?*

Natalie sits there with me in disbelief at what she's hearing. I can't blame her. I'm struggling with all of this, and I'm the impulsive and irrational one. I think her logical, practical brain is about to burst at the seams. It doesn't help that she doesn't trust Hyda one bit either.

"We will meet here every day for a couple of hours to train you, Mia." Hyda puts a plan in place. "Remember, child. You can't tell a soul about your magic. The world doesn't know magic exists, and we have to keep it that way." With that, Hyda concludes the conversation. I nod

"Got it. Not a soul." *Not even my parents.* That realization breaks my heart a little.

Chapter 15

Xavier

Eterna

It's been a week since our last mission. We've been racking our brains to come up with a plan to get back in the Elders' Castle without getting caught. We've used every resource we had, yet we came up empty-handed, which leads to why I'm sitting under an old abandoned bridge. It's dark and cold. As I walk to blend into the shadows, I swear I'm stepping on some kind of carcass because the air around me is a noxious mix of sewage and death. This is the last lead that may be useful before we hit a dead end. You'd think I'd be immune to such surroundings and that I've seen everything in my life at this point, but this place still gives me the creeps.

My attention shifts to the opposite side of where I'm standing as I hear slow, light footsteps approaching. I take a careful, measured step forward, trying to assess whether this is the person I'm supposed to meet. Then, a low, rough voice echoes from the shadows asking the secret question.

"Why do you come?"

"To light what's dark." I answer.

"You're seeking entrance to the Elders' Castle?"

"Yes. Can you help me?" I approach the figure until there are only a few feet between us. My eyes have already adjusted to the dark, but the man in front of me is cloaked in black. He's short and I can't make out his features, but I can tell that he's an old man. He has a cane to help him walk. He hands me an envelope.

"Here's a map of the castle. Be very careful. This is a dangerous task you're seeking."

I pocket the envelope and thank him, but before I can say anything else, he's gone. I make my way back out of this dump. It's a nice feeling to come out of the dark into the fresh night air.

As I head back home, I take in how beautiful this night is and how the city of Eterna is illuminated with a beautiful golden glow. Memories of my mother rush through my head. There are days where I just miss her and try to recall whatever little things that have stuck with me throughout the years. I miss the days where she used to come home late from work and take me up on our rooftop to look at the city. She'd tell me all sorts of stories about magic and the blessings we were given to be part of this land. The stories of her training, becoming a general and a warrior to protect Eterna and our people, is what used to fascinate me the most. I can't remember everything in detail, but I remember the feeling of how she used to make me laugh and look forward to another day of her stories.

At the end of each night, she'd hold me in her arms until it was time to send me to bed. With a frustrating ache in my chest, I say out loud to absolutely no one, "Where have you been, Mother? What kept you from me all these years?" Those questions never seem to leave my mind, no matter how hard I try to move on. I hold my necklace and lift it. The cool feel of glass and metal grazes my lips as I kiss it and whisper a prayer to see my mother one day. The night is so quiet. My only companion is the sound of crunching pebbles under my boots as I continue my walk home.

Happy with what I acquired from tonight's contact, I run up the stairs to our home two steps at a time. I open the old rustic wood door to a dark living room. Laughing, I shout, "Children, I'm home." I've always teased them with this since I'm the oldest. Cerene peeks out of her door with disheveled hair, as if she was pulling on it. Gideon comes out of his room rubbing his eyes. It seems that I've woken him from sleep. They both trudge to the living room.

Yawning, Cerene asks, "Was your last lead beneficial?"

I nod and that seems to sober them up. They both look at me, eyes wide open, anticipating my next words. I pull the map from my pocket and wave it in the air. "We have a map of the whole castle. We'll need to craft a very good plan because we are going in to investigate."

"Yes! Now we are talking. Some good old action," Cerene says excitedly, as if I just told a child I have candy.

Gideon, on the other hand, reaches for the map in my hand, ready to inspect it.

I stop him by pulling the map out of his reach. "Not tonight. Sorry I woke you up, but I couldn't keep this to myself, we all needed this news. Now that we have this map, we all need clear minds in the morning to plan something solid. Let's all get some rest. I hand the map to Gideon because I know he will want to look at it first thing in the morning. I say goodnight to them both. They go back to their rooms as I close my own bedroom door.

Come morning, the sun is high up in the sky and hitting my face through my window. I've always loved to sleep with the window open. At night, I hear the owls hoot and during the day, I hear the birds chirp. It is something my mother had me get used to doing. She taught me how to listen and focus on my surroundings. Sometimes, it calmed me and other times, it alerted me when there was danger coming. I drag myself out of bed and grab my dark green towel from the hook hanging behind the door before opening it. Gideon is already up and inspecting the map he has placed on the table. I mumble "good morning."

He just waves his hand while he keeps his eyes glued to the map, fully engrossed in studying it. I head to the bathroom quietly to take a quick shower and get ready for the day. Once inside, I turn the faucet on and let the hot water run for a minute, letting the steam fill the room while I take off my clothes. I step in the shower and let the water slide down my body as I just tilt my head back to enjoy the feeling. I grab the shampoo to find it empty, so I reach for the soap instead and start lathering up my body and hair. Once I'm satisfied that I'm all clean and fresh, I step out of the shower. As I start drying my hair, Cerene's knock on the door is followed by her grumbling. "Aren't you done in there? You know there are other people who want to use the bathroom, too."

"Almost done." The moment I open the door, she shoves past me and practically kicks me out as she slams the door.

I let out a laugh and shake my head at her childish behavior. Gideon laughs from behind me and says, " morning grump."

"She wouldn't be Cerene if we didn't have to deal with her attitude." I say as I reach to open my bedroom door, I hear him respond.

"As long as she doesn't drown us in our sleep." Then he turns his attention back to the map.

I crouch behind the crumbling stone wall, map in hand, dirt streaked across my hands. We've been running around for hours, mapping the grounds and studying everything that surrounds the Elders' Castle. It's a mess of blind spots and patrols, and it's wearing on both of us.

"It's a complicated mission," I mutter, mostly to myself. Gideon glances over, sweat glistening at his brow despite the shade.

"Every damn entrance is crawling with guards."

He's not wrong. I scan the outer walls through a narrow gap in the brush. Each gate is sealed tight, reinforced by layers of magic. No way we're getting in that way. I look back at the map, tracing the faded lines that wind beneath the castle like veins. There, an underground passage, all tunnels, snaking beneath the main structure and branching into different wings.

"That's our way in," I whisper, tapping the parchment.

"Assuming it still exists," Gideon says.

I sit back on my heels. The truth is, we still don't know what we're even looking for. If the Elders are hiding the Vega family, where would they keep them? Where do we start? The castle is massive. If we try to search every corner, we'll burn out long before we find anything.

"We can't do this alone," I say quietly. "We need to narrow down where the information is. Which rooms are worth the risk." Gideon nods, eyes narrowing as he thinks. Flying in on a Zarka is out of the question. We'd be spotted before we even hit the ground. No one goes to the Elders' Castle anymore. There was a time when the townspeople came here freely, for guidance, for healing. Now? No one's allowed in. The Elders have locked themselves away, drunk on their own power. They don't care what happens to us.

They shut the gates years ago. Anyone who gets close is imprisoned. All that remains are the drop points, impersonal boxes where citizens leave their pleas, their pain. And no one answers. I shake my head.

"We have two choices. One, we disguise ourselves as guards, try to bluff our way in." Gideon raises an eyebrow.

"And two?"

"We take the tunnels. It's a gamble, but if we don't try... we may never know what the Elders are hiding. Or what they're planning. Something's happening to the magic, to Eterna itself. If the Vega family is still alive and imprisoned..." I trail off.

"And if the tunnels lead nowhere?"

I fold the map, sliding it into my pocket. "Then everything we've done is for nothing. Another dead end."

Silence hangs between us for a beat too long. Then Gideon straightens.

"Tunnels. We take the tunnels." There's conviction in his voice now, and I cling to it. The passages don't appear guarded, and they're ancient, we're guessing no one knows they exist. If it wasn't for the map, we wouldn't have known they are even there. I glance toward the castle one last time before we slip into the brush to head back home.

I sit alone on the sandy brick rooftop of our building. It's a place I like to hide away when I'm thinking. As I hold my hourglass necklace and look at the starry night above me, I wonder why we are putting ourselves in danger to go face-to-face with the Elders. Then, I have to remind myself that Cerene's magic is at stake. We simply don't know what will happen to her if her magic is lost. There are old tales we were told as kids, stories about the Elders, how they slowly lose their magic, how it fades until they grow weak, sick, and eventually die. Just thinking about it makes my heart pound. I can't let that happen to Cerene. We have to keep going. We have to see this mission through and get to the bottom of what's really happening.

Chapter 16

Mia

Brookstone

The first day of training is rough. I stand in the training room agitated and pretty much annoyed. My arms ache. My jaw is tight. I raise my hands again, fingers trembling, trying to conjure something, just a flicker, a spark, anything, but nothing happens.

"Again," Hyda says from the corner of the room. She's seated on a simple wooden bench, arms crossed over her chest. Looking at me, observing how my body moves, and that look in her eyes says she's seen more battles than I can imagine.

"I'm trying," I mutter, heat rising in my face, though it has nothing to do with my fire.

"Trying won't help you when it's real, trying doesn't stop the Elders from hurting you."

I turn to face her, frustration spilling out of me. "I don't know what you want me to do! It won't come when I ask. It hurts. I feel it, I just don't know what to do to bring it to life"

She watches me in silence for a beat. Then she stands and walks over, her boots tapping steadily across the wood floors.

"You think I don't know what that's like? To have something inside you that you can't control? I may not be magical, but I've helped your mother before. Everyone struggles with their magic when it is awakened. You need to concentrate and control it in your mind first. Then will it to life. Now try again."

I look down at my shaking hands. "This doesn't feel like a gift, It feels like something I'm not supposed to have."

She nods slowly. "Most power feels like that at first."

I glance at her, searching her face for mockery, but there's none. Just that steady calm she wears like armor. She kneels beside me, lowering her voice.

"I'm not here to make you feel safe. I'm here to make sure you survive this. And you will, but you need to stop fighting yourself."

I clench my fists, then release them. "It's easier said than done."

"Everything worth doing is," she says. "You think I was comfortable the first time I held a blade? I nearly took my own ear off."

Despite myself, I let out the smallest laugh.

"There it is," she says, with the hint of a smile. "You're not a weapon. You're just someone who hasn't learned how to hold the fire without letting it hold you." I nod, slowly. She's right, even if I don't want to admit it.

"Now," she says, standing again and backing up a few steps, "one more time. No fear. No forcing. Just focus."

I square my stance, take a breath, and close my eyes. The heat comes, not wild, not angry, but quieter this time. Like it's listening. Like maybe, it wants to be understood. Then I feel it. Once I open my eyes, the flame is sitting in my palm, dancing as if waiting for me to command it. I smile, turning to look at Hyda who has the biggest grin on her face.

"And that is the lesson for the day. Get some rest, we'll try again tomorrow.

The next day is the same, training early in the morning. I go back home, eat, and paint.

Now, I'm lying on the couch, eyes closed for just a minute, needing a break before I head to the shower for the night.

Darkness engulfs me. I blink a couple of times. Stars surround me, bright and brilliant, scattered across the sky. My hair dances in the wind as it brushes against my face. I'm standing in the middle of a beautiful field. Even in the dark, the flowers glow with vivid colors. I take a deep breath, savoring the air and the sweet, earthy smell of everything around me. It feels like I've stepped into a heavenly place. Then I hear it, the soft crunch of grass. I turn.

The same man from my dreams is there, perched against a tree about ten feet away. I feel his eyes on me. Watching, but just like always, I can't see his face. The tree's branches cast shadows that block my view. I take a few slow steps toward him...

Then I jolt upright with a gasp as Natalie closes the door to our apartment.

"Damn it," I mutter, wiping the sweat off my face.

She sets her bag down immediately and hurries over. "Hey, another dream?" she sits beside me without hesitation. I nod, still catching my breath. Without a word, she reaches for the blanket draped over the back of the couch and wraps it around my shoulders. Her hand rubs slow circles across my back, grounding me.

"Are you okay? Do you need anything?" Her voice is soft, her brow furrowed with concern.

"I'm fine, don't worry," I force a small smile. "It was just another dream. And it wasn't a bad one."

She doesn't press me. She never does. Just listens, as I tell her what I saw, the stars, the glowing field, and the man near the tree. I ramble a bit, piecing it together as I speak, and she stays right there through all of it, nodding. When I finally trail off, she nudges me gently.

"You know, you could be a dream chronicler with the way you describe these."

I laugh under my breath. "Maybe in another life." I rise to my feet, finally ready for that shower. As I head to my room, I pause in the doorway and glance back at her.

"Hey, I left you some food in the oven."

Her face lights up, already pulling her shoes off.

"Thanks. You're the best."

"No," I say, with a tired but honest grin. "You are."

I stop counting the days of training. They all blur together now, one after the other, carved from the same schedule and stitched with the same aches. Every morning begins the same. Hyda is already waiting in the training room when I arrive, standing near the far wall with her arms crossed and that unreadable look on her face. We've had enough time to bond. She's not as odd as I first thought, not once you get to know her. Her gruffness hides something warmer, something real.

The training starts with pushups. Always pushups. My arms burn before I hit twenty, but I push through because I know she's watching. Next come the daggers. She's placed two worn targets on the far wall, wooden boards, battered and cracked from years of use. I throw the blades over and over again. Sometimes they stick, sometimes they clatter to the ground. Every time I miss, she doesn't scold me. She just says,

"Again."

Then we move into close combat, maneuvers to disarm, to block, to hold my ground. I'm terrible at it. My movements are too slow, too stiff. I flinch when I shouldn't and hesitate when I need to strike. I can see the frustration tighten in Hyda's jaw, but she never yells. She just circles me like a wolf, corrects my stance, and says,

"Start over."

After that, it's time for the part I both dread and crave: magic. Even though Hyda has no magic, somehow, she still knows how to help me find it. She teaches me to quiet my thoughts, to breathe, to feel for something inside me. It doesn't always work. My hands stay cold. My mind stays loud. It takes a couple of tries till the flame answers. It flickers to life, small, shaky, but real. I stare at it in awe, I'm still not used to it no matter how many times I summon it. Hyda just nods, a satisfied look on her face.

It's all so much to adjust to. My body aches constantly, shoulders tight, legs sore, fingers bruised from gripping too hard or blocking too slow. I've always been active, but never like this. This is survival, discipline, transformation. We end every session with jumping jacks and more pushups. By the time Hyda is done with me, I'm drenched in sweat, starving, and dreaming of nothing but a hot shower and a quiet bed.

Some days are harder than others. Some days, I want to quit. My arms ache, my legs feel like jelly, and my patience wears thin. But Hyda never lets me fall too far into frustration. Her dedication is relentless, it keeps me grounded. During water breaks or while we stretch, she talks. Not always, but when I need it most.

"You know," she says one morning as I collapse onto the mat, "your mother used to fall flat on her face during training too."

I glance up at her, panting. "You're lying."

Hyda smirks. "Wouldn't dare. She once tripped over her own feet during a footrace and knocked over two spectators like bowling pins."

I let out a tired laugh. "That sounds... strangely believable."

"She was stubborn, even though royal women don't typically train in Eterna, but she always attended combat training with me." Hyda says, leaning back against the wall. "Thought she could outfight her exhaustion. Sound familiar?"

I roll my eyes. "Okay, fine. Maybe a little."

She tells me more, small things, moments that feel like pieces of another life. Stories about my biological mother and father, how the three of them used to sneak into the training hall after hours to practice or play pranks on the instructors. I listen closely, hanging on every detail. She tells them like they're fairy tales, full of laughter, rebellion, and wild-hearted adventure. Every time, her eyes drift, just a little. She stares past me like she's watching something I can't see, something long gone.

"Do you miss them?" I ask quietly.

She doesn't answer right away. Then nods.

"Every day."

It's quiet for a moment, the air between us thick with everything unspoken.

"I wish I knew them."

"You're more like them than you realize."

I don't know her well, not yet. But I'm starting to. There's a softness in her that she hides beneath all that discipline and sharpness. It shows in moments like this, in the way she talks about my parents, in the way she shows up every day, without magic, without obligation, just to help me become someone stronger. And for that I can't help but love her for it. I know she says she swore her life to protect mine, but that was ages ago.

I know it's only been a short time since I met her, but I can feel her care for me. There were days I fell asleep on her couch after a long day of training, only to wake up covered with a soft blanket and a plate of cookies and water on the small side table. Those little things made me smile. The more I saw her, the more she started to act like a loving mother who really cared about my well-being and safety. A few days ago, I brought my blanket back. I asked her about the stitching and the letter C. At first, she hesitated but then revealed that it was my initial. It stands for Celestia. My real name. The name my biological parents gave me the day I was born. I was so overwhelmed with emotion and didn't know what to do with that information. When I got home that day, I sobbed until I fell asleep.

Today I'm distracted, splayed on Hyda's floor as sweat covers my body.

"I don't know if I'm cut out for this training. I'm not one to back down from a challenge, but I haven't slept well and I'm tired."

"You will continue your training to build the muscles you need before we have to go to Eterna. I don't know what kind of danger you will be facing. The prophecy was not clear about that. Why aren't you sleeping well?" she asks me from the corner of the training room.

"Besides the constant disturbing dreams, flashes of light around the streets, and..."

I'm cut off by Hyda's reaction. She drops all the daggers that she was training me with in a loud *clunk* on the floor. "Flashes of light! What kind of light?"

I dust my pants off and stand up, "I don't know. Some days, it's a blinding light, other days, it's like a ripple in the distance, or sometimes objects around me just seem to have a glowing halo around them. I can't really explain it. It could be my imagination or something wrong with my eyes."

"No… No… No… We are running out of time. We have to leave. We have to go to Eterna. This is bad. Really, really bad." Hyda is talking to herself again. Mentioning the flashes of light clearly has triggered her.

"Hyda, what's going on? You're mumbling."
She turns to me, eyes wide open. I didn't think her eyes could look any bigger than they already are.

"Make haste, my child. We have to go to Eterna as soon as possible. Go home, prepare yourself, and meet me back here in two days. Take care of your life here. Inform your parents that you're going on a trip. Make sure no one is left worrying about you while we are gone. I'll be waiting for you."

She leaves me standing there, sweaty and out of breath. Bewildered, I gather my things.

On my way home, I call Natalie.

"Hey, I have an update. I'm leaving for Eterna in two days."

"WHAT?" Natalie screeches. "Are you insane? I thought you were training and still have time."

"Apparently not. I was telling Hyda about having dreams and seeing flashes of light, then she just flipped out and said we have to leave."

"Okay, I'll meet you at home in an hour."

After I hang up with Natalie, I call mom and dad, but no one answers, so I leave them a message to call me back.

Chapter 17

Freya

Eterna's Prison

I place my fingers between the cracked tiles of the prison cell. I've moved and broken these tiles years ago to access the earth underneath it—willing all my power to feel my children's magic. I've done this every day for the past twenty-one years. It has always been the same as today. A very faint wave of magic comes through my body, but nothing significant that tells me they are alive and well, or even if they are actually here in Eterna. I let out a groan and sit back on the old worn out bed with sheets that have turned yellow with time and pillows that long ago lost their defined, fluffy form. A luxurious prison considering all the other ones. A special treatment for who we were.

Silas glances at me. "Keep trying," he says in a hushed voice.

I look at him with rage running through my veins. "This is all your doing. It has always been your fault. That damn plan was not crafted well enough. What if... What if we lost our babies?" A sob escapes me. It's a question I've asked him a million times now. My dreams of ever seeing them, holding them again are long gone. I've waited year after year, full moon after full moon, hoping and praying to the highest power out there to bring them back to me, but to no avail.

Silas rushes to me. "Honey, we did what we thought was needed to keep them safe. Remember, they would've taken them away, too. They were the prophesied babies." He talks to me as if I've lost my mind and can't remember what happened.

He places his hand on my back, making slow circular motions to soothe me. He can't know how a mother's pain runs so deep. With every day that passes by, I grieve that I didn't get to hold them, didn't see their first smile or first steps... So many missed opportunities and milestones. Everyday, I think my tears will dry, but they still fall until I have no power to cry anymore. I don't think anything will take away the ache that resided in my heart the moment I handed them to Hyda.

I remind him, "I don't have magic, Silas. I can only sense it and draw it to me to feel their well-being, and I haven't been able to do that at all."

He stands up and asks me to try again as he walks around the small cell .

I go back to my corner of broken tiles, taking in my familiar surroundings of the worn out paint on the walls and a small rusted faucet in the corner where we wash up every day. A small window that lets in the sun's rays in the daytime and the moonlight in the night, my only source to the outside world. I'm just thankful we have a small door in the cell that separates the restroom from where we sleep. I go back to my task and dig my fingers in the dirt, close my eyes and try to channel the magic into the earth and focus on the bond I have with my babies. Minutes pass by and I keep drawing magic to me to sort through it, looking for their power.

My memories go back to that wretched day, the day the rebellion decided they had had enough loss. The day they decided they no longer wanted to wait for a change and took matters into their own hands. Silas said we would be okay, but he was so wrong. I see it now. Hyda was supposed to take the kids to safety through a portal so no one would detect them and their magic, but only for a couple of days and then come back for us. Instead, the Elders found us accomplices to the rebellion. They locked us up and forced Silas to work for them. People think we are dead. Little did they know, we have the prophecy still hidden. They would come and take Silas every day to help them figure out what was happening to Eterna like an errand dog. I hate all of it. They can't kill us because we're the last of our bloodline. We know too much precious history and information. As for the rebellion, they all went into hiding, and whoever was captured that day faced horrible punishments. I resent waking up and breathing not knowing where my precious girls are. My anger makes me dig my fingers deeper in the crooks of the earth, feeling hard stones go under my fingernails.

I snap my eyes open as I feel a strong wave of magic crash through my body. I don't just feel it, I can smell the power. Its sweet scent, accompanied by vibrant colors of purples, blues and reds. Joy floods through me. I know what this means. A ripple of power blasts through all Eterna.

Silas comes barreling toward me, yelling, "What did you do?" The next thing I feel are his hands holding my arms, shaking me. "Freya. What did you do?"

I look him straight in the eye. "Nothing. They are finally here, Silas. My babies are here. I can feel them." I sob the last of my words, not believing I've finally sensed them for the first time in twenty-one years. A speck of hope ignites inside me.

Chapter 18

Xavier

Eterna

We are armed to the teeth, wearing our scouting gear, along with black jackets that help us strap most of our daggers and weapons to our backs, legs, and arms. We didn't want to waste our limited supply of Bazer to feed the Zarka to fly us to our destination, so we simply decided to leave our home before sunrise and walk to the Elders' Castle. After lots of sneaking around and surveilling the castle, we crafted a plan the best we could. We agreed that the tunnels would be our best route. We kept an eye on the guards, knowing exactly when the next rotation would be. They were very efficient. They change guards every hour, and there are fifteen minutes left until the next rotation. All we need to do is slip by with a distraction in place. There are four guards posted. Two at the entrance gate and two on the side where the tunnels are. If you didn't know the tunnels actually existed, you'd think that the guards are just resting or taking a break from their shift on the side wall of the castle entrance.

Gideon and I keep watch of the guards while Cerene is gathering her magical power, preparing a gigantic water ball to throw at the ones near the main gate. I see her flexing both of her hands in front of her, bringing one up with her palm facing the sky as she summons water. First, a couple of drops appear as she wills them to grow in her palm. With her other hand, she's making circular motions on top of the hand holding the now small ball of liquid, coaxing it to grow. She continues her motions for a couple of minutes. I never tire of watching her, mesmerized and in awe of what she can do. As of late, her magic has not been as strong, and I see the toll it's taking on her every time she uses it. I see the smirk on her satisfied face once she's happy with how she has crafted that giant ball of water. She's taking her ready stance, pulling her hands backwards and pushing with all her might, throwing that water at the guards. The moment she hurls it at them, a giant wave rushes at them as if it was a raging wave of the sea. They cower back, not knowing what to do as they scream in surprise.

The other two at the entrance of the tunnels run to see what all the commotion is. While they are busy, I tell Gideon, "This is our cue" as I see Cerene running our way. We come out of our hiding place in the shadows and run towards the side of the castle while all four guards are trying to determine where the flood of water came from. Cerene and Gideon are stationed at both sides of the entrance, scanning our surroundings, while I move away layers and layers of twisted green vines that have covered the entrance to the tunnels. Unable to remove some of it with my bare hands, I grab one of my daggers from my belt and make quick work of cutting some of them away. I try not to disturb too much because we'll need the entrance to look somehow untouched.

Under the vines is a small square, iron door with a latch that has long rusted from centuries of enduring changes in the weather.

"Hurry up," Cerene urges me.

"I'm working as fast as I can," I grunt. It takes me another minute before I free the door. We manage to all go inside one after the other in a rush. I close the small door behind us, making sure the vines fall back into place so no one would suspect an intruder. It is so dark here and it takes a minute for our eyes to adjust. I can feel Cerene's back touching mine.

"As exciting as this is, I pray there aren't any rats in here," Cerene says between dry heaves from the rotten smell.

"Gideon? I think it's time for that light of yours, man," I whisper as I try to figure out what is taking him so long to get it lit.

Once he gets the small torch going, he's sitting on the ground, his boots are tangled and trapped in some vines. Cerene steps forward to help him get out of them and take the torch out of his hand. Her face looks pale from drawing so much from her magic. I place my hand on her arm.

"Are you okay?"

"Yes, I'm fine," she answers with disdain.

"Okay let's keep going." I urge them to follow me as I start taking my first steps into the narrow path. We had a map, but there is no telling if these dark, moldy walls and floors have ever been used. The entrance was guarded for a reason. I cough and my eyes tear up, the smell is so potent, I feel it burning my insides. I can almost taste it. We've started smelling the rot in different parts of Eterna, signs that the magic and the land are dying.

With the occasional huffs that come from Cerene, I know she's weak and tired. Gideon, on the other hand, is always so quiet, and I know in his head, he's probably counting and measuring how long we have been going in the same direction. We just keep going straight with nothing ahead and no sound whatsoever. We've been walking for a while now, stopping a couple of times to drink some water. It should be daylight by now, but down here, surrounded by nothing but stone, it's impossible to tell. Even with the torch Gideon is holding, the darkness feels endless. As if reading my mind, Gideon says,

"It should be around noon."

Sweat trickles into my eyes, and I wipe it away with the back of my hand. I reach for the canteen at my side and take a long swig, the water warm but still refreshing. All of a sudden, we feel a rumble. At first it's very small, like small rocks falling, but then it gets louder. We look at each other, feeling something strong rattle the tunnels—an energy coming at us. Cerene clutches my arm tightly, and I feel her shaking. I turn to her and hold her. I feel her body lean into me, I'm trying to figure out what is happening when a gust of power hits us from all directions like a ripple that knocks us on our backs. I go tumbling down with Cerene in my arms. Our torch is long blown away. I hear Gideon somewhere beside me ask. "What the fuck was that?"

Chapter 19

Mia

Brookstone

Two days. That's all the time I have to prepare before we leave for Eterna. And somehow, it's already here. I sit cross-legged on the floor of my room, phone in hand. The speaker crackles slightly, both of my parents' voices overlapping, concerned and sweet in that way only they can manage.

"We just want to make sure you're safe, sweetheart," my mom says for the third time.

"As long as you're safe and happy, we're okay," my dad echoes, his voice softer now.

They've been giving me space lately, just little texts every day to say hi, or send a dumb meme, or remind me to eat something green. I really love that about them. It makes the guilt sting more. I swallow hard and rest my head against the side of the bed.

"I promise I'm okay," I say.

It's only half true. I haven't told them about Hyda. I haven't told them about the magic burning in me or the hours spent training until my arms shake. I don't mention the dreams and the man in them, or the fact that I don't fully know who I am anymore, but none of that changes how I feel about them. I'll love them forever.

Natalie sits across from me on the rug, mouthing "you got this" with a supportive grin as she peels the label off a water bottle.

"We're going to a wellness retreat," I say, trying to keep my voice light. "Just a few days to breathe, regroup, and disconnect from everything. I'll call you when we get back." There's a pause on the other end of the line. Just long enough to make my stomach twist.

"That sounds really nice," my mom finally says, though I can hear the hesitation in her voice.

"We're proud of you," Dad adds. "Let us know if you need anything, anything at all."

I hang up after a few more rounds of I-love-yous and please-be-safes. The second the call ends, I set the phone on the floor and let out a long breath I didn't realize I was holding. Natalie leans over and nudges my shoulder with hers.

"We sounded almost convincing."

I laugh, even though my chest feels tight.

"If we'd been face-to-face, they would've seen right through us."

She nods, pulling her knees to her chest.

"Good thing phones don't show lies."

Now comes the next tough thing, convincing Natalie to stay behind.

"You still need to go to work."

Natalie rolls her eyes and gives me the *seriously?* Look.

"Mia, quit trying. There is no way I'll let you head into the unknown alone." She hugs me and mumbles into my shoulder, "We are in this together, bestie. You jump, I jump."

Pulling away from her embrace, I ask,

"What if I drown?"

"Then it's a good thing I'm a nurse. I can revive you," she says, wiggling her eyebrows at me.

I laugh. "There is no changing your mind, is there?"

"Nope," she answers back, popping the P.

"Okay then, let's get ready. Call whoever you need to call and pack a backpack."

She salutes me. "Aye aye, captain."

I shake my head at her playful response and mumble under my breath,

"Eterna, here we come."

I tried to sleep, but I kept getting up throughout the night to pack and unpack my backpack again and again, not knowing anything about Eterna. What is the weather like, and what is the whole atmosphere? What would be essential? Too many unanswered questions. Natalie called it "heading into the unknown." I settled on one pair of black pants, a black jacket, a couple of tank tops, and underwear. If I'm going to be needing anything else, I'll have to improvise. Call me crazy, but I did pack my lucky paintbrush. Okay, so it's not really lucky, but I wanted to have something with me from home. The sun is up and we should be heading to the Auracle.

I pick up my backpack and phone, not knowing if there is any service in Eterna, then look around the room. *This is insane. Why am I scared? I'm going to be back. This is not goodbye.*

I glance at my nightstand, and our family picture stares back at me, so I rush and grab it and shove it in my backpack just in case. With that, I move and open the door to leave.

I find Natalie standing in the middle of the living room, staring into space wearing blue jeans and a red blouse, with her honey blonde hair in a high ponytail. She's carrying a brown backpack that is so full it looks like it's about to burst. I can't read her features, but I think she's as nervous as I'm. "Good morning, Nat."

She turns around startled, putting her hand on her chest.

"Oh, you scared me. Good morning. Are you ready for this?"

"Honestly... no. But I have to do it." I start walking toward the door. "It's time to go."

She nods as she adjusts the backpack straps on her shoulders and starts walking behind me.

Standing in front of the Auracle again is like deja vu from the first day I found this place. I'm nervous, looking at the dangling E of the shop name gives me a strange feeling, like starting the first day of school, anxious but excited at the same time. It's chilly, and my exhale has puffs of breath steaming in the cool air. I give Natalie a look.

"Is it too late to get some hot cocoa and cuddle on the couch?"

She presses her lips together and takes a deep breath. She tugs me forward, and we both enter the shop.

Inside, we find Hyda ready to go. I assess her as she waves us to the back of the shop. She doesn't have a bag and isn't carrying anything at all, which strikes me as odd. Inside the lit room where I've trained the last couple of weeks, the shelves that once held all those daggers and grenades are now almost empty.

"Child, is Natalie coming to Eterna?" Her voice is uncertain.

"Yes," Natalie snaps back at her before I can say a word.

Hyda looks at me to see if I'll say otherwise. When she sees my indifference, she clears her throat. "Very well then."

She comes closer to the door where Natalie and I are standing, and hands Natalie a dagger.

"Here, this is for you, just in case." Natalie takes it with trembling hands. Hyda then turns to me and extends something wrapped in a white cloth. I stare at her in confusion as she unwraps the dagger that was put up on display—the one with the ruby on the tip of the hilt. "This is yours now. Your mother gave it to me as a gift the day I became a general. I always carry it with me. It is one of a kind. I want you to have it."

I stand there, not knowing what to say. "Hyda, this is too much. I can't take this, I—"

Before I can finish what I wanted to say, she takes my hand and places the dagger in it "I want you to. For good luck. Consider it an early gift welcoming you back to Eterna."

I feel the dagger in my hand. The weight of it is perfectly balanced. I wrap my fingers around the hilt and turn it from side to side, watching as the light catches on the metal, reflecting the light. I realize it has an engraving on it. I read it aloud. "For better or for worse. Together always." Hyda's eyes light up when she hears me, and the woman smiles! *I never thought I'd see her smile this big, happiness apparent on her face.*

It takes a couple of minutes for Hyda to strap more daggers to her side and around her belt. I realize she's carrying a small bag under her hooded cape. "Okay, girls, let's go." Natalie and I start to turn around to go out of the main door, but Hyda stops us. "This way." She points at the now empty shelf that was holding all the daggers. She takes her final steps toward it while Natalie and I wear the same expression of confusion. Hyda slides her hand behind the shelf, fumbles with something that makes a clicking sound, then the whole shelf shifts to the side. *I would have never in a million years thought there was a hidden walkway behind that shelf.* I stride toward the now open walkway.

I feel Natalie hesitate behind me with slow steps. I glance at her, and she adjusts herself and starts following. Once all three of us are inside, Hyda clicks a button on the side and the shelf moves back in place. The walkway is narrow—barely enough space for one person to walk in—so we follow each other one by one. Hyda is in front of me and Natalie behind. I brush the walls with my hands on both sides as we follow Hyda, feeling the wall of the tunnel to ground myself. There is a cool breeze that blows every few minutes.

"Where does this tunnel lead, Hyda?"

"To the forest, my child," she answers me with ragged breathing. It feels like we are going downward, then the walkway looks like a winding road as we ascend.

"How did you find this place?" I ask, intrigued.

She carries the hem of her cloak trying to walk faster as she answers me. "Years ago, I got tired of going to the forest in the cold. Being torn between two different worlds was not easy. I knew I couldn't leave you here alone, but my heart and soul was on the other side. I kept going to the same spot we crossed over from, in hopes of feeling a little bit closer to home. I needed time to heal, and this was my only solace. So I mapped out the distance and dug this tunnel. It took me years to finish it. What you walk on now took me three years to construct and build." I was concentrating on her story, listening and marveling at the dedication she had to build this, not realizing she stopped walking, I bump into her and feel Natalie crash into my back as well.

I apologize as Hyda adjusts herself and says, "we are here."

I realize we have come to a stop at the end of the tunnel, and there is a small door obstructing our exit. Hyda brings out a key to unlock an old rusted padlock. Removing the lock from the clasp, she pushes the small door outwards. The wind is so strong it pushes the door back in on us, so I step forward and help her push it open. Hyda squeezes her body out and starts dusting the invisible dust from her clothes. Once I step outside, I hear the crunch of the dry leaves under my boots. I turn around and lean on the door to help Natalie out.

As we catch our breath from the walk, I start to take in my surroundings. We are in the heart of the forest at the edge of the city. Tall, old trees surround us—trees that look hundreds of years old. Their leaves are dark and light yellow and brown, and their full branches sway from side to side as the wind blows. The fresh air soothes my soul as I breathe it in.

Natalie steps beside me. "This used to be a park back in the day. People used to come out for walks and picnics. No one knows why it was closed." She talks quietly. We both turn around at the sound of Hyda dropping her bag next to us on the forest floor.

She bends down to retrieve a small, crystal vial. As she moves it in her hand, my eye catches how the liquid inside swirls and glitters with a purple, blue, and silver glow. It looks so mesmerizing. Without any warning, Hyda hurls the crystal glass. It lands about ten feet away from where we are standing. The glass shatters in the dirt, and its contents spill in a manner I haven't seen before.

The liquid swirls and moves in a circular motion around and around, getting bigger by the minute, until it becomes a round, silver orb floating just one foot above ground. The portal is big enough to let us all through, and bewilderment fills my senses at the sight. An actual portal is opening right in front of my eyes. I'd never believe it's actually real if I wasn't standing right here. Staring ahead into the unknown makes me feel scared and excited at the same time. This can't be real. Yet here I am, waiting to step through the portal.

I turn feeling Natalie's hand holding me, grounding me. As I trail my gaze toward her face, I see the fear in her eyes. The uncertainty is visible. We are both snapped back to reality as Hyda approaches the silver orb.

"This is a magical portal. I summoned it with a portal key, and this is our way to Eterna."

Hyda is looking into the portal as if checking things are okay on the other side. Natalie and I are stiff as a board, rooted in place, unable to take another step. I can feel Natalie trembling beside me. Her body is shaking, making me tremble with her. Hyda turns to face us. "Girls, it's time. The portal will close soon. I'll pass first, then I need you to hold hands and pass together. It can transport only two people at once, and I assume you don't want to pass through alone, so I'll go ahead of you," she explains quickly.

I force my feet to move forward, dragging Natalie with me. Standing in front of the portal, I hesitate, then take a step back. Stomach churning, I'm feeling like I'll empty my stomach, even though I couldn't eat anything before coming. I still feel nauseous nevertheless. I let go of Natalie and Wrap my arms around my waist, trying and failing to compose myself. I keep taking deep breaths to give myself the courage to move forward. Natalie beside me, a bundle of nerves, mirroring my own feelings. She hasn't uttered a word until now. Her voice comes as a whisper.

"Mia, are you sure about this?"

"No." My response comes quickly and frantically.

I start to pace, try to breathe and calm myself. *I can do this... I can do this... Come on, pull yourself together. I went skydiving for god's sake. This is just another adventure. So snap the hell out of it. So what if it's completely uncharted territory?*

I look at the portal. Hyda starts to step in, and before she goes in all the way, she turns.

"Hurry up. We are losing precious time." I shake my head, not ready yet to follow. Her words register in my mind as she says, "Aren't you ready to go search for your parents and meet your other half?" Before I can respond, she disappears into the pulsing portal.

I'm shocked at her last confession. She didn't mention anything about my other half until now. This woman keeps surprising me. She's definitely full of secrets. I chase all my fears away for the time being. Turning to Natalie, I extend my hand to her and say, "Let's do this." A nod is all the response I get.

The moment we step into the portal is like jumping off a cliff. The world shifts and turns, and I feel as if I'm floating, surrounded by a blinding light. I squint and try to tolerate the light assaulting my eyes but it's no use. I squeeze them shut. I can't feel the ground under my feet. I still feel as if we are on a roller coaster, dipping from a great height. It's very cold at first. *Not cold. Freezing.* Natalie and I are shivering, holding onto each other's hands for dear life. Then, a soft breeze grazes my skin, comforting, like the first day of spring. It still feels like we are walking in a loop, as if we are in the heart of a twister as it goes round and round, the wind lashing at us from all directions. I don't know how long we are in that state, but it feels like forever, and I don't like the feeling one bit. Suddenly, everything stops as our feet touch land.

Chapter 20

Hyda

Eterna

The moment my feet touch Eterna's soil, uncontrollable tears stream down my face. I kneel down to the ground and dig my fingers in the dirt. Grounding myself, not believing after twenty-one years of loneliness, I'm back home. I kiss the soil, the place I was born in and intend to die in. The air is different and clean. I take a deep inhale, giving my body and soul the comfort it needed all these years. *Home at last... I never thought I'd say the word again. HOME! I'm finally home and can't wait to find everyone I love.* I lay my trembling hand on my chest, feeling my erratic heartbeat. My next task is to find *him*. Without him, my heart will be lost. I lay there, sobbing, forgetting about the girls who haven't stepped through the portal yet. *Maybe it's a good thing. They gave me a few minutes to collect myself before I have to put on a mask of courage again. I'm also human, I remind myself.* I stand up again, remove the dust that my black pants have collected as I bring the hem of my cloak and wipe my tears away.

Glancing back at the portal, it ripples as Mia and Natalie step forward, holding each other's hands as if their lives depend on it. Both have their eyes closed while stepping into the unknown. I have to say, I feel accomplished to have them here, having Mia back home where she belongs. The moment her feet touch Eterna's soil and the portal closes behind them, a strange wave of power erupts all around us, knocking me back down to the ground.

Chapter 21

Mia

Eterna

It takes me a minute to feel the blazing light disappear. Still holding Natalie's hand in mine as if we are grounding each other in place, I slowly dare to open my eyes and turn in her direction. The moment she opens her eyes, she heaves and lets go of my hand and steps aside to empty her stomach. I stay standing in place, letting the dizzy sensation fade away. I take a couple of deep breaths, then look at where I'm standing. I try to check on Natalie, but she waves me off as she coughs and continues to empty her stomach.

Hyda is a couple of feet away from me, getting up from the ground. Once my head stops spinning and I'm no longer disoriented from coming through the portal, I look up at the horizon and gasp at the beauty in front of me. It's a sight to behold. The sun is up in the most alluring clear blue sky. The sunrays are shining on everything around me, giving it an ethereal feel. The land in front of me is a mixture of stunning colors, as if I'm standing in the middle of an enchanted painting made of dreams and wonder.

Blossoms of purples, pinks, and reds surround us. Blue bushes that I've never seen before in my life are tucked in between the blossoms, giving the whole bunch a unique combination of colors. There are no people around. It looks like we're far away from the residential area. In the distance is a city with high columns and domes decorating the beautiful skyline. It's like a vision of Agrabah, the famous world of Aladdin. Something inside me blooms, and I'm suddenly intrigued to go explore this land. Something is calling out for me to do so. I'm overwhelmed with the feeling of joy and peace. I've seen many beautiful places like Paris and Rome, but nothing compares to this. I'm in awe of it all and it takes my breath away.

As I turn around to observe the rest of my surroundings, I frown to see the other side of where I'm standing is yellow and bare, almost completely dry, as if this land has been long dead. It makes my heart ache at the sight. I hear Natalie's footsteps as she approaches me.

"Mia, this is such a beautiful place. I still can't believe we made it through the portal, even though my stomach was not happy with that trip."

"Oh yes. This place is stunning. But look at this land over here," I say sadly.

I feel Hyda's hand on my shoulder. "It's worse than I thought it would be." Her tone matches my own. Her face is etched with pain and something more that I can't decipher.

"We have to start moving. The portal draws too much power and magic. I've seen this happen in the past, when I opened a portal years ago to cross over with you. It didn't take long for the Elders' guards to come swarming in, looking for the source of magic. Plus, the moment you entered, something happened. A wave of power erupted all through Eterna. It knocked me on my ass, and I'm sure everyone else felt it, too. We need to go somewhere and lay low," she continues.

I'm interrupted by a shift in the light. Darkness suddenly takes over as the sun is completely blocked above us. My eyes widen in shock and fear to see three big birds, wings spread wide over us, circulating overhead, as they start descending. The wind picks up and the grass starts to move from the sheer force of the birds flapping their wings. My hair slaps my face from every direction, despite my effort to shield my eyes.

They land about twenty feet away from us. This majestic creature is so familiar, the more I look at it. Realization hits me like a storm making my heart race. It's the same bird I saw in my dreams, but now I'm standing face to face with it. Its head bears the delicate shape of a blue robin, with captivating golden eyes now fixed on me. Despite its size, its face holds a friendly, gentle expression. Its colossal body moves with surprising grace and elegance. Each step is like a hush of wind in this land. Phoenix-like wings unfurl behind it in a radiant arc. Its feathers are vibrant shades of royal blue, and they catch the sunlight as it adjusts them, making them shimmer as if dusted with glitter. Tall, muscular legs that end in four gleaming, golden talons shake the earth as it makes its way towards us. I step back, reaching for Natalie's hand, finding her frozen in place as she watches in horror.

Hyda, on the other hand, has a knowing smile on her face, looking at these birds with joy. She simply says, "Zarka, how happy to see you again."

The closer the birds come to us, the more horrified I get. Then, the three birds stop right in front of me, tuck their wings and bow to me. *What the hell is happening right now?* Alarm bells ring in my head and tell me to run away. I'm rooted in place, watching, waiting to see what comes next. Then, something strange happens in my head. I hear a voice. Not my own, a sweet voice like a melody. Smooth and steady. "Welcome to Eterna. You're one of the prophesied children. We have been waiting for you. We need you. Eterna needs you."

"Who said that?" I ask out loud. Both Hyda and Natalie look at me.

"What's wrong, Mia? Who said what?" Natalie asks, confused.

"That voice, telling me welcome to Eterna."

Hyda's brows furrow, assessing and trying to figure out what I'm talking about.

"Celestia and Cerene. Only you can hear us," the voice says.

I speak louder, responding to the voice again. "Who are you? Who is Cerene?"

"I'm Zarka. We are bound to you, but we haven't sensed you since after your birth. Your magic and ours are bound together. We are here to serve and guide you when you need us. You don't have to feed us to make us transform into our magical form. All you need to do is summon us in your mind. We are linked to you. You both bear our mark."

Confusion washes over me as the voice floods all my senses. I don't hear Hyda nor Natalie speaking. I cry out from a pain in my shoulder. I put my hand on my birthmark as it continues to burn me. Scorching pain radiates down my shoulder as I grunt and hold back more cries. The voice in my head says, "This was never meant to hurt you, but you have been away for too long. It will only take a second for the pain to subside. Your mark is awakening."

I feel Natalie holding me in place, pulling at my tank top, trying to see what is the matter with my shoulder. "Mia... Mia... Oh my god, your birthmark."

"What the hell is wrong with it?" I mumble.

"How can this be? Your birthmark has completely transformed. The unidentified shape it used to be is no longer there, it's..."

"It's what, Natalie? What the fuck is it?"

"It's a gorgeous blue wing!" She fumbles with her things and brings out her phone to take a picture, then she hands the phone to me. I'm in shock at what I'm seeing. Yes, it is stunning. Before I can say a word, we hear people approaching in the distance.

Hyda starts urging us to find a place to hide. I hear the Zarka again in my head. *I don't know if I'll ever get used to this.* "Fear not, they are friends, not foes."

I turn to Hyda and tell her, "The Zarka says they are friends, not foes."

"Can you hear the Zarka speak?" Her eyes widen in surprise. I nod. She stops taking a stance as if ready for battle, then she puts both of her hands on her daggers, ready to draw them at the first sign of danger. Hyda pulls Natalie behind her. I simply stand next to the Zarka, as if it's the most natural thing to do. *I might still be in shock from all this and will need to process it later.* We wait as three people approach us.

Chapter 22

Xavier

We stumble in the dark tunnel, trying to regain our footing. "Did that wave come from the tunnel?" Gideon asks.

"No. It's from outside. Something shifted. My magic is flooding my senses. I need to get out of the tunnel now. I need air. I can't breathe here," Cerene's pained voice answers. I'm still holding her, and I can feel her body still trembling. It is terrifying me. I try to speak as calmly as I can.

"Okay, change of plans. Let's get out, regroup and see what that blast of power was. Then we can reassess the situation."

"But we have been walking for a while. It's going to take us twice as long now that we don't have our torch," Gideon responds.

"I have an idea, but both of you will have to hold on tight to me," Cerene says. I nod even though no one can see me, then tell her, "Okay." Gideon and I manage to hold her from both sides, with her being in the middle. Without warning, we hear water trickling underneath our boots, growing slowly until it becomes a massive wave pushing us forward toward the way we came in. Being always in control of things makes the sensation of drifting away uncomfortable. Being unable to control the wave Cerene commands feels unsettling. I've seen her work her magic a million times before, but this is new.

After a few minutes, we slam hard against the iron door as it bursts open, throwing us out of the entrance. We land hard, coughing and spitting up water, trying to catch our breath from the rush of the wave. We're soaking wet, as if we dove in the sea fully clothed and armed. To our surprise, there are no guards on site. *Something did happen for the guards to leave their post.*

Once we get our footing and are ready to see what's happening, three Zarkas land in front of us, and the next thing I know, Cerene is clutching her shoulder and crying out in pain. I've never seen her in such a state. *Was all this because she was using a lot of magic? How can I help her when I don't understand a thing about how her magic works?* I walk close to her to see what's hurting her, I remove her hand from her shoulder to look at the unidentified shape of her birthmark, the one I always thought was something interesting. To my shock, the birthmark has transformed into a stunning blue wing. I don't understand what's happening right now. I'm brought back to Cerene's face when she asks, "Who is Celestia?"

Gideon and I answer together. "What? Who are you talking to?"

Cerene lets go of her shoulder and stands up to walk towards the Zarka, stroking one of the birds' heads. Turning back to us, she says, "Boys, I can hear the Zarka talking to me. We have to leave. It seems we have some visitors from another place." Confusion is an understatement for how I'm feeling right now. *Zarkas fully transformed; we didn't need to feed it! How is this even possible?*

"Cerene, what do you mean?" I ask, confusion lacing my voice.

"Something about the prophesied children. The Zarka will help us. Will explain later. We need to leave now," she says as she starts to climb the bird.

We each mount a Zarka and we take off towards the south of Eterna. The closer we get, the more uneasy I feel. We're heading to a place that I know too well—a place I've visited a million times before, in hopes that I could find her. I tighten my grip on my necklace. *Could it be her? After all these years?* Hope fills me, but I'm unsure. From this height, we can see three other Zarkas in the distance. We land a fair distance away from them.

Cerene descends from her Zarka first, even though she's just a couple of feet away from me, her mind seems to be miles away.

"What's going on, Cerene?" I ask her as Gideon and I dismount the Zarkas and the birds fly away, leaving us behind in a cloud of dust.

"The Zarkas are speaking to me, mindlinking with me, and they want me to meet someone—Oh my god!" Cerene says as she takes off running. Gideon and I exchange a look and start running after her. As we get closer, my heart starts to pound fiercely in my chest. It is becoming harder to breathe as I see a black cloaked figure and something in me stills. I don't recognize her, not really, but there's a pull, deep in my chest, like a thread tugging loose. It doesn't make sense. It's been twenty-one years. Twenty-one years without a word, without a face to hold on to. And yet, some part of me knows. My mind hesitates, but my gut says it's her. My mother.

Cerene stops in front of three Zarkas and three other women. She says something, but I can't hear her over the sound of my heart pounding in my ear. Catching my breath, I come to a stop behind her as she embraces another girl that seems to be her age, half a foot shorter, with longer wavy brown hair. I'm puzzled by the whole interaction. Where does Cerene know these people from? Before I can assess the situation any further, a surge of power hits us and we are again thrown, landing on the ground from the impact. It is the same as when we were in the tunnels. *What's causing all this?* I glance behind me and see in the distance an Elder with guards approaching, probably wanting to investigate what that ripple of power was. I'm sure they can see us, but we need to escape now.

I stand up as fast as I can, extending my hand to help Gideon up, then take charge of the moment and tell them, "RUN. Guards are coming. We all need to hide." The three Zarkas seem to understand what is going on, and they kneel down to let us mount them. Gideon and I get on one Zarka, while Cerene and a girl ride another. A second girl with honey gold hair and the cloaked woman ride the last Zarka. With that, the Zarka takes off flying back to the city, taking us back home, away from the guards. *We are safe for now.*

Chapter 23

Mia

The Zarka speaks to me again as three people land in the distance, "Celestia... Cerene... it is an honor to witness your reunion. Your concealed birthmarks are fully transformed into wings to connect you both to us."

Then another voice asks, "Who is Celestia?"

Confusion strikes me at having a second voice in my head.

"Who said that?"

A rumble of the bird's voice comes in again. "Celestia, we know you're confused and this is all new to you, but Cerene is your twin sister. We have been waiting for this. Together at last."

The girl comes running and arrives first. She looks around my age. She has straight, brown hair with cherry red highlights. It's just a couple of inches below her chin, plastered on her neck and face, and it seems like her hair is wet. She's taller than me by half a foot, slim and fit, and wearing all black clothes along with black leather boots. She has daggers strapped everywhere on her legs, arms, and back. She looks like a warrior who just came back from battle, but for some reason, she's soaking wet. She comes to a stop in front of us and says, "Hello. I'm Cerene... How can this be? The Zarka said you are my twin sister." She hesitates but then she embraces me, and something inside me shifts. A power surges between us and fire ignites in my chest. *My power is flooding all my senses and it wants to burst out of me. I feel it growing.* The moment I return the embrace and put my arms around her, something sparks in my chest, a feeling like it was the right thing to do. An energy surrounds us, wind blowing and everything blurs around us.

Once we both step away from each other, we see Hyda, Natalie, and both guys on the ground as if they were knocked over by something. Cerene and I watch, stunned at the scene. "Did you feel that?" I ask her. She opens her mouth to say something as the others regain their footing and stand up, but she's cut off by the two approaching men. One is running and shouting for us to "RUN" then saying something about the guards.

The moment Hyda hears that, she has us all scramble up to ride the Zarkas. Natalie protests about going on the bird, but Hyda grabs her by the arm and has her ride next to her. I end up riding with Cerene, and with no warning, the bird takes off. My stomach drops and dips with every sway the bird takes, and my ears pop once we are high in the sky. I don't have time to sort through emotions right now. I'm functioning on pure adrenaline. Everything is happening at lightning speed, giving me no warning to try to adjust to the situation. Sometimes I have to remind myself I'm awake and this is really happening. But everything is so surreal.

While I'm still on the bird's back, holding onto Cerene in front of me, I try to assess her. She seems like she knows what she's doing, and is taking control of the bird like she has done it a million times before.

"She grew up here in Eterna. She has been on our backs many times." The voice of Zarka comes back in my head. *Is it going to answer all my questions, even when I don't voice them?*

"Celestia, you will have to learn to direct your question to me when you need answers and to block me when you don't want me to hear you," Zarka continues.

"How can I do that?" I say out loud and Cerene slightly turns her head to me.

"What?"

"I was asking Zarka how I can block them from talking in my head."

She chuckles. "Oh, you hear them too. They are mindlinking with you."

"How? It's a strange feeling. Do you always speak to them like that?"

She shakes her head. "While we do have a potion to mindlink people, this is the first I've heard the Zarka doing it. Today, after that wave of power that hit Eterna, they spoke to me, too."

"You both are the only ones who can hear us. You're the prophecy children," Zarka informs us.

Realization hits me. I'm connected to Cerene. I feel it in my soul, and I can't wait to land and have a conversation on the ground. Looking down from high up here, it's beautiful, yet I'm terrified I'll somehow fall and break my neck. I take a deep breath and close my eyes.

I take it all in. The wind is blowing on my face, and the sensation is like complete freedom. Then I realize I feel... oh my god... I feel whole! The love of adventure and danger has always soothed me to the core. This is a deeper feeling. Was my soul seeking to be back here all my life? Was my inner self always wanting me to come back to this place? Now that I'm here, what does Eterna have for me?

I'm lost in my thoughts until I hear Cerene's voice. "Brace yourself, we are landing." Then, I feel the Zarka dipping forward, and my stomach churns, but I tighten my grip on Cerene's waist and feel hard muscles under my hands. *She must be a warrior of Eterna. That would explain her clothing.*

The Zarka lands, once again producing a big cloud of dirt. I cough from the unexpected dust entering my nose and mouth. Cerene dismounts the bird and extends her hand to help me down. *She seems nice. Something about her makes me feel safe.*

The moment everyone is off the Zarkas' backs, the birds take off and transform in the sky to regular sized birds and I'm stunned to see the transformation in front of my own eyes.

"Yes. that never ceases to amaze me." Cerene says laughing. I look around and we are all standing in a clearing, bare land ahead of us, in total awkward silence.

The two other guys with Cerene seem to study us with intent. One of them speaks.

"Hello, my name is Gideon." He's tall and muscular. He overshadows me by a good foot. I have to lift my head to actually look at his face. He's good looking, with dark brown eyes that sparkle in the light and give contrast to his dark brown complexion. He smiles at me as he points at the other guy beside him.

"This is my brother, Xavier. Our home is not too far from here. We need to get off the streets. The guards will be looking for whoever made that shift in power, and I have a feeling that you're the reason for it."

I look at Natalie. She doesn't look like she's doing so well, and I feel guilty for not checking up on her, but she seems like she's sticking by Hyda for now. Hyda, on the other hand, has a look I can't decipher. Her big blue eyes are welling up with tears as she stares straight at the guy called Xavier, but she hasn't said a word.

"You can trust us. I think we are all looking for answers here," says Cerene. Hyda nods, and we all end up following them.

I soak in the feeling of being in this new world and where we are heading next. Excitement burns within me at the prospect of the unknown. My companions all seem to walk in silence. No one says a word as we pass through these strange, yet fascinating streets. After walking for a few minutes away from the place the Zarka dropped us off, narrow streets come into view. The streets are crowded and buzzing with people going about their days. Market stalls on both sides of the street make it impossible to pass without bumping into other pedestrians. The smell of food being cooked out in the open makes my mouth water and my stomach growl. The smell of spices is pungent in the air. Colorful flowers dangle down from every window of the buildings behind the stalls. It's a small town where people seem to be familiar with all this buzz.

The whole atmosphere floods my senses. I'm overwhelmed with it all. I stumble on something and lose my footing, but before I fall flat on my face, Xavier's hand wraps around my upper arm and pulls me up to steady me. I look at him and get consumed by his big blue eyes. *Wait, I've seen those eyes before.* But he lets go of me and smirks, rolling his eyes in annoyance.

What the hell? I don't get to say anything as he strides ahead of us and rounds the corner. I start walking next to Natalie.

"Are you okay?" She nods and gives me a small smile.

"I've been better." I reach and hold her hand.

"It's all so overwhelming," I whisper. "The bird spoke to me, Natalie." She looks at me, a question in her eyes.

"That girl, Cerene, is my twin sister. That's what the bird told me." I tell her, not believing what I'm saying.

"What! The bird talked to you?" she asks.

I shrug, not knowing what else to say. She wiggles her eyebrows. I giggle under my breath and shake my head at her. Natalie will always surprise me with her behavior when she's uncomfortable. Situations like these make me love her more because this girl will always put me first above all else. For that, I'm forever blessed. She was my chosen family, and I'll do any-thing to keep her safe.

We reach a three-story building with sand-colored brick, giving it a dusty look. Flower pots sit in rows at every window, making the building look alive and lived in. There are vegetable stalls on this side of the street too, with merchants still shouting and ushering people to come and buy from them. Cerene opens an old rusted iron gate that makes a squeaking sound, then motions for us to enter.

We climb the steps all the way to the third floor. At the top, there's only one door. Cerene turns the handle to the wooden door of their home and enters, then holds the door open for all of us to go in after her. Once we are all inside, Cerene closes the door and starts shrugging off her jacket and kicking off her boots.

"Please make yourself at home. It's not much, but this is our par-adise." She says to all of us with a kind smile.

Hyda seems anchored in place, hesitating, still looking at Xavier for some reason. Natalie asks to use the restroom and is guided by Gideon to a door on the left side of the living room. The walls are all painted light grey, with one navy blue accent wall where they have a painting of the three of them. It's sitting in the middle of the mantle on top of an old fashioned fireplace. Their couches are made of wood and beige cushions. Small side tables sit next to the couches, their wood old and scratched. It is very simple, yet has character. It looks like they have been living here for a long time. In the middle of the couch sits Xavier, his tall legs spread and his elbows resting on both of his knees. He has his head tucked between his hands. He seems to be lost in thought, looking down at his feet.

I walk slowly as I hear Hyda clear her throat before saying, "That necklace you wear, where did you get it from?"

I notice that sentence brings the attention of Gideon standing at the end of the room, and Cerene stops in the middle of unbuckling her armor from her back, as if they were all in sync waiting for Xavier to answer. I feel myself holding my breath as he lifts his head from his hands and stands. His fingers circle the pendant he's wearing. At that moment, I notice how tall he is—a wall of muscle, his black shirt hugging every piece of him. His bronze-toned skin glows under the light and his sharp jawline gives him a striking look. A slash across his left eyebrow adds a hint of danger—just enough to give him a bad-boy look. Full lips that make me wonder how they feel. *And I'm staring. What's wrong with me?* Oh God, he's gorgeous. His eyes are a striking deep blue. *I see it now. His eyes are familiar because they are the exact replica of Hyda's.*

Chapter 24

Xavier

I strode ahead of everyone after catching that clumsy girl before she fell on her face. I didn't give her the time of day in my haze and didn't care if I seemed rude. I wanted a minute to breathe, a fucking minute to calm my racing heart. That cloaked woman with big blue eyes, *my blue eyes,* is my mother. I don't know what to say. Did she even recognize me? I'm sitting in the middle of our living room, not remembering how I got up here, holding my head between my hands. I'm trying and failing to control my racing heart that's about to pop out of my fucking mouth. I hear them all enter as Cerene tells them,

"Make yourself at home. It's not much but it's our paradise."

I feel my mother approach the living room, cautious and calculating. She's now standing three feet away from me. She clears her throat and addresses me with a question.

"That necklace you wear, where did you get it from?"

I feel everyone freeze around me, holding their breath to hear my answer. Cerene and Gideon both know the answer to that question, and if she recognizes it, then I'm certain she's my mother. I lift my head and stand tall in confidence, like how she taught me years ago.

As my eyes meet hers, I notice how much time has passed. How life seems to have taken a toll on her. She's older now, with wrinkles surrounding her eyes and mouth. Her hair is grey and silver surrounding her face. She's hunched down a bit even though she's standing as tall as she can. Her stance and how she carries herself hasn't changed. Her kind eyes sparkle with hope as I circle my fingers around the hourglass pendant around my neck. I see her waiting and anticipating my answer.

I try to sound confident, but my voice comes out as a whisper.

"My mother gave it to me twenty-one years and thirty three days ago." *Yes, I've counted every second my mom was away from me.*

At my response, my mother falls to her knees. Tears fall down her face as she extends her arms, reaching for me.

"Xavier. My boy. My love. My heart. Ohhhh... my heart. I ached for you, so many years and..." Her voice breaks and a loud sob escapes her.

Her words stab me like a knife through the heart and I can't get a hold of my emotions. I lunge at her and gather her in an embrace. Kissing her head, her cheeks, her hands. I feel moisture on my face and realize I'm crying with her. Tears held for too long. The vulnerability that I hide from the world all comes tumbling down, and I'm in pieces. I'm finally holding my mother. *My mother!* Despite all my hopes of seeing her, I never thought it was going to happen. But now it is true, she's here. I let my head rest on her shoulders, and I'm transported back to being the little boy hugging his mother before she leaves for work. Giggling with her as she tickled and kissed my cheek before she went out the door. I hold on tight to her this time and never want to let go.

I lose track of time, soaking in the feeling of my mother's embrace. But when I finally open my eyes and wipe the tears I've shed, I look at my mother and her face reflects the same emotions as mine. Love, hope and the feeling of being complete.

"I've missed you. So much. Words will never explain how much I needed you, Mother. But I kept her safe, as promised." She raises her eyebrows in question. "Cerene. My sister, I kept her safe."

She turns her head to look at Cerene, who is sobbing silently in the corner with one boot on. Then she turns her attention back to me.

"Oh, my dear boy. That was never your burden. I'm so sorry. But I'm happy to see you stuck together," she says as she cups my face in her hand. I lean into her touch, grounding myself, letting my inner self believe she's actually here and alive.

Where was she all these years? I need answers, but for now, I hold her and help her stand back up.

"Okay, we all need to wash up, eat, and get better acquainted with each other." I speak to everyone even though I don't want to move an inch away from this precious woman.

My mother smiles.

"But first, Mia..." she calls to the girl with the wavey brown hair, who perks up at the sound.

"I'd like you to meet your twin sister, Cerene." With that revelation, both girls look at each other unsurprised. A memory slaps me in the face. *Me, standing behind a tree, holding a baby in my arms, while my mother walks away from me, holding another baby.* Fuck, there were two babies. *How did I miss that?*

Chapter 25

Mia

Hyda knew. This whole time she was with me, she knew I had a twin sister and didn't tell me. But why? Cerene and I lock eyes and smile as I start to connect all the dots. How the Zarka spoke to both of us. I was distracted at first and stunned by the sequence of events from the moment we went through the portal. Hyda did say, "Don't you want to meet your other half?" I forgot about that once I was out of the portal. But now, I'm standing in front of my sister.

I have to steady myself. I extend my hand and reach out to hold on to the couch's back, slowly lowering my body to the floor. I'm tired of getting ambushed with the truth. *I wish people would start just telling me the whole truth at once so I can deal with it all in one go.* Cerene approaches Hyda and asks her,

"Is this true? Zarka spoke to us and told us we are twins, but where was she all my life?" Before she can hear Hydra's response, she comes and sits next to me, then holds my hand and says.

"Celestia? That's your name, right?"

"No, I'm Mia."

She narrows her eyes at me. "But Zarka didn't call you that."

"I know. It addressed me as Celestia, my birth name… But that is not my name. My parents named me Mia, and that is the only name I go by."

Her kind eyes sparkle. "You had parents? Our parents?" she asks with hope in her voice.

"No. My adoptive parents." *I hate the disappointed look I see on her face.*

"Oh." That's all the answer I get as she looks at our linked hands.

Hyda comes into view. "My dear girls, I'll explain everything to all of you. It seems everyone has unanswered questions. It's all been a big misfortune, really."

"Are we going to address the elephant in the room?" Gideon asks, getting everyone's attention. He makes an explosive gesture.

"The blast of power. Where did it come from? No one puts me on my ass for no reason. I was blasted twice with that thing and I need to know what caused it."

Cerene collects herself. "It doesn't matter. What matters is that I have a sister and I love that." She squeals as she throws her arms around me, crushing me in an embrace that is so strong yet comforting. She's better at this than me. I've never been good at receiving new information. I just don't know how to process my feelings in the moment.

Natalie finally comes out of the bathroom, and her hair is fixed in a messy ponytail. I can tell she washed her face because she looks refreshed. She takes in her surroundings, trying to figure out what she has missed.

"Do I need to cry or scream with joy?"

Gideon laughs and responds while pointing at Natalie, "I'm going to like this one."

I shake my head and motion for her to come sit next to me and Cerene. Once she's sitting, I say, "Cerene, meet Natalie. My best friend. I hope you two can be friends. Natalie, meet Cerene, a sister I didn't know I had."

Natalie smiles as she says, "I can see the resemblance."

Cerene nudges Natalie's shoulder. "Of course. We are twins, after all."

I look at her and reply in a sad tone. "Yes. Twins, and we know nothing about each other." There's a beat of silence before she reaches out and takes my hand, her grip firm, grounding.

"We have all the time in the world now."

That one sentence unravels something tight in my chest. My eyes sting, but I blink the feeling away.

We sit for a long time, just the three of us, cross-legged on the floor, the quiet around us settling like a blanket. Cerene and I start talking, at first cautiously, like we're feeling our way through fog. We begin with the birthmarks, those strange mirrored shapes on our shoulders that transformed into blue wings. Proof that we were connected before we even knew.

"I used to think mine meant something was wrong with me," Cerene says. "No one else I knew had one."

"Mine stings from time to time, but I was always curious about what it looks like," I say.

We start sharing bits of ourselves, things we've never told anyone else. I learn she hates thunderstorms but loves the smell of rain. That she hums when she's nervous. Her favorite color is deep green, like the forest at dusk. She has a habit of sneaking out just to feel the wind on her face.

"I used to sneak up to the roof," I admit. "Whenever the world felt too loud. I'd bring my sketchbook and just... be. It's the only place I felt like I could breathe."

"I remember that." Natalie says with a smile.

Cerene leans her shoulder against mine. "We were doing the same thing. In different places. Without knowing it."

We all laugh, light and full, as we bond over how much we hate being told what to do. It's the kind of laughter that softens the edges of everything else, the danger, the secrets, the weight of the unknown waiting for us just outside this room. For a while, we forget about Hyda, Xavier, and Gideon. Right now, I just want to sit here and enjoy the company of Cerene and Natalie.

Chapter 26

Hyda

I'm sitting in complete bliss, taking everything in as if it's a dream. From spending years sitting alone in Brookstone, to sitting in a cozy small apartment in Eterna. Some days, I didn't even speak to anyone. I thought I'd eventually lose my mind. Now I'm surrounded by the kids... Well, they are all adults and no longer kids. That thought brings me sadness. We have lost so much time with each other, and I don't know who to blame it on. I did watch Mia grow up, always close yet so far, but to see Cerene and Xavier be these wonderful people, sticking together and caring for one another, brings me joy. Cerene is so sweet. Her personality has a bit more spark than Mia's. I think my son has rubbed off on her growing up. He was always an active child who loved adventure and stories of mysterious events. He'd wait for me to come back from a long day of work, ready to hear about my day and what tale I'd tell him.

I watch them getting acquainted with each other. The girls settle into a quiet corner, chatting and catching up. Everyone has a chance to wash up and get something to eat. Xavier seems to have made this a home for Cerene, Gideon, and himself. Looking at him, my heart swells with pride. He can act like he's collected and put together, but I can see the vulnerability behind those blue eyes that mirror mine. So many of his features resemble his father's, and as happy as it makes me that he took a piece of each of us, my heart aches at not knowing if Mateo is still alive somewhere. If he is, then why hasn't he taken care of his son?

Cerene comes in carrying a tray, calling for everyone to gather to have some tea, and I take that opportunity to tell them about what transpired years ago and what will need to happen next. I clear my throat and say, "Now that everyone has rested as much as we can, given the circumstances, I'd like you to all sit and listen to the story of how we got separated and what brought us here. You will need every piece of information to be able to fix Eterna and handle the Elders."

"This should be interesting," Gideon says, approaching to sit on the couch facing me. Xavier comes out of his room with disheveled hair as if he has been running his hands through it, wearing grey sweatpants and no shirt. What catches my eye is the tattoo he has running from the side of his neck down his chest, ending at his waist. It's a realistic image of lightning engraved in his skin like veins. *I have to ask him when he got that tattoo.*

He takes long, lazy steps toward the living room, then throws himself onto the couch next to me. He then leans in close and plants a kiss on my cheek, and I close my eyes to savor the moment, allowing my crumbling heart to be soothed by the love of my child. *How many times have I dreamed of moments like these?* I tap his leg in assurance. Mia and Cerene walk side by side with Natalie behind them. I smile seeing the girls finding comfort in each other's company. They settle on the fluffy carpet on the floor. Cerene hands everyone a cup of tea, and I watch Mia closing her eyes and taking a whiff of her cup before smiling. Xavier beside me chuckles and Mia notices him mocking her and stares back at him in defiance. *I have a feeling these two are going to be a handful.*

"Okay. I'll start at the beginning, back as far as I can remember." I see all of them look at me, anticipating the story I'm about to tell.

"Twenty-one years ago, just a week before Cerene and Celestia were born, the seer Otto who was working with the rebellion died. He was the last of his kind who possessed the magic to predict the future. With him gone, the rebellion lost hope. Silas and Freya Vega were the royals who led and protected the rebellion." I take a deep breath as I look at Cerene and Mia, letting them know, "Silas and Freya are your parents."

I take another sip of my tea and continue as they all listen to me in silence. "On that day, Silas Vega called for a meeting with all those involved in helping and leading the rebellion. I was there with them. I was the general of the royal guard. Mateo, my husband, was my second in command. Silas and Freya were more than royals to us. They were our best friends, and we would live and die for each other and for the safety of our homeland. We had met to discuss things. With Otto gone, we heard rumors that they were going to appoint Edith in his place. She was a wretched woman, a widower whose husband died from drawing too much power from the land. She was also hungry for that same power and seemed to put herself before anything else. She had said she was willing to sacrifice her daughter to gain the ability to be a seer like Otto. Eterna couldn't afford such corrupt people in power. At the time, the people of Eterna were struggling to find food and shelter. The plan was to leave harmless explosives around town and the Elders' Castle. While the Elders' guards went looking for the source, all the Royal guards who served the rebellion, along with me and Silas, would go into the castle, surround them and force them to step down and let the people vote for the new leaders." I take a deep breath to collect my thoughts again before I continue the story.

"Freya helped behind the scenes. The common people and Elders hadn't seen her in a long time. When she was just a few months pregnant, she went to visit Otto the Elder when she heard he was sick. They were good friends. He was her mentor. Freya didn't have magic, but she was able to always sense it and know who that magic belonged to. She was a great asset to the Elders. Before she left him that day, as he embraced her, he sensed her pregnancy and told her to go into hiding because he saw her carrying the prophecy children."

Cerene cuts in. "Our mother went into hiding to protect us?"

I nod.

Mia asks me another question. "Who are the Elders again?"

Xavier huffs in frustration at the question.

"The Elders are families who have magic abilities in their bloodline. No one knows how they came to be, but they were blessed with it by the land of Eterna. They are the powerful people who made our government. They made sure things were in order and just in the past, but just like any other government, with time greed takes over," I explain briefly and continue.

"Freya knew of the prophecy, as it was handed down in their family from one person to another for over fifty years. Until it was entrusted to Silas. Little did he know that his own children would be the ones the prophecy talked about. I personally didn't know much about its details. To me, it was like a legend being told from a past generation. When Silas and Freya confided in me and told me they had the scroll of the actual prophecy in their possession and it was true, I was perplexed but didn't push further for information. For the safety of all, it was best hidden. The only one who knows where it is hidden is Silas." I pause and ask them to hand me a glass of water. I haven't talked this much in one go for a long time. Gideon hands me one from the tray Cerene set on the small table. After taking a sip and swallowing it, I continue the tale.

"Silas was a strong royal leader. People respected him and loved him for his generosity and kindness. He could have been a great Elder, but he didn't possess any magic. He was often not on the same page with the Elders because they were gaining more power from the land in unnatural ways. Too much magic corrupted minds, and they tortured civilians in search for more power. They were turning evil. Hungry for power, always wanting more than they were given. Silas wouldn't stand for it and hated the inequality, and that's how he became the head of the rebellion. Wherever Silas and Freya went, Mateo and I followed, and we wouldn't have it any other way. Then the twins were born on the same night that the prophecy indicated. We were certain it was true. Freya was able to feel the magic hidden in her babies.

"Three days later, Silas, the royal guards, Mateo, and I executed the plan with some of the rebellion members. To our surprise, the Elders had anticipated all our plans. We don't know how they discovered all that. They didn't have a seer in their ranks. The only explanation was that we had a mole. That mole cost us dearly. Explosions erupted on time, but everything we planned didn't." A tear trickles down my cheek at the memory, and I wipe it away. "The Elder's guards were ready for us. The harmless explosives ended up causing damage because someone tampered with them and changed their locations. The damage was painful, not to them but to us. They attacked us with speed and force. Smoke was everywhere in the city. They had the element of surprise on their side. Innocent lives were taken."

I turn to hold Xavier's hand. "I lost your dad that day. One minute Mateo was next to me, having my back, and the next, I couldn't see him in all the chaos." My voice is only a whisper now. I see Mia, Natalie and Cerene wipe tears from their eyes. "I looked everywhere for him. He simply was gone. I called to all our guards, or at least, what was left of them, to retreat and go into hiding, then ran as fast as I could to check on Freya and Silas. I needed to carry on with the plan, the one thing Freya didn't want to happen." I cover my face with both my hands. I hated reliving this part. This part of the plan was what made me lose everything I hold dear.

"Mother, do you need to take a break?" Xavier's rough voice asks me sweetly.

"I'm fine. Just heartbreaking memories, my child." He squeezes my hand and lets me continue my story. "When I got to Silas and Freya's house, I found them both in the bedroom. Silas made it before I did, and the moment I saw him, I broke down in tears for what I had to do next, as I told them I couldn't find Mateo." I take a deep breath as I continue to tell the room about that fated night twenty-one years ago and how it changed all of our lives.

"Freya knew she wasn't able to go with the kids because the Elders had their doubts about the prophecy. If they had known about the kids, they would have made sure that they wouldn't live. So she had to do the hardest thing a mother could do—let her babies go. It was supposed to be for only a couple of days. To lay low and then regroup. Silas handed me both babies a box of portal keys, and I knew what I needed to do. I ran so fast inside the secret passageways of the house. Once I was out in the midst of all the chaos, no one saw me. I ran back home, grabbed Xavier and headed to South Eterna, where I knew the portal keys would work."

Xavier interrupts me, his voice etched in sadness. "This is where you left me and Cerene hiding behind a tree. You were supposed to come back but never did."

I nod as my tears keep falling down. *I need to stop crying. This changes nothing of the past.* "Yes, my son. The portal keys are a tricky thing. They let only two people through at once, and all of you were little. I opened a portal, crossed over and found myself in a park, a garden that had people walking around. I set Mia on the grass and came right back for you and Cerene. I was too late. The guards had found you and were walking away.

I had to go back for Mia. It took me a couple of minutes before I was able to make it back to her. When I got there, a couple had already found her and were walking away with her. I was so disoriented from crossing into this new world, I didn't know what to do. So, I followed them back to a police station and waited until they got out, then went to a hospital. In the end, they took Mia home. I was devastated to have lost all three of you. I slept in the streets, hiding, to see what they would do with her. They ended up adopting her and raising her as their own. I wanted to take Mia, raise her and come back when the time was right, but I was in a new land with nothing to offer other than my protection. So I let them give her the best life they could give, while I watched from the shadows."

Mia and Natalie watch me as I exhale. "Once I knew she was safe, I used another portal key, came back and looked for you and Cerene, but I couldn't locate you. There were many orphanages for me to scout through. I discreetly looked for Mateo, Silas, and Freya, but people knew who I was, and I had to be very careful not to get caught. Edith was looking for every single one of us. The people of Eterna said the Vega family were executed. Elder Edith took control of the Elder families. I just couldn't believe the change that took place in Eterna in just a couple of days. I wasn't able to confirm any of it. I sneaked back home and took what I needed to survive. I was hoping to find your father, but he wasn't there and didn't seem like he ever came back home for you or for me. I had to make my peace with losing him. The only option I had was to go back through the portal and watch Mia grow from a distance until she noticed me." I set my shaking hands in my lap, letting out a deep breath. "I did everything I could, given the circumstances."

"How do those portal keys work and how many do you have?" Gideon asks.

I'm taken aback by that question, I hesitate to answer him. "I don't really know how they work. Silas gave them to me and taught me how to use them. There were six of them, but only two left." He nods, but I see him calculating.

"What does this mean for us now?" asks Mia.

"We need to find your parents," Gideon responds instead of me.

Chapter 27

Xavier

Listening to my mother tell us a brief vision of the last twenty-one years of her life was heartbreaking. I didn't know which one was worse, her leaving me or watching over Celestia from afar. That girl had it all. She had parents who took care of her and had my mother as her guardian angel. And here we were, Cerene and I, struggling all alone. We've been fending for ourselves and growing up with no support system. I want to scream at the top of my lungs. Albeit, she's Cerene's twin, but why? Why did she have a better life than we did? Jealousy fills me. I try not to stare at her. She seems infuriating to deal with. Cerene is happy and smiling, so I'll need to keep to myself and interact with her only when needed.

Everyone is still sitting in the living room, trying to figure out our next move. I need some space. I want to go up on the roof to think and clear my head. Before I do that, I take my mother's hand and let her know she can rest in my room. She nods and lets me guide her. As she enters, I see her observing everything. "My bed is comfortable. You should be able to get some needed sleep," I tell her, trying to break the silence.

"Thank you, my child. I'm trying to take it all in. Here I was thinking, once I reach Eterna, I need to search for you. I'm glad the universe had you waiting for me the moment I stepped back in Eterna."

She reaches to cup my face in her hands. I lean into her touch and let my eyes close, savoring all her love with that simple touch. *It's true what they say: nothing can soothe your heart like a mother's touch. And God knows how much I longed for this.* "I'll need one thing from you, Son."

I open my eyes, eager to give her what she wants. "Anything."

"I saw how Cerene carries herself and that she's well trained. I'll need you to make sure Mia is ready, too."

I close my eyes and take a deep inhale. "I don't have time for her. She doesn't need to come on the mission to find her parents. She'll be a liability. Training takes time and effort, and she doesn't look like she's cut out for that, Mother." I know I sound like a scorned child, but this is how I feel.

My mother presses her lips together and looks at me. I know that wasn't the answer she was expecting. "Son, she's as stubborn as you, and she'll want to be included. She's one part of the prophecy."

I nod in acknowledgment. My mother didn't change much and won't rest until she gets what she wants. "Okay, mother, I'll do this for you. But know that I'm not happy about this."

She nods and smirks at me. "We will see. Now let me get some rest."

I give her a kiss on the cheek and walk out of the room. The living room is now quiet and empty. I guess everyone went to get some rest too. *Good. Now I can think alone for a bit.*

I cross the living room, straight for the door and up one flight of stairs to the roof. Once I'm up, I brace myself and clench my hands into fists. *Fucking hell, what is she doing in my thinking spot?*

Chapter 28

Mia

As we sit in the living room, I watch Xavier take Hyda into his room to rest. Gideon retires to his room as well. Everyone is very overwhelmed and deep in their own thoughts after Hyda finishes her story. The room is quiet now, but not the peaceful kind. It's the kind that weighs heavy, pressing into our chests. I can't believe she actually went through all that and still watched over me all my life. It is so admirable, her dedication and honor. Natalie doesn't look so well; her face is pale. Cerene sees it too. She offers to give Natalie some clothes and a clean towel so she can shower and go back to her room to get some sleep.

I feel suffocated with the amount of information dumped on me all in one day. I stop Cerene before she can walk out of the room and ask, "Hey, Cerene, where can I go to just take a moment to breathe?"

"Just walk out the door, and you will see some stairs on the left. Take them up, and you will find yourself on the roof. I'll help Natalie and follow you," she says with a smile.

She's so friendly. Her smile radiates kindness. "Thank you. See you in a bit then," I respond as I walk towards the door.

Once I'm outside, I realize that this building has only one apartment on each floor. It's like single homes stacked on top of each other. I spot the stairs to the left and start climbing. The roof is flat and you can walk on it without slipping. It is also made of brick, and it has a fence surrounding it, no higher than a foot. It doesn't look quite complete. Some bricks are out of place and on the ground. There is a lot of dust on the surface, and as I walk further to the edge, I feel the sand crunch under my boots. My eyes are glued to the horizon, and the sun is setting, creating a magical, purple landscape. The castle in the distance, with its high columns and domes, looks like a floating house in the sky. I close my eyes letting the last rays of the sun touch my face. I savor the moment and memorize it to put it on canvas once I'm back home.

I clear my head and take a deep inhale, stepping closer to the edge of the roof, I take a seat to soak in the sight before me. The town is still buzzing with people and sound. Merchant stalls are still open. I'm consumed by this new feeling I have inside me. A feeling of warmth. *Could it be my fire? Is it the idea of being one step closer to seeing my biological parents? Or is it that I'm not alone, and I have a twin?* I know I was never alone. My parents and Natalie have always been my family. My thoughts are interrupted at the sound of crunching sand under someone's boots.

I turn around with a big smile, thinking it's Cerene. Instead, I lock eyes with Xavier's deep blue, stunning eyes, and my smile falters at his expression. "Oh, hi. I thought you were Cerene."

He bunches his brows and clenches his fist. "What are you doing in my spot?" The words are spat like venom.

I turn back to face the city and think of how to respond. "I needed to breathe. Cerene told me I could come up here, so I did."

"Cerene had no business sharing my spot." His voice is angry and he's starting to get on my nerves.

"I don't see your name written on it," I respond as I chuckle. He stands next to me, almost invading my personal space. *For a man with his gorgeous looks, he sure is an ass.*

"Listen, Celestia. You don't get to walk in here and take everything you want. Some things, like this spot and my mother, are off-limits. Isn't it enough you had her watch over you all your life while I was in the streets?" His words are laced with hatred.

What did I do to him to deserve this? I certainly didn't take his mother. I stand up and face him. "First, my name is not Celestia, it's Mia. Second, I'm not taking anything from anyone. I'm as much a victim as you are." He growls as I take a step towards him. "If anything, your mother was stalking me. I had no idea she even existed till after my birthday."

Before either of us get to continue this argument, Cerene's voice comes from behind us. "Mia... Oh, Xavier, I didn't know you were up here, too." He turns and gives her a sweet smile. *He smiles! Such a prick.*

"I'm ready to get some sleep," I tell her.

She walks towards me and holds my hand. "Let's go then. I'm dying to hear more about you." I tighten my grip on her hand and start walking with her.

From behind us, I hear, "Goodnight, Cerene." He pauses, and then, "Goodnight, Celestia."

I don't respond to that. He's insisting on calling me Celestia! He laughs out loud as we walk through the door to go downstairs. By the time we reach the apartment, I can still hear his laughter. I ignore him and go with my sister to rest.

Chapter 29

Freya

I wait for Silas to come back. Elder Edith summoned him after the second surge of power. I'm sure she wants to know what it is. She thinks he'll speak. After being in this cell, she really thinks he'd actually help her. She's delusional.

Silas can be so charming, and he has her convinced that he has no connection to the prophecy. I know she needs me, but I'd never bow down to her. She knows I can sense magic and can connect the powers to individuals, but Edith will never know the extent of my power. Only Otto knew exactly what I can do. He was my mentor and I miss him dearly with every day that passes by. His loss was a great blow to Eterna—the only one working with us towards the benefit of the people. Once he was gone, and our so-called takeover failed, all hope vanished.

I hear the guard talk to Silas in a hushed voice as they approach our loathsome cell. Once they come into view, Silas is accompanied by one of the old guards, Hayes, a face I see often. He always brings Silas back to the cell. At least Hayes is nicer than the other ones. When he sees me, he nods at me. I smile at him in acknowledgment.

"Good day," he says as he locks the door after he lets Silas in.

I walk slowly towards Silas, locking my eyes with his, wanting to know if it's safe to talk since Hayes still lingers in the hallway. I wait a few minutes till Hays is out of earshot, then whisper, "What happened? Does she know anything?"

He shakes his head. "Everyone felt that power, but they are confused. They are sending guards to investigate and see if there is anything amiss," he tells me in a hushed voice.

I clutch his shirt as I face him. "Silas, I need to see my daughters." His eyes are tired, bloodshot, and weary. "What did she have you do this time?"

He pats my hand. "I've been searching all the old tomes for her. She's looking for anything that has to do with the prophecy and what that surge of power could be," Silas explains.

I step back and smirk. "She'll never know. Only I know what that power was. Now tell me, how can we find them?"

He walks towards the bed and sits on it while he scrubs his hands over his face. "I'm working on a plan. I hope it will give me a chance to find them, or at least contact them. They need to know we are alive. I need to give them the key."

I sit next to him and feel the bed dip under me. "Tell me when you plan to do it so I can sense how far they are." He nods and we both sit in silence.

Chapter 30

Mia

I feel the sunlight on my face as I open my eyes, then wince at the pain in my neck from our sleeping arrangement. Natalie chose to sleep on the carpet with a pillow and a blanket while Cerene and I shared her full-size bed. She's sprawled on the bed as if I'm not sleeping next to her and hogging all the covers. I haven't slept in a place other than my own bed lately, and sleeping on someone else's bed has always been a problem of mine. So saying I'm uncomfortable is an understatement, but I'm not going to be ungrateful. They were generous enough to let us stay with them. Hyda, on the other hand, took Xavier's room. I have no idea where he ended up sleeping. I didn't really see him after our roof encounter.

I sit up slowly, trying not to disturb Cerene. The moment I put my feet on the floor, I hear her mumble, "It's morning already? Ugh..."

Of course she's sleepy. We talked most of the night. We exchanged our experiences of our powers. She wields water, while I wield fire. She was trying to catch up on twenty-one years of life in half a day. I was practically listening with one eye open. Then she gave up and finally let us fall asleep. The plan was to wake up in the morning and decide what's next.

I keep thinking of Natalie; she doesn't seem to be adjusting well. She was dizzy and disoriented all night, even after she rested. It looks like traveling through the portal doesn't sit well with her.

I step out of bed and walk to where she's now sleeping. I crouch down and rub her back. "Natalie... Natalie... wake up, sleepy head." She stirs awake and opens her eyes. I notice they are bloodshot and her face is pale.

"How are you feeling?" I ask, concerned.

"Mmm... not too great."

"What do you feel?"

"My head is still spinning. I'll try to get up, wash up, and see if I feel any better."

I nod and give her time to get up. As Natalie and Cerene start getting up from their beds, I seize the moment to use the bathroom ahead of them. Once I step out of the room, I realize I'm wearing a sleeping shirt that barely covers my butt. I peek to the side and see Gideon hunched down over some papers. I don't think he'll see me if I dash to the bathroom.

Concentrating on my target, I take off to the bathroom as fast as I can. I reach for the door as it flies open, and I crash straight into hard muscle and lose my footing. I fumble and claw at the air, desperate to grab onto anything to regain my balance. My hand finally latches onto what feels like a towel, but it's too late. I fall back and land on my bottom. Flustered, I look up, only to find myself staring at a fully naked Xavier.

He holds both his arms up and looks down on me. "Heavens, woman. Watch where you're going." I concentrate on his eyes. It takes me a second to salvage the situation and mumble, "Sorry." I extend my arm up, passing him back the towel.

He looks at me from head to toe, his eyes rest at my thighs and almost bare bottom. He clenches his jaw and swallows. I freeze in my spot, unable to move under his gaze, heat rising under my skin. He then gives me half a smile and says, "You like what you see?" He fastens the towel around his waist and walks past me. He stops for a second. I jump back to my feet and rush inside the bathroom. Before I close the door to hide my shame, he speaks again. "I hope you enjoyed the show."

Anger bubbles inside me. "You wish." With that, I slam the door.

My face is flushed from embarrassment. I've always been confident around men. Xavier infuriates me with the way he looks at me. It's been a tough couple of days, and he practically told me he hates me last night. He definitely knows how to get under my skin with simple words. I wash up as fast as I can, knowing everyone needs to use this bathroom. This time, I open the door slowly to make sure I don't run into one of the guys again. I see Hyda sitting on the couch with a smile on her face. No one is there with her. I sigh in relief and continue my exit.

"Good morning, Mia. I hope you girls got some rest last night."

"Good morning, Hyda. We did get some rest, but Natalie seems to feel unwell," I tell her as I pull at my shirt from both sides.

"Okay, go change and have her wash up, then let's see if we need to take her to the healer." I nod and go back to change. As I'm about to close Cerene's door, I hear her say, "Be prepared to continue your training with Xavier after breakfast."

Fuck!

Chapter 31

Xavier

After breakfast, we each get started on the tasks we discussed. Cerene takes Natalie to the healer to see why she's feeling ill. Gideon and my mother are going around town to investigate what news is circulating. I'm stuck with Celestia and her training. I don't think she likes this arrangement any more than I do. We walk in silence out of the apartment. She's walking beside me but trying her best not to look at me. She's wearing black leggings that hug her curves in all the right places and a white tank top. Her brown wavy hair is loose, swaying with the wind as we walk through the street to our personal training room. It's not too far from the house. I rented this place from its owner. It used to be a storage room for an old library. When they cleared it, I knew it was the perfect place for us to train.

I see her taking in our surroundings. I'm almost tempted to ask her about her world. She looks like a tourist, and we don't have many of those, given the fact that we are shielded from the rest of the world because of our magic, which brings me to our next problem. Celestia doesn't blend well. It's not just the way she carries herself, too careful, too composed, but there's something else, something in her eyes that doesn't quite match the rest of us. With time, people will start to notice.

I try my best to take the road that is mostly quiet this early in the morning. People are just starting to wake up. Merchants are just about to start piling their goods into stalls for the day. I come to a stop in front of a big, black sliding door. I insert the key in the lock and slide the door to the side. "Illuminate," I say and the whole place lights up. I turn around to see a surprised Celestia. "The owner has magic." I motion for her to enter, not caring to explain any further and slide the door closed after her entrance.

The place is big and open. I didn't add much to it. I put up a wooden wall on one side and propped some targets for our dagger throwing. The second wall has a cabinet where we keep most of our weapons: swords, daggers, knives, axes, and arrows. We learn and train with various weapons, but at the end of the day, we all prefer our daggers above all. The other wall has a bench to rest. In the corner we have a small bathroom. I start taking off my jacket and watch Celestia from the corner of my eye lowering her backpack.

I turn to face her. "Are you ready to show me what you got?"

She eyes me as she opens her bag and pulls out a dagger. It's a blade I recognize very well. I'd know that ruby anywhere. Of course, she has my mother's dagger. She stands up and walks far from the wooden wall. Choosing a target, she takes a ready stance as she lifts her arm up, angling her dagger. She throws the dagger as hard as she can, and it lands on the floor. She closes her eyes, her face flushes red. I assume she's annoyed at her failure.

"Of course!" I scoff. She turns her head so fast to look at me, fury in her eyes. I lift my eyebrow. "To throw any blade accurately and quickly, you need to find the balance point. Hold it between your fingers, blade up. Tilt it back slightly as you bring it up, then push your arm towards the target and release as it fully extends, letting your wrist snap forward ever so slightly as you do. This will keep your dagger aligned with the target and keeps your spin predictable." I speak as I demonstrate with my own dagger.

She looks from my hand to the wall as it hits the bullseye. She rolls her eyes at me.

"Show off," she says as she walks to retrieve her dagger and stands to give it a second try.

I hate the way she stands—too proud, too sure of herself. She's had things I've yearned for my whole life and never got, safety, parents that cared for her, the luxury of believing the world can be fair. I tell myself that's why she gets under my skin.

I step behind her to correct her stance and her grip. Her hip brushes my thigh, a hot unwelcomed spark coils in my gut, the kind that makes me want to pull her closer and shove her away in the same breath.

"Not like that," I snap, forcing the hilt upright in her hand. "Blade up, or you'll gut yourself before you touch your enemy."

"Maybe I'm not cut out for this."

A bitter laugh escapes me before I can stop it. "You're not cut out for a lot of things... but here you are." She glances back over her shoulder, eyes bright with defiance, and damn me, she's beautiful.

"You sound like you'd rather I wasn't."

My jaw tightens, but my hand stays on her wrist. "I'd rather you didn't need to be."

Her mouth curves, not quite a smile. "Is that concern... or something else?"

I lean in, close enough that my breath brushes her ear. "Both." My voice comes out low, rough. "Now, try again before I change my mind about teaching you."

She throws the dagger and misses and tries again and again and again and again. I stop counting. She doesn't land one successful hit. I see the frustration in her, and she's exhausted. She keeps flexing her arm. Sweat coats her forehead. I know she's tired, but I'm a stubborn bastard, and I take my training seriously.

"You're a mess, drenched in sweat, failing at every move, and somehow, I can't stop watching."

She jerks her shoulder back, shaking off my comment, letting her hair swing over her face, hiding the flush but not the fire in her eyes. Am I being an ass to her? Absolutely. She looks too soft, and her hands look delicate, with manicured nails. She doesn't look like she's had a hard day in her life. She's hopeless, but damn, the way she keeps going is maddening in ways I don't like admitting.

"Take a break. Drink water. We can try something else next." She tucks the dagger in her waistband. She pulls a bottle of water from her bag as she sits on the bench. I see her eyes roam over me as I throw several daggers at the wall.

I try to focus on my target when I finally hear her voice. "You can be a little nicer, you know. For the record, I really didn't have a hand in Hyda leaving you behind," she says as she takes another swig of water from her bottle.

"I think I liked you better when you were quiet, Celestia."

"Ughh... for the millionth time, my name is Mia."

I ignore her annoyance. "I see my mother didn't train you to throw the dagger correctly."

"Has anyone told you before how annoying you are?" she seethes. I laugh at her remark and see how frustrated she gets as she caps her bottle of water and puts it on the bench. She walks towards me like an elegant cat, ready to attack her prey. Once she's standing just inches away from me, she lifts her hand and ignites fire in her palm. "No, she focused on this instead." She lets the fire in her hand sit there between us for a minute, then closes her hand, snuffing it out. The whole time, she watches me with intent, satisfied at my surprised expression. She steps back. "So are you going to train me more or are we done for the day?"

"Why? Do you have better things to do with your time?" I counter.

"Yes, actually. I'd rather spend the time exploring and getting to know my sister better."

"Hmm... Well, show me what my mother trained you to do, then after that, I'll release you for the day."

Chapter 32

Mia

Lying on the couch my eyes close but my mind is racing with thoughts of earlier today. I barely survived the first day of training with Xavier. He has been rude and hateful. He kept challenging and teasing me like it was a game. He was definitely trying his best to rile me up. He wanted a fight, but for what outcome, I didn't understand. Every sharp word, every impatient glare made me want to storm out, throw the daggers and walk away. He thinks I have a hand in why he was an orphan. He needs to work out these issues with Hyda. I don't know why he was taking his anger out on me. Despite all of it, I was satisfied with his stunned expression when I drew my flame and let it rest in my hand between us.

He didn't know I also have powers like Cerene. I liked that I was able to shock him with something. Damn him, he looked so seductive throwing his daggers one after the other as they hit the bullseye. I couldn't stop noticing the way his jaw was so perfectly chiseled, and the tension in his shoulders when he moved. I loath that it made my pulse quicken, I know he was trying to intimidate me. I really hate men like that, he's infuriating, impossible and ridiculously, unbearably attractive but I'll have to tolerate him and take everything he's able to teach me. I just need to make sure I can keep my frustration at bay. I hate him. I've never hated a person I just met, but it seems the feeling is mutual.

The way he guided me back to the apartment was truly annoying. He was trying to hide me as much as possible, dashing from one street to another making sure it was not crowded. He simply didn't want to be seen with me. I didn't make things easy for him. Not on purpose, at first. I really was fascinated with the whole town and was just enjoying the buzz of the street. I've always loved watching people go about their day.

I need to stop thinking about Xavier. He has been in his room since the moment we arrived at the apartment while I lie here and wait for the others to return. frustration fills me, my feet hit the ground and I start roaming around the living room, finding some papers sitting on the dining table along with maps of Eterna and a couple of pins and pens. I take a look at one specific map. It is old, and the parchment is yellow and brown around the edges. It looks ancient. It looks more like blueprints of a house or a villa, and I'm just curious about it all.

I manage to find a clean piece of paper and pencil. I sit there and start sketching. I want to occupy myself while I wait. I'm tired from training but eager to know more about this place. More about my sister's life, my birth parents, and how we can find them. As I start to sketch, I hear music—a guitar melody drifting through the apartment, enchanting me with its tune and tugging at something deep in my soul. It's a sad melody, and it makes my heart ache. I lose myself in it, my hand sketching as if it's guided by its rhythm.

I don't know how long I've been sketching when the apartment door opens. Cerene and Natalie say hello as they head towards where I'm sitting, but I don't think Natalie is feeling any better because she looks paler than before.

"What happened? Did the doctor... I mean, the healer tell you what's wrong?"

Cerene pulls out a chair for Natalie to sit. "The healer tried, but results were not clear. She seems healthy despite what she's feeling," she explains as she settles next to me.

"So what do we do next?"

"I need to rest. I've never felt this way before. I feel so weak and drained," Natalie responds.

It breaks me to see her like this, so fragile and unlike the vibrant, fun person she is. I reach for her hands and try to help her stand. "Let's get you to bed. If you stay this way, you're going back home."

"No, Mia. I'm not leaving your side."

"We will discuss this later, after you rest."

Cerene watches us as we talk, not interfering in our conversation. Yet, she helps me take Natalie to her bed. After we make sure Natalie is comfortably tucked in bed, Cerene and I exit the room and head to the kitchen. She starts rummaging through the cabinets in search of something to eat while I quietly prepare myself a cup of tea. She grabs a box of cookies, satisfied. "Found them!" The corners of her mouth lift in a smile that reaches her eyes. I chuckle at the sight of her happiness I think we are more alike than we know.

"So, how was training with Xavier?" she asks between bites.

"Ughh... don't ask." I mumble in frustration.

"Oh no! That bad?" But I don't even answer, just give her a look of affirmation.

"Look, I know he can be—"

I cut her off. "An ass?"

She laughs. "Well, difficult, but he's really nice deep inside. He cares too much at times. He shows his pain in different ways. God knows we have had our arguments. He's overprotective." She watches me as I digest her words.

"Overprotective? No. He is harsh, angry, and cold. He just hates me. Only God knows why."

We are interrupted by Hyda and Gideon coming back from their exploration trip. They seem to be engrossed in a deep conversation.

"Since Edith is the leader of the Elders, I can see why Eterna would crumble. Magic will falter because she's power hungry and will stop at nothing to gain other people's magic. Her husband did it before her. So that doesn't surprise me," Hyda states.

Gideon looks furious. "Yes, but they could have easily recognized you getting that close to the old city of Eterna. That part of town used to belong to the Vega family. Now it's just an abandoned palace, and they have eyes and ears to see who dares to enter it." He slides his hand into his hair. "I'm just glad I grabbed you before you got any further."

With that, I hear Xavier open his door and walk out to see what all the commotion coming from the kitchen is all about. Gideon, Hyda, and Xavier discuss the situation at hand while Cerene and I listen. Xavier keeps telling his mother, "It's foolish to underestimate Elder Edith," assuring her that they will make a plan to get to the abandoned part of town. "Going without a plan is suicidal," he continues. Hyda listens to him, but from the short time I've gotten to know her, I've seen she has a will of iron and will not be persuaded.

Chapter 33

Xavier

After training, I choose to hide in my room and play my guitar instead of having to interact with Celestia any longer. I have to admit, she's strong-willed and stubborn as a bull. I admire her dedication at making things hard on me on the way back. She kept swaying away from the path, wanting to see the town. After spending some time playing my music in peace, I hear Gideon's voice, meaning my mother is back, too. I gently place my guitar in its usual corner beside the bed and step outside.

As soon as I open the door, I hear Gideon reprimanding my mother for being hasty. I come into the room to understand what is happening and how my mother tried to go back to the Vega Palace. When she left this morning, she didn't mention that was her plan. My mother is a sneaky general and I can't underestimate her. I trust her judgment, but she's been away from Eterna for a long time, and things have changed around here since then.

"Going without a plan is suicidal."

She presses her lips and looks deeply in my eyes. "I know Silas and Freya are alive. Edith wouldn't kill them. They're too important. I want to see if there are any signs of them there."

"Mother, no one has been in that part of town. I scouted that place many times before they completely closed it a couple of years ago."

I notice Cerene and Gideon look at me with wide eyes. I choose to ignore both of them and continue. "I remember our house. I know exactly where it is. I recognize the roof we used to sit on, me and you." My mother's eyes soften when she hears that. "I went often, in hopes of finding you." I confess as I look at Cerene. This is something I've never mentioned to her. I didn't want her to cling to any false hope. *I didn't tell anyone; it was mine to feel alone, mine to swallow the ache that claws at my chest.* I shrug my shoulders and address her. "Sorry, I didn't tell any of you." She nods in understanding. I lock eyes with Celestia, who is piercing me with her gaze. I see a flicker of sadness, something tender, almost... pity. My chest tightens, and I can taste the bitterness rising. *I don't want anyone's pity, especially from her. From her, it feels like a blade. I don't want her feeling sorry for me, not her.*

My attention is drawn back to my mother, who is now standing in front of me, gently reaching for my hand to hold. "Oh, my dear boy. I'm so sorry... I'm sorry for not being there. I hope you understand there was nothing I could've done to change this outcome."

I don't respond. I have nothing to say to that statement. *I'm a grown man. Why does it hurt so much to hear her say those words?* I close my eyes and say, "Okay, let's all sit and agree on a plan for the next few days."

We gather around the kitchen table where Cerene and Celestia are already sitting. Air thick with tension, I watch Celestia eyeing me as I take my seat, her big, brown eyes rimmed with thick, long lashes. She's sipping on a cup of tea, trying her best to look calm and collected. They all watch me, waiting for me to come up with a plan. Instead, I ask, "What does everyone have in mind?" Celestia opens her mouth to say something. I raise my hand before she can say anything. "You need training. There is nothing you can do." I see the fury rising in her eyes.

"How would you know what I was going to say? Douchebag."

I smirk at that. *"Douchebag."* How funny. I should be offended, but heat flares through me, sharp and satisfying.

She turns to address my mother. "Hyda, Natalie is not doing well, and despite her protests, we have to do something."

My mother looks at her with loving eyes. "What did the healer say?"

Cerene pouts as she drums her fingers on the table and answers. "Nothing really. Her symptoms are rather strange for a healthy person. He asked her to rest."

My mother narrows her eyes, the gears in her mind are turning. "I've heard old tales, but I'm not sure of their accuracy." *She always knew how to get everyone's attention. Those tales she always told me as a child.*

"Ages ago, when Eterna was first shielded from the rest of the world for its magic, individuals who were not born in Eterna started to get sick. Slowly, people who had magic helped transport them to the other side of the shield. It's some sort of side effect. That's how they started to separate people and recognize Elders and royals. It's as if the land recognized bloodlines with magic. With time, only people born in Eterna were able to live here. No one ever knew the reason." My mother continues, "If that's the case here, we have to get her back home, but we'll need to figure out how to get more portal keys."

"I don't care how many portal keys we have left. Natalie needs to go back home, and that's not up for debate," Celestia snaps back at my mother.

"I'll have to agree with you, my child. I'm sorry. I knew this was a possibility. But I also knew you'd never agree to come through the portal without Natalie. It was a risk I had to take." My mother agrees.

I suggest taking one vial of the portal keys to Jake to see if he can replicate it. Or at least find the components to its power. My mother agrees to that, too. "None of this brings us close to finding out where they are keeping the Vega family," I point out.

My mother stands from her seat. "I'll take Cerene and Mia with me. I have a plan. You can go see about the portal keys. Gideon, stay and take care of Natalie," my mother orders. The person I knew as a child shines through those big blue eyes. I missed hearing her command a room.

Chapter 34

Mia

It was difficult to wrap my mind around everything. I did make my peace with the fact that magic exists, and my flames, but for magic to affect Natalie? That's something I wasn't prepared to deal with. Natalie is my family, and I can't let anything happen to her. *Damn it, this is all my fault. I should have insisted she stay back home. What was I thinking, dragging her here with me? I know she came willingly, but I should have prevented it.*

My mind is riled up. Cerene's voice interrupts my raging thoughts. "Mia, everything will be okay. We'll figure out how to solve this."

I appreciate her sentiment, so I just smile at her. "Hyda is waiting for us to get ready. Let's just go…" I hesitate. "And Cerene?" She looks at me with love in her eyes, waiting for my next words.

"Thank you."

That puts a smile on her face, and I notice how her eyes light up. "Of course. What are sisters for?" she responds with a voice filled with joy.

We wait till sundown, until the streets are silent and people are retiring to their homes for the day. Dressed in all black clothes, we exit the apartment to go with Hyda. She doesn't tell us what her plans are. She just wants us to follow her in the dim lights of the now dark city. For the first time since I met Hyda, I notice how her moves are swift and precise, she's like a whisper of a ghost, blending in with the dark as if she were the shadows herself. *No wonder I never spotted her all the years she was watching me back home.* I look around. We are in an abandoned, old part of town. Windows are dark and covered with dust. Some of these houses are nothing but skeletons. *Is this where my parents and Hyda used to live?*

Hyda leads us along the streets with intent, knowing this part of town like the back of her hand. She motions for us to slow down as we come closer to a large house. Two grand, cracked stone columns frame the house, giving it a grander look, lost to time. The windows are dark and covered in dark green vines. A heavy-looking, dark brown gate is blocking the entrance despite the crumbled wooden door behind it. The blown up, broken, half brick fence surrounding the house indicates the amount of damage this house has taken in the past.

Hyda leads me and Cerene around the house, and we walk in utter silence, following her steps. At the end of the street, what looks like almost fifty or sixty feet away from the house, stands a small tomb-like stone, rooted in the ground and surrounded by trees. Hyda stops in front of it and starts checking all our surroundings. She stands behind the tombstone and pushes it to the side, revealing a small staircase leading into the ground.

"I'm not going in there," whispers Cerene.

"You can't stay out here," Hyda says as she starts her descent. *What is it with this woman and tunnels? Whenever I have to follow her, it's a hidden passageway.*

Cerene eyes me and I shrug. She smiles. "After you, sister."

I start to go down the stairs in the dark passageway. This is unlike Hyda's passage back at the store. It's old and humid, and the smell of wet dirt overwhelms my senses. It doesn't smell bad, it smells like fresh rain on dry land on a hot day. It's a short flight down the passage, and I hear Cerene try to shift the stone to close the entrance as she comes down behind me. I'm met by Hyda at the end of the steps. It's pitch dark right now. I don't see anything, but I can feel Cerene and Hyda beside me.

"Mia, we could use your flame, my child," Hyda whispers in the dark. I nod even though I know they can't see me. I take a deep breath and concentrate on my inner flame. It's a feeling that I learned to get used to. It's a heat wave at the back of my mind. I coax it to bubble up, then urge it to come to life. The flame illuminates the dark around us.

"Oh my God! Your magic is even more mesmerizing than mine," Cerene says with a giddy voice behind me. I turn to look at her for a minute and see the reflection of my flame in her eyes, giving her a beautiful glow.

"Let's go, girls." Hyda gestures for us to continue walking.

Under the light of my flame, I can see moss around the edges of the floor and ceiling. The only sound is our footsteps. There are small puddles of water on the floor. "Where are we going, Hyda?" I ask, wondering why we have to take this road underground.

"You will find out soon enough," she answers me between panting breaths as the passage takes a turn to go upwards. Oh God, how much I hate Hyda when she doesn't give me a straight answer. Everything is a mystery with her. She has to keep me intrigued as if I haven't followed her without question to Eterna in search of my family. After a few minutes, we come to a stop as a massive wall that seemingly ends the passage. I give Cerene a questioning look, and she just shrugs.

Hyda steps forward, extending her hand. She presses her fingers against the cold, rough stone wall, feeling the uneven surface beneath her touch, and carefully moves away the moss and dirt clinging to the crevices, revealing faint seams.

"What are you doing?" Cerene's question echoes in the passageway.

"Shhhh..." Hyda responds quickly. Her movements are slow, deliberate, every scrape and brush is a search for a hidden latch. We hear a soft *click*. "Help me push, slowly and gently."

We both come close to her. I snuff out my flame and start pushing the wall inwards. It makes a squeaking sound as it opens into a dark room. Once the opening is big enough for us to go through, we stop pushing at it.

Hyda enters first and we both follow her. The only light in this room is what little moonlight is able to come through the dirt-covered window. Tattered curtains hang around three big windows. Everything is covered with a blanket of dust, undisturbed cobwebs at every corner. Crooked, grand tapestries hang on the wall. The room looks like it was frozen in time.

I try to summon my flame to see better, but the moment it ignites, Hyda says, "No light. They will see it." So I let it die in my hand. Now I know she doesn't want anyone knowing we are in here. Cerene and I both observe the room. A king-sized bed sits in the middle, draped with dust-covered linens. Two small bassinets sit about four feet from the bed. On either side of the bed, matching wooden cabinets stand. An armchair lies overturned, legs up in the air, as if knocked over in a struggle. Clothes and personal items are scattered across the floor, the entire room is in chaos, signs of a life once lived, now abandoned.

Hyda is still looking around the room as if she is searching for something specific.

"What is this place?" I whisper.

"Girls, this was your parents' room... Your room," she says gently as she turns to look at both of us. "This is the Vega house. Your house, if things hadn't gone up in flames." Her voice is laced with vulnerability.

I look at Cerene, my eyes brimming with tears, realization hitting me like a bulldozer. *I'm standing in what was supposed to be my home, where I should have grown up and made memories. Memories with my parents and sister.* Noticing Cerene's features mirroring my own, I go to her and hug her as a sob bubbles out of me, overwhelmed with emotions I can't place. I have no memories here, but the feeling of loss of what could have been breaks my heart.

I feel Cerene's embrace comes to an end. "What the fuck, Hyda? You could have given us a heads-up. Bringing us here without even giving us a clue is foolish. Didn't you think we would be overwhelmed by it all? We both long to know about our parents, but springing things this way is not kind. We need time to process all this." Cerene is angry, and I understand that feeling very well. I look at the room one more time, and an overwhelming feeling rushes through me. I clutch my chest as pain suffocates me. Before I can say a word, everything goes black.

I'm standing in the shadow, hidden in a place I haven't seen before. Two people are talking to each other in hushed voices. A man and a woman. I try to walk closer, but something is holding me back. I'm shackled to the floor. Confusion and panic takes over me. I want to get out of these restraints. I shake and kick my legs around, wanting to find a way to see if there is a lock I can break. Forgetting about the man and woman in the corner, I summon my flame, but it doesn't come. I try to scream to ask them for help, but my voice doesn't come out. They can't see me. They don't know I'm here. It looks like only I can see them. Are they also trapped? They continue to talk to each other. The woman turns, and I can see her face now. She's an older woman with brown eyes. She's still addressing the man. "The other key is still in the house." I try to listen more, to get closer to them. I try to move my body forward, but it's in vain. The shackles still hold me in place. The feeling of being trapped makes my chest constrict. I can't breathe... oh God, how I hate this feeling... I can't breathe.

Hands grip me tightly, pulling me upwards. My vision is blurry. I see someone's face in front of me. "Mia... Mia... oh God! Mia, please wake up." I try to talk but my throat is dry. I start to make out the voice talking to me. It's Cerene.

"It's okay, child. This happened to her the other day when her flame was activated."

"What do you mean? Why is she unconscious now?"

All I hear are hushed and concerned voices. Although, Cerene is more panicked than Hyda. The fog in my vision clears, and I can see them hover over me. "Thank God you're awake. I was terrified. What happened?" Cerene asks me.

I swallow, trying to ease the dryness in my throat before talking. "I'm okay. Another dream took over me."

She scrunches her eyebrows. "What kind of dream?"

"I don't know how to explain it. My dreams don't feel like dreams at all; they're fragments of places and faces I've never seen. They're sharp and vivid, but I can't hold on to them. Some of them feel urgent and some of them fade, it's like watching moments I was not meant to witness," I try to stand up from where I was laying on the floor. My black clothes are completely covered in dust now. "I'm assuming it's something connected to my newly awakened powers, but I can't make sense of it." I continue explaining as I try to dust off my pants and tell them what my dream was.

"Those dreams are part of your gift, Mia," Hyda says.

"Wow, how perfect. A gift that sends me to places where I feel like I'm stuck in a bad dream."

"Can't you see, my child? Your magic is guiding you and us to what we seek."

I'm confused by her last statement. *What is she trying to say?*

"So the woman in your dream said, 'the other key is in the house?'"

"Yes." I'm uncertain where this conversation is going. Cerene is standing very close to me, trying to make sure I'm really okay. I look at her and smile. "I'm fine. Don't worry."

"Says the person that was just lying flat on the floor unconscious."

I chuckle. "Fair."

Hyda steps away and starts looking at things around the walls. "Your dad was a clever man. He never left things for anyone to be able to find them easily." She huffs. "Good thing I knew you so well, my dear friend, Silas." She's talking to herself, mumbling those words.

"What are you looking for?" I ask her.

"A key."

I look at Cerene and echo, "A key?"

"Yes.. yes, my child, a key and maybe a map... If we don't find your parents, we'll need to search this room upside down to find what we need to get to the prophecy. This is the only way I can help you save Eterna and possibly your parents." Cerene and I follow Hyda's lead and search all the walls and furniture.

"What are we looking for exactly in the walls?" Cerene asks.

"Anything that looks different or out of place, yet not too obvious. Some things are hidden in plain sight, yet we can never see them." We search in silence for what feels like forever.

I'm tired now and covered in dust. I sit on the big bed to rest and take in my surroundings once more in hopes that something stands out to me. That's when I see it, a glittery flash as the moonlight hits one of the small bassinets. It's like starlight caught in mid air, pulsing softly in the shadows. It feels less like light and more like a whisper made visible, a secret meant for us to find. "Cerene. Hyda. I think I found something."

They both stop their search and come to stand next to where I'm sitting down on the bed. I point with my finger to the exact spot I see the shimmer. Cerene walks towards the bassinet. Crouching down, she starts to take all the bedding out of it and tries to pull on the wooden corner of the small bassinet, but it doesn't give. She picks it up and tries to shake it, but nothing falls out. Hyda and I walk up to her to see how we can help. There is definitely something in there.

"May I?" Hyda says to Cerene, extending her hand to take the bassinet from her. She places it back on the floor and runs her hand around the edges. She finds nothing. Then she places her hand on the spot I point to and twists it in different directions. It suddenly pops open. An old silver key falls out. She laughs as Cerene and I watch her in astonishment. "Oh Silas, how I miss you and your games," she says to absolutely no one.

Chapter 35

Xavier

My mission for tonight is to go to Jake's shop and hope he can figure out a way to replicate this magical portal key. It's always so odd to walk the empty streets of Eterna at night. Usually buzzing with people, now so quiet. There are things you don't pay attention to in the crowd—the beauty of the street. Every wall of the market is covered with lush green vines bursting with multicolor blooms, making the brick wall come to life. I see why Celestia kept marveling at it all when I was trying to guide her back home after our morning training. I always appreciate the quiet of the night. It is the perfect time to actually see the magic of the city and its beauty. Magically lit lanterns adorn every corner, illuminating and giving the street a cozy hue. The sweet, floral scent drifts on the cool night breeze, while glittering stars in the night's clear sky shine down on me like fulfilled dreams, making the walk all the more enchanting.

I'm not surprised to see Jake's shop closed when I come up in front of its entrance. I knock on the wooden door, then I wait a couple of minutes and knock again, but there seems to be no one inside. That's very strange given the fact that Jake lives at the back of his store. I round the side of the store, peek into the dark window, and confirm no one is there. *Where would Jake go?*

Deflated, I rake my hand across my face, trying to figure out where to find him or whom to ask. I start walking back home. I need to consult with Gideon. Maybe we can find another person for this job. I always look for Jake first, simply because I trust him. He's efficient and discrete. I never have to think twice when it comes to him getting things done. The farther I get from Jake's shop, the more frustrated I become. Anger bubbles inside me for not accomplishing this task. *In situations like this, I feel useless; not being able to come up with a solution to solve a problem. It is always so complicated when it comes to magic.*

Before I know it, I'm climbing the stairs to our apartment. As soon as I open the door, I hear their chatter. My mother is talking to Cerene. Celestia, Natalie, and Gideon are in the middle of it all. Seeing Gideon baffled between the babble of the four women around him makes me smile. He's definitely overwhelmed. His eyes are wide open, looking from one woman to the next, trying to catch up with their conversation.

I clear my throat and they all turn around to look at me. "Finally, you're here," Gideon says, relieved. "Please help me out here. They want to take Natalie back home. She's not feeling well. Hyda thinks magic is causing all this, but we have only two portal keys. If we use one of them, then we'll have only one left."

I run my hand through my hair, calculating an appropriate approach to inform them that Jake isn't home, and I have no way of finding him. "Okay, there is no good way to say this."

Celestia folds her arms across her chest, waiting. Her eyes settle on my lips as she nervously bites the corner of her lower lip.

I exhale loudly. "Jake is gone. I can try to see in the morning if he opens his shop again. This is the first time I haven't found him when I need him. It is very strange. I can't help feeling that something is off."

My mother nods in understanding. Gideon's eyes are fixed on me, and I know he's thinking of the worst-case scenario. So am I. Things are not right lately. The more I press on finding information about magic or what's going on, the more uneasy I feel.

"Great. We are back to square one. I won't put Natlaie's life on the line. She needs to go home, and I don't care even if it's the last portal key we have," Celestia says.

My mother sits on the couch while Natalie protests about wanting to stay, but I look at her, and sure enough, her face is so pale, as if life has begun to slip away and take the glow she had when she first arrived. As much as I hate to agree with Celestia, I think Natalie has to go home. At least she'd be able to recover where she belongs. "I agree. Natalie needs to go home," I say and watch the surprise evident on Celestia's face.

Her mouth hangs open and her brows hitch up, her voice barely a whisper as she says, "Thank you." The girls scramble away, helping Natalie get ready.

Once they are out of earshot, I ask, "What's the plan, Mother?" She fills me in on what happened with them tonight. I'm stunned at the key she's holding in her hands and at the power that Celestia holds. *Who would've known a city girl from another world can hold this much power?*

"What does it open?" I'm lured by the glow of the silver key.

"Silas was good at many things, but the best thing about him was his ability to keep things hidden. Whatever this key opens, it will be one step closer to the prophecy and to helping these girls fulfill their destinies."

"Why didn't you tell me Celestia had magic?"

"Why would it matter? You found out in time. Besides, I thought you were smarter than that, Son. If Cerene has magic, why would her twin not have any?" She responds with mischief in her voice and continues, "We have to take Natalie home, but someone will need to help her get to the portal entrance. She's not in good shape. Then we can focus on what this key opens." She taps me on the shoulder and walks back to my room. Before she shuts the door behind her, she tells me, "I believe you know what to do."

Interlude

Somewhere in Eterna, in a cave that is long forgotten by people, its floor uneven and damp, carrying the stale scent of decay and death, lies the grave of many who have perished in the dark without anyone remembering them. The floor is littered with bones. They are my companions. I'm pretty sure I lost my mind a long time ago when I started talking to the remains. "I need every shred of power. It must be mine. I must seek that ripple of magic and its source. It may be the only way to find them and get my revenge."

I dig my fingers in the dirt of this hollow cave that has housed me for the past twenty-one years. My only visitor is the occasional guard, sent by Edith and her evil need for more magic. She may think I'm helping her, but I'm helping no one other than myself. "It is imperative that I get my revenge and find them." Power surges through my body, draining the land of its magic as my fingers dig deeper in the earth. I look at my arms as my veins turn black. I know the meaning of this, but I won't refrain from taking more from Eterna, because it took everything from me.

Chapter 36

Mia

Cerene and I guide Natalie back to bed as she protests about sending her back home. "Mia, I came here to help you and be with you. I might not have magic and feel like shit, but I won't leave you alone."

"I don't want to lose you. You need to understand, I won't let anything happen to you here. You will listen to me and go home. I'm not alone here," I tell her as we help her sit on the bed. She shakes her head at me. "Natalie, please, if you stay, I'll worry and won't be able to concentrate on finding my parents. If you don't go, I'll have to just drop this and come home with you." I try to persuade her. She stays quiet for a minute.

Cerene intervenes. "Will it help if I promise you she'll be okay? I know you guys have been together all your lives, but I care about her too. Nothing will happen to Mia as long as I breathe." I hear the truth in Cerene's words, and Natalie hears it too.

Natalie nods. "How will I know what happens to you? Will you come back home later? You know our phones don't work here."

"Natalie, I swear it. I'll come home as soon as I see this through. I'll figure out a way to contact you," I assure her even though I know she's not fully convinced.

Cerene walks from the bed to the corner of her room. There is a white wooden closet where she keeps all her clothes. She opens it, riffles through her clothes, and retrieves a small vial. *What is it with this place and vials? Do they use them for everything?* She clutches it with her hands and brings it to us. "I swear Xavier will kill me if he knows I'm giving you this." She hands it to Natalie and continues explaining. "This is a Klinxer potion. If you take a small sip, it will allow you to speak to anyone you want in their mind. Problem is, they will hear you, but you won't be able to hear them back unless they drink the potion, too. Take it and use it wisely to let Mia know you're okay. I was supposed to use it for emergencies. Because, as you heard Xavier, if Jake is gone, then we have no way of getting any more of anything."

Natalie takes the potion with wide eyes.

Cerene reminds her, "Remember, very small sip." Natalie nods. I feel a warmth spread in my chest at the interaction between my best friend and my sister.

I reach out and clasp Cerene's shoulder, squeezing very gently. "Thank you for this."

Natalie hides the potion in her pocket as I turn around and start putting Natalie's things back in her backpack. I hear her say under her breath, "So much for being a nurse and saving you. It looks like I'm the one who needs saving right now."

I chuckle. "Oh Natalie, I never needed saving... but I definitely always want your support." I finish zipping up her backpack, carry it over to the bed, and hold Natalie's hand, preparing to tell her what I've decided I want her to tell my parents once she's back home.

"Natalie, I'm sorry to have to put this on you, but I'd like you to go to my parents and tell them the truth about Eterna. I don't know how long I'll be here. I don't want them to be worried. I want them to know I'm safe. Tell them I'm with good people." I glance at Cerene and smile. "Tell them I found my twin sister."

Natalie looks at me with tears in her eyes. "Is this you breaking up with me?"

We both laugh at that comment, then she continues to assure me that she'll do what I want. After a few hugs and tears shed, I gather myself and say, "Cerene, we are ready."

Cerene hops out of the chair she was occupying, and she quickly wipes a tear from her eyes, hiding her emotions from me as she cheerfully says, "Alright." We help Natalie back up from the bed. In the living room, we find Xavier and Gideon talking, but they stop their conversation the moment they see us.

Xavier is looking at me. I feel those dark blue eyes bore into me, reaching for my soul. My breath hitches as I watch him lick his lower lip. I'm lost in my thoughts, like I'm under his spell. *Oh God, why does he make me feel this way? I hate him. He's insufferable. Why is he looking at me that way? He hates me. I know what he's doing... He's trying to intimidate me with his looks.*

I blink fast and come back to reality as he speaks. "Gideon and I were discussing opening the portal in a different place than where you guys came through. The only problem is we don't know where it will take you on the other side."

Cerene asks the question I was going to ask. "Why not the same place?"

Gideon answers this time. "They have guards posted there right now. We suspect they felt where the powerful magic was coming from. Elder Edith doesn't miss a thing."

Hyda comes out of her room slowly, her steps soft and steady, and says, "Edith will always be a thorn in my side. Maybe try a place along the same side where we came in. As far as I know, that area is the border of the shield between our worlds." Xavier and Gideon nod in acknowledgment.

"Aren't you coming with us?" I ask her.

"No, my child, I need to attend to something tonight." *Can she be any more vague?* She approaches Natalie and gives her an awkward hug. "Take care of yourself, Natalie. If I'm right, you will feel better the moment you step out of Eterna."

Natalie presses her lips tight together and nods back at Hyda.

We walk out of the apartment together. My chest tightens at the thought of not being able to talk to Natalie for a while, but her well-being comes first. If Eterna is hurting her, she needs to go back to her life where she's safe and healthy.

Chapter 37

Xavier

Concern is etched on the girls' faces as we walk through the dark alleys. Every time a sound comes out of one of the houses we pass, they jump. The more we walk, the more I notice exhaustion overtaking Natalie. I stop them at one of the corners and tell them, "We can't continue like this. I don't want her to faint." Both Cerene and Celestia agree with me.

Gideon offers to pick Natalie up for the rest of the way, but Celestia says, "Hey, didn't the Zarka say if we needed help to just call upon them?"

Cerene answers her. "Yes, you're correct. I totally forgot they mentioned that."

"How do we call them?" Celestia asks.

"I'll try to concentrate and call them. Same way I mindlink Xavier and Gideon on the missions." We stand for a couple of minutes in the corner while Gideon supports Natalie.

It takes Cerene a little longer than I expected, but then she says, "Okay, they are on their way to us." The Zarkas are very fast birds. It takes them less than five minutes to find us. As two of them land, the wind shifts around us, and I hope to God we are not being tracked, though it wouldn't be unusual to spot Zarkas gliding across the sky. They are massive, perfect for anyone to follow us if they had reason to. Gideon carries Natalie and rides one, while Cerene, Celestia, and I ride the second one.

Cerene is in the front, leading the bird, while Celestia is clutching her sister as if her life depends on it, clearly not used to the height we are at. I, on the other hand, sit behind her and try my best to hold on with my legs and not touch Celestia at all. The wind blows her hair everywhere. Some of it gets in my face, and I can smell the sweet scent of coconut. It beckons me to lean in, and I catch myself sniffing her hair. *What the hell am I doing?* I pull myself as far as the bird allows me.

As we reach our destination, I tell Cerene, "Make sure to land a good distance away from the guards. Though guards don't look twice at Zarkas, they're used for trade runs, patrols, and messenger flights. No one bothers to track them; as long as we don't raise suspicion, we are just another shadow among many."

The Zarka descends in a sweep of wind, its massive wings stirring the dust into a whirling dance in the dark. The landing is as quiet as it can be, given its size. Shimmering gold talons curl into the earth with graceful precision as it kneels down for us to dismount. Cerene pats the bird as it inclines its head to her. I still don't fully understand that sudden connection between the twins and the Zarka.

We walk silently in the open field, dark green grass crunching under our boots and the scent of roses in bloom blowing in the night's breeze. We walk as close as we can to the edge of the barrier. We were never able to see it. It always felt like a power or force that pushed us away from it, preventing us from physically passing.

I grab the portal key from my pocket. "Are you ready? Once we open it, we need you to pass fast. I hope it will close quickly behind you. But we won't leave until it does, just in case the guards come. We'll ensure no one goes after you."

Natalie drags her feet as she turns to Gideon. She gives him a hug. "Thank you. You're really nice, and I wish I could stay and get to know you better."

My friend's eyes twinkle as he smiles back at her. "A pleasure, Natalie. I hope I'll get to see you again. Get home safely."

Cerene and Celestia sandwich Natalie in an embrace. I see Celestia's face contort with sadness. I can almost see a tear dance in her eyes under the moonlight. I feel something in my chest, a feeling I can't place. My chest tightens at her unhappiness.

They whisper their goodbyes and tell me, "Okay, we are ready."

I throw the key at the invisible wall and watch in disbelief as the portal opens in front of me. It's something I never thought I'd witness in my life. Having my mother live all that time on the other side makes me curious to know how things are over there.

The portal snaps open, revealing a flickering, swirling, silver-blue energy. It pulses and hums. I feel it vibrating in my bones. As the glow expands big enough to let anyone of any size pass through, I'm concerned this glow can be seen from miles away. Maybe it was a mistake opening a portal at night. I bid Natalie goodbye as she steps inside and waves goodbye to Celestia. We watch her as she disappears into the void.

The portal does not close as fast as I thought it would. Gideon is keeping watch from one side, and I'm on the lookout from the opposite. Cerene seems to comfort Celestia for having to let her friend go. I think she feels alone in this new world without her best friend. I can't relate to her feelings, though. None of us has ever left Eterna. I assume it feels strange to be in a different place that is not what you're used to. I watch the girls walk towards the Zarkas that were still waiting for us. As the portal starts to slowly close after what feels like forever, I hear slow steps approach behind me. The crunch of the grass underneath their shoes alerts me to their presence. I slowly and discreetly draw my dagger out, readying myself for the person approaching. Before they can ambush me, I make a swift turn to find two guards coming at me. Their attention is drawn to the remaining small opening of the portal which gives me the opportunity to attack first. I call, "Guards!" to let Gideon and the girls know we have company as I land the first hit on one of them. The second guard lunges at me, ready to strike, but Gideon rushes to my aid, ready to fight dirty. We both deliver calculated hits straight to the face. The sound of crunching bones and flesh echoes in the night as the guards cry out in pain. The guards do put up a good fight, but we are faster and stronger. We take them out in minutes, and we run back to mount the Zarka the moment the portal closes shut completely, leaving the unconscious guards on the ground.

Chapter 38

Mia

It's been a couple of days since I sent Natalie home. It still feels so strange to not be able to talk to her. I hope she's feeling well and back to her normal life. I was hoping she'd use the potion Cerene gave her. Despite being busy with training day in and day out, I miss her a lot.

Cerene is so kind to me, and I can see how life would have been so different having her around. We have so much in common. We are both outgoing and active, and we like to find trouble because it adds action and excitement to our lives.

She's tougher than me, I have to admit that. She told me everything about growing up in an orphanage. I felt horrible for her. I can't begin to imagine how hard it was. That rough life made her stronger. She's a fighter. I'm glad she has Xavier looking after her. Albeit he hasn't been nice to me, but he loves her and he's her family.

Gideon is so resilient when he puts his mind to anything. He goes above and beyond to find information and facts we can use, even though they haven't let me go on one single mission with them. I hate being left behind, and I know they put me in this bubble because Xavier doesn't think I'm ready. Little does he know that the minute I stepped through that portal, I felt like a butterfly emerging from her cocoon, seeing the light of day for the first time.

I'm again left in the apartment to look over some books about the history of Eterna. One of the books explains how the land was enchanted with magic, though no one knows the main source of it. All they know is that it is in the land itself. The prophecy is mentioned briefly, but nothing indicates what it foretold. As I brush my hands down the old pages, I feel a sinking feeling in the pit of my stomach, like I'm free falling. I close the book, trying to get a hold of myself, but something is happening to my body. I look at my hands. They're trembling as the feeling of flames consuming me starts flooding through all of my senses. I feel sweat trickling down my spine. I try to blink, but all I see are flashes of light. A voice startles me.

"Celestia, breathe. You're letting your magic consume you."

"Zarka?" The bird hasn't spoken to me since the day I arrived. "What is happening to me?"

"Your body is not used to all the power you have. You have to recognize when a vision wants to come to you." The Zarka's voice rumbles in my head as it continues to explain. "You're almost ready. We feel your flame growing. We'll soon need your help." With that, the Zarka's voice disappears, and I feel my body relax.

A vision? Is that what's been happening to me all this time? Not dreams, but visions of things that might happen? If this is true, I need to revisit my dreams and see if I can find any clues in them that can lead us further into our mission.

I'm startled when Gideon, Xavier, and Cerene come barging in the apartment, laughing and teasing each other. They're joking around, talking about what transpired on their mission, oblivious to my existence in the room. I look at them with envy. They make a great team. Their dynamic and how they complete each other in everything makes me want to be part of it all. To be one of them.

Chapter 39

Xavier

It's been a couple of days of mission after mission, with each one giving us a small glimpse of hope of finding something bigger. Today was a successful one. Despite our shattered, wet, and dirty clothes from the amount of time we crawled in the tunnels to map out our next move, we came back home content. It was all worth it because we finally found a way into the Elders' Castle without being detected. Cerene, Gideon, and I walk all the way home laughing and making fun of each other about how Gideon and I got stuck in the narrow tunnel at one point and needed Cerene to flush us out with her water power. We enter the apartment in the same state of laughter with tears of mirth in our eyes.

Gideon and Cerene continue to relive the scene from the tunnel as I notice Celestia sitting at the far corner of the apartment, books surrounding her as she looks at us. Envy is etched all over her face, and I know that look too well—a look of wanting to be included. She notices me looking at her and tries to compose herself by flipping the pages of the book sitting in front of her at the table, pretending she's busy. I almost feel like I want to give her a hug. I'm surprised at that thought. *She's winning my traitorous*

mind with her innocent doe-like eyes. If I'm being honest with myself,
she's growing on me. I like how resilient she is. No matter what I throw
at her, she seems to always resist.

As Cerene and Gideon go to their rooms to get changed, I cheerfully
say, "Celestia." She rolls her eyes at the use of her birth name.

"It looks like it's time for you to join us on our next mission. We
finally found a way in."

She jumps out of her seat in excitement, and her eyes light up before
she even speaks. "FINALLY." Her voice is breathless, unguarded, and
something in me tightens. "Are you serious?" She asks seeking confirmation.

I nod calmly though my pulse is already betraying me. Before I
can stop her, she's moving closer, wrapping her arms around me in
a sudden, impulsive hug. I can feel the heat of her body, the curve of
her chest brushing mine, and I swear the world narrows to nothing
but this, her heartbeat, my own, and the dangerous closeness of our
bodies. I'm aware of everything: the scent of her hair, the sound of her
breathing, the almost-hush of the room. My hands hover, wanting to
touch, needing to, but trying not to. She tilts her head slightly, and my
own shifts instinctively. Our mouths are a breath apart, the kind of
proximity that promises more than either of us should allow.

The apartment door swings open. My mother steps in and the moment shatters. She doesn't glance twice, she's clearly occupied with her
inner thoughts. Celestia jerks back from me, eyes wide. I step back too,
heart still hammering, aware of the tension that lingers between us even
as we both turn to face my mother, pretending the hug didn't happen.

Before my mother can say anything Celestia speaks as if trying to
shift the moment into something else. "Hyda, we have good news, they
finally found a way to enter the Elders' Castle through the tunnels."

My mother looks up at us, her eyes sharp. "I have some news too. I've been visiting the local bars, listening for whispers. I've been leaving hefty tips for the barkeep, encouraging loose lips. Rumors say Edith is keeping Silas and Freya alive, using them to uncover why the magic is fading."

"Good," I reply. "That confirms your theory; she kept them alive."

"Yes, but there's more," she continues, leaning forward. "There have been sightings… at least of Silas. He's reportedly been seen with guards on the abandoned roads of the old district, being escorted to and from the main prison."

I can see the gears turning in my mother's mind.

"Mother, we can't risk going there. It's heavily guarded, and it would put everyone in danger. We need to scout first," I insist, but I can feel it, there's no way to convince her otherwise.

"No. There's no time for scouting. If this is true and he's been spotted, Edith will soon realize people have seen him, and she'll change the routes she takes. She won't risk loyalists catching on."

Her gaze locks onto mine, unwavering. "We go tomorrow. If there's any chance to see Silas and confirm he's alive, we go. We can head to the old district first, then the Elders' Castle tunnels. We'll be exhausted, but if you refuse, I'll go on my own."

I clench my jaw. I won't let her go alone. There's no talking her out of it. "Let me discuss this with Cerene and Gideon too."

"Do what you must, but with or without you, I'll be going," she affirms.

"Fine," I say, the words tasting bitter. "We go."

We continue training aggressively late into the evening. I don't want to take Celestia with us and have her compromise our mission, so I do my best to make sure she's ready. She's not great with her dagger, but she's finally getting control over her magic and fire, and according to my mother, this is the most important part of training. Celestia needs full control over her magic to be able to defend herself, save Eterna, and fulfill the prophecy.

We are both tired and covered in sweat. She drops her dagger on the floor and lies down, spreading her arms above her head as she takes deep breaths to relax. I collect all the daggers from the floor and put them back in their places. I watch her chest rise and fall, hair clinging to her neck, and can't help but want to go over and remove those stray strands and touch her. I continue to watch her as she reaches for her bottle of water while still lying down, uncaps it, and splashes some of the water on her face before drinking it. I catch myself wetting my dry lips, following the trail of water drops at the corners of her mouth, then down her chin and neck with my eyes. She's a sight to behold. I shake my head to clear my mind and concentrate on the task at hand. *What the fuck am I thinking? She seems to have some power over me with the way she's splayed on the floor drenched in her own sweat.* I try to distract myself by making sure each dagger is right where it belongs, but my brain keeps taking me back to Celestia. My body is reacting to her; my feet seem to take calculated steps towards her, as if they are moving of their own accord. I just want to go near her, grab her, and lick all the sweat from...

"Hi. Are you guys done for the day?" Cerene's voice comes from behind me and cuts off my train of thought.

I nod and smile back at her. *Damn it. She sure saved me from making a big mistake. Celestia is distracting me. I didn't even hear Cerene come into the training room because I was consumed with my inner fantasies and the things I'd do to make her scream my name.* I compose myself as I watch Celestia gather her things to go back home with Cerene.

Chapter 40

Mia

Tonight Hyda checks on me after training as if she knows her son is taking his frustration out on me. I'm honest and explain that I dread every minute I'm spending with him, and I think he feels the same way. I can't wait to be done with this training. We are growing more civil with each other, like professionals working together except for my awkward hug moment earlier today.

I just want to prove myself, but I didn't expect that. Not him. Not the way he looks at me, sharp and infuriating, like he can see every corner of me that I try to hide. I keep replaying it in my mind, trying to convince myself it is just the excitement, just the relief of finally going on the mission with them. Nothing more, but my heart doesn't listen. It's still pounding, still remembering the close feel of his body, and I feel a little dizzy just thinking about it. I tell myself I'm imagining things, I just need to focus on the mission and not him.

My feelings are conflicted. I try to push the memory away, forcing my racing heart to settle. Slowly, I let my mind drift to other things, safer things. I miss home so much. I catch myself wondering what my parents are doing at this time of day. What would my mom cook for dinner this weekend? What kind of stories did my dad bring back from work? And if Natalie is safe and sound and is in contact with them. I'm still anxiously waiting for her to use the potion at some point. Has she told my parents the truth of my whereabouts like we agreed before she left?

I love being here, too. Eterna is like an adventure to me right now. I'm on a mission to solve a mystery. I keep going back to my inner feelings. I don't know what I'd say if I ended up seeing Silas. I'm still unsure of how to feel about that, but I know I'm excited to participate in tomorrow's mission. I want to prove them wrong and show them that I'm ready. I won't compromise them and the mission at hand. I'm determined to be one of them and not have to miss out on all the thrill. I know this is not a game; it's a matter of life and death, but I'm more than capable. I'll just have to show them how strong I am, and what I'm made of.

The next morning, I look at myself in the mirror as I strap my dagger to my thigh and tighten the belts of the leather harness across my shoulders.

Cerene gives me a pep talk. "You got this, Mia. I've seen you train, and you're as ready as any of us can be. Don't let Xavier intimidate you. He's an ass sometimes, but trust me, he always has a reason. I even hate him most of the time," she says as she looks me over.

I give her a warm smile. "I don't care what he thinks. I'm confident that I'm ready for this." I double check that I'm not missing anything as I glance one more time in the mirror, not recognizing the person I see. I feel like I've come a long way to get to this person I am today, with hard work, sweat, and tears.

"Shall we?" I ask her as I take my first step toward exiting the room.

"No pressure, we just might get to meet our father today if we are lucky." I hear her boots stomping on the wooden floor behind me until I feel her hand squeeze my shoulder. "Let's roll. This is going to be interesting." I look at her and see a wide smile spread across her face. *At least she's put together and isn't twisting with nerves like me.*

Outside the room, we find Xavier, Gideon, and Hyda ready and waiting for us. They're all dressed in black and strapped with as many weapons as they can carry. Hyda gives me a kind look and nod as if she's proud of me. As I continue walking, I catch Xavier ogling me as I pass him. I take my chance and throw his comment from the first day I was here back at him. "You like what you see? I hope you're enjoying the show." He clears his throat and says nothing, but I hear Gideon and Cerene laugh under their breath as I walk out the door.

Chapter 41

Xavier

T he moment Cerene and Celestia come out of the room, my eyes follow Celestia as she walks to leave the apartment, wearing black boots and tight cargo pants with her dagger strapped to her thigh. Her pristine white tank top is contoured by her black leather harness, her daggers sheathed high along her back, the handles peaking just over her shoulders. She carries herself differently today, confident and strong, because today is not just any mission, it is *the* mission. I cannot take my eyes off of her. The whole room goes quiet around me, and I'm mesmerized by her beauty. I snap out of it when she brushes past me saying, "You like what you see? I hope you're enjoying the show."

I clear my throat to answer but refrain when I realize she's throwing my comment back at me. I chuckle silently. *Smart girl. She saw an opportunity to get back at me and took it. I'll find a way to get back at her.* I hear both Gideon and Cerene laugh, so I give them a stern look as we all walk out of the apartment.

We descend the stairs and walk around the building, to a back alley. I whistle to call a couple of Zarkas that are flying just above us. Once they land in front of me, I pull a couple of Bazer from my pocket only for Cerene to tell me they don't need it. I put the Bazer back in my pocket as I take a couple of steps back to let the birds transform. The girls and my mother mount one bird, while Gideon and I mount the second. The birds take off as Cerene and Celestia communicate with them.

"So, I have to ask… what was that back there?" Gideon asks me.

"What do you mean?" I answer him, not knowing what he's referring to.

He laughs then continues, "Come on, man, I could cut the tension with a knife with the way Mia talked to you."

I take a second to respond and wish he'd drop the subject. "There is no tension. I hope I don't regret bringing her on the mission today."

Gideon presses on with his questions. "I've seen the way you look at her…"

I cut him off before he can say anything else. "There is nothing there. She's just a person my mother asked me to train, and she happens to be Cerene's sister. Is she beautiful? Yes, any man would think so. We also despise each other, if you haven't noticed. So there is definitely nothing there."

He chuckles and responds, "Okay. If you say so."

I grew up with Cerene, I took care of her like a sister, but Celestia is nothing like the girl I grew up with. They share the same blood, but that's where the similarity ends. Her eyes, the tilt of her head, the way she carries herself has an edge that's sharp and impossible to ignore. I barely know her. And yet… I can't stop the way she draws me in.

I'm relieved when he stops talking because we are finally here and about to land. I don't need to be thinking about Celestia any longer. My main focus is on the mission and making sure that we all come out unharmed.

The Zarkas land smoothly a few miles away from the Elders' Castle. We dismount in a hurry to avoid being seen by any guards as the birds transform back to their smaller size and fly away. We walk through the green fields of Eterna until we reach the abandoned old district. As expected, my mother takes the lead as we follow behind her. I feel warmth spread in my chest. *As a child, I always wished I was with her on one of her missions.* We pass through ruins of the past, buildings and homes long deserted and forgotten still standing here as if waiting to be discovered. It feels like ghosts still linger here, I can't help but wonder how beautiful it must have been once upon a time.

My mother gestures for us to follow slowly, and I realize I'm not used to taking orders from anyone. Yes we work as a team, but this feels strange to me. Nevertheless, we follow her, until she stops. Satisfied with the location for us to set up our stakeout. We crouch behind the broken wall of what used to be a market stall, the cold stone pressing against my back. The ruins of the old city stretch around us like the bones of something long dead, buildings cracked open, windows gaping like empty eyes, streets drowned in dust and silence. No one lives here anymore. Only the city guards remain, patrolling, looking for any magic they can find to report back to Edith. We wait.

Cerene sits beside me, her arms wrapped around her knees, eyes sharp and unblinking. Gideon leans against a fallen column, mind busy as always calculating what might come next. Celestia presses herself low into the rubble, completely still, her gaze fixed on the street ahead. None of us speak. My mother is just assessing everyone and everything like a hawk. We've been watching for hours. Then, a figure appears far down the road. Tall. Broad-shouldered. Dragged by guards. My heart catches in my throat. I shift forward, barely breathing.

"Is that... him?" Cerene whispers.

We all rise slightly, just enough to see over the crumbling edge of the wall. The guards are pushing him around. Then he turns.

"Mother. Is that him?" I ask, hopeful that we finally found Silas.

She takes a minute to look at him and lets out a breath. "It isn't him."

The hope inside me collapses like a tower knocked loose at the foundation. Cerene exhales sharply and drops back behind the wall.

"It's not him," she says, her voice low, raw at the edges.
Gideon curses under his breath.

"We're wasting time. He's not here." I say addressing my mother in hopes, she lets us go forward with our original plan.

"We can't leave. Not yet. We give it more time. I need to know for sure."

Cerene looks at me, exhausted, but she nods. Celestia doesn't say anything, still watching the road as if he's going to materialize from thin air.

Gideon sighs. "We stay the night then."

The sun is already slipping behind the broken skyline, casting the ruins in rust-colored shadows. The city feels even emptier in the fading light, a graveyard of stone and silence. We set up camp a little further away from where guards patrol. Everyone pitches in to set up the little supplies we got to have something to eat and get some rest. While we take shifts at our earlier post to make sure we don't miss Silas if he truly is being escorted by any of the guards. I take the first watch of the night. I keep my gaze glued to the horizon. Somewhere beyond the next street, the guards continue their frequent patrols, searching through a dead city for traces of magic that no longer exist. My heart gets full of hope at every sight of them in hopes that Silas is with them, but we've only seen one prisoner so far, I have clear instructions to alert my mother if any other prisoners are spotted.

My eyes burn, gritty from being awake for too long, but I keep them on the road. Footsteps crunch behind me. I don't turn. *Light but uneven... that's her, she thinks she's being quiet.*

"Shouldn't you be asleep?" I ask, voice low.

"I tried," she says, lowering herself next to me. "Didn't work. I thought we could trade shifts."

"Trade? You? I'm not so sure you'll be able to stay awake." Her eyes narrow. *There it is. The little flair. Too easy.*

"I can stay awake and keep watch just fine," she snaps.

"Mm-hm. Until you get distracted counting stars."

She sighs and moves getting ready to get up. Maybe I pushed too far. I was trying to keep myself awake and not drive her away. I grab her elbow, gently tugging her to sit back down. *Careful. Don't let your mouth outrun your brain.*

"Look if it helps, I don't mind the company. You can stay and help me stay awake."

She faces me and blinks, like she wasn't expecting me to cave. Because I'm too tired to hold it in, I say, "If there is any chance to find your father, it's all worth it. It'd make me feel lighter."

Her brows pull tight. "Why?"

I rub my hand over my face. *Lie. Make something up. Or... screw it.* "Because I talked to my mother before we left; she's almost certain my father is long dead." My voice feels rough, even to my own ears. "So if there is even a sliver of hope for yours... maybe it's selfish, but it feels like I'm doing something that matters. For her. For me."

She doesn't answer right away, eyes searching mine like she's trying to read between the words. *Great. Now she's going to feel sorry for me.*

"Thank you," she says quietly.

I nod and look back to the street where the guards are still moving. We stay in a comfortable silent for the rest of the shift. She doesn't say much, but it's better than me sitting alone with my own thoughts for company.

Throughout the night we change shifts, each getting a couple of hours of sleep. Once the sun is up we are all back to the stakeout location. We are all exhausted and this mission feels like a bust. Suddenly, we hear voices in the distance that grabs our attention. We all look to the street in alert, that's when we see guards dragging another prisoner. We look to my mother for confirmation, and she holds her hand up, indicating to move closer slowly without alerting them. We shift carefully and strategically towards the guards using the old buildings for cover.

Once we are close enough, I slowly move my hand and unsheathe my daggers, turning my head around to see Gideon, Cerene, and Celestia do the same. We are ready to defend ourselves. We can easily take the guards. As they approach, it's confirmed we have to deal with a few well-armed guards and one prisoner. It looks like this prisoner is being escorted to the castle. What catches my eye is the way this person is dressed in elegant, fine clothes. His attire is one of the old royal outfit styles, navy blue pants, a white shirt and a darker shade navy blue jacket with gold embroidery on the shoulders and sleeves. They are covered in dust from this place or maybe a struggle. He's about my mother's age with salt-and-pepper hair. He looks very tired, catching his breath as he walks along with the guards. Only one guard is holding him, but it's more in support rather than a guard pulling on a prisoner.

We are all crouched behind a half collapsed wall, my mother's feet shift and she turns her head to look at me with wide eyes. I can't make up my mind if she's indicating danger or if she recognizes him as Silas. She finally gives a silent command to take out the guards only. Gideon and I step out of our hiding place to surprise them. The guards scramble for their weapons as we begin our assault on them. We flush them away from where we were hiding. The guard's blade whistles past my ear, close enough I feel the air split. I duck low, slam my shoulder into his gut, and a grunt bursts out of him. Behind me, boots scuff and a sharp clang rings out, that's Cerene, parrying hard. A curse follows, not hers. She's holding strong. My guard shoves me back and comes in fast. I twist, catch his wrist, and drive my elbow into his temple. He staggers but doesn't go down. To my right, Gideon got his opponent by the collar, smashing him into the wall. The guard swings slow, then stops entirely as he crumbles.

My guard lunges again. I sidestep, hook his leg, and send him crashing to the ground. One quick strike with the hilt and he's out cold. Celestia's voice cuts through, sharp, commanding, and I turn just in time to see her plant her knee into her guard's chest, slam him back, and drop him flat. He doesn't move. We've got this batch down, I'm sure there'll be more to follow.

I breathe hard, knuckles throbbing, I turn to look for my mother. I find her frozen in her spot. I don't know her to be a woman who backs from a fight, but she seems to be in shock. As she's standing in her hiding place watching the scene unfold.

"This is going to be a problem when the guards don't return to the castle." I hear a man behind me say.

My mother rushes out of the side of the building towards him as if his words broke her spell. The man turns around to face her as she takes down her hood and reveals her face to him. Tears are brimming in my mother's eyes looking at him as a smile spreads across her face.

The man spreads both of his arms, ready to hug my mother. His face is mirroring the disbelief my mother has on hers. We watch them, as they finally let themselves collapse into each other. Their arms wrap tight, faces buried, and I can hear the quiet hitch of breaths I know are full of relief, fear, and everything in between. I don't move. I don't look away. I just let them have this, because I know it's rare, this kind of peace.

They both compose themselves and wipe the tears from their eyes. My mother finally speaks. "Heavens, Silas, I never thought I'd lay eyes on you, my dear friend. I'm glad Edith kept you alive."

Silas answers her back, "I could say the same to you, Hyda, protector and general of our order."

My mother lets out a soft chuckle as she looks around and realizes we are all still watching them. The tears haven't fully stopped, but she wipes them away with trembling fingers. Her voice is tender, almost reverent, as she turns to him and says,

"Silas... these are your daughters." She pauses, her gaze lingering on each of us before adding, "And this is my son, Xavier and his friend, Gideon."

I try to collect myself to meet the man of the hour. The man we are in search of. The famous Silas, father of Cerene and Celestia. The holder of the prophecy. I turn to look at Cerene and Celestia. If I'm stunned, then how must they be feeling to finally meet their biological father?

Chapter 42

Mia

Hyda's words come crashing down on me like a current, freezing me in place. "Silas... these are your daughters." *She said Silas, I'm not imagining things,* I think to myself.

My heart is beating so fast I can feel it in my throat. I take slow steps along with Cerene beside me, toward the man who is our father. He's about six feet tall, broad shoulders, with brown and grey hair complementing his features. His kind, light brown eyes resemble Cerene's, glowing in contrast with his tanned skin. He's looking at us both in disbelief. His eyes are brimming with tears as he closes the distance, taking us both in a tight embrace. I'm torn inside. I don't know this man, yet I feel something for him. Maybe love, but nothing like the love I feel towards my adoptive father. I can see Cerene sobbing in his embrace. This means more to her than it does to me. She had to grow up without a father, and that just breaks me.

As Silas's embrace loosens, he takes a step back and looks at us, and with a choked up voice says, "Your mother is dying to meet you. She senses your presence and has been wanting a way out to come find you." When none of us says anything, he continues, "I've been dreaming of this day for years now, regretting the outcome of many things. I'm sorry you girls had to grow up without us, but you need to know that there wasn't a day that passed by without us longing for you."

I'm trying to register his words and say something to him, but Gideon says, "I hate to ruin this family reunion, but it looks like more guards are coming this way."

Hyda and Silas exchange a look. Cerene is still recovering from her emotional state when Silas tells Hyda quickly, "Only the Zarkas know where the prophecy is hidden. The girls need it. Go to the old tunnels. You will find clues there to follow. I've never been there; it's a place meant for the prophecy children to find. Be very careful. The tunnel is guarded by ancient magic, and it feels everything."

I hold onto his arm. "Come with us," I tell him.

He smiles and puts his hand over mine. "You're warm to the touch. You're the one with the fire magic. Celestia, my girl." He plants a kiss on my forehead as he takes off his ring and puts it in my palm. "You will need this to open some of the locks you will encounter on your journey. Take it and protect it. Without it, you won't be able to reach where you need to be." He then reaches for Cerene as he says, "Come here, my water wielder. Your mother will be so proud to see both of you." He wipes a tear from her cheek and kisses her on the forehead as well.

I assess the ring in my hand. It's so vintage and masculine in appearance, looking like a seal in a way. It has wings engraved at the center of it, along with a very small ruby nestled between the wings. I slip it on my index finger and watch it size down of its own accord to fit me perfectly.

Silas looks at us one last time and turns to clasp Hyda's shoulder. "Hyda, your duty is still to protect them with your life. Make sure they combine their powers at the entrance of the old tunnels. I'll have to find a way back to the cell of the castle and tell Freya that you're all fine and maybe buy you all some time to fulfill the prophecy."

Hyda looks deep in his eyes and asks him one last question. "Mateo?"

He shakes his head in a response, and I see the sadness contort her face.

"Knock me out and leave," Silas tells Hyda. She nods, salutes him with one hand, and hits him on the head with the handle of her dagger with the other.

We watch Silas's massive body hit the ground as Hyda gestures for us to hurry up and follow her to the old tunnels, wherever that is. As we follow Hyda, Cerene and I both look back at our unconscious father on the ground, and we also notice several unconscious guards along the way, realizing that Xavier and Gideon have been taking care of the guards while we were talking to Silas.

We keep running for a few minutes before we stop in front of a very old, collapsed building. Confusion washes over me and Cerene. There is no entrance here, just wreckage.

"What are we supposed to do?" I ask.

Xavier says, "Mother, are we sure about this? The place is full of guards. This is uncharted territory. We don't know what we are looking for." She dismisses him with a wave of her hand and turns to me and Cerene. "You heard Silas. Combine your powers."

Cerene and I look at each other in bewilderment, not knowing how that will work. Cerene asks Hyda, "How? It's fire and water. How on earth are we going to combine them?"

Hyda instructs us, "Cerene, summon your water. Mia, ignite your flame." We follow her instructions as she continues, "Now, my guess is as good as yours, since I've never seen this happen before, but bring them together."

Cerene and I step closer to each other and try to bring our hands close to one another as Hyda tells us to will our powers to combine. I concentrate and will my flame to combine with Cerene's ball of water. To our surprise, both of our elements combine in front of our very eyes, a floating orb, half flame and half water, surrounded by a silver glow. This shouldn't be possible, yet it is, and the result is too stunning to describe in simple words. The orb floats around Cerene and me as we are anchored in place, in shock at what's happening. Suddenly, the orb comes crashing down three feet away from us, illuminating an invisible door with a single lock that has the shape of wings engraved on it.

I'm snapped back to reality as I hear Hyda's voice. "Mia, quick, use the ring Silas gave you." I hesitate as I take a step towards the door, pulling Cerene by the hand with me for support. I take a deep, ragged breath to calm my nerves, then gently place the ring top on the lock. It makes a faint *click*, and the lock dissolves along with the door to reveal a blue-lit passage leading to a staircase. I turn around to look behind me and see Gideon, Hyda, and Xavier with their jaws dropped in awe, but they quickly recover when Hyda asks everyone to pass through. Once we're all inside the passage, the door disappears as if it never existed.

Chapter 43

Xavier

W e are all cramped up in an enchanted passageway, unsure where it'll lead us. This is the first time in my life I feel dumbfounded. I'm always prepared for what will happen next. There's always a plan in place for me and the team to follow. As for the magic I just witnessed, if I wasn't physically standing there, I'd never believe it could be possible, from how Cerene and Celestia combined their powers to the invisible door appearing from nowhere. I'm trying to collect myself to go forward and deal with what's to come.

Cerene breaks the awkward silence by saying, "Now what? Do we go down the stairs?"

My mother is fidgeting and looking around the walls as she says, "Silas said there will be clues for us to follow, so keep your eyes open."

Without a word, Celestia ignites her flame one more time and takes the first step down, taking the lead on this. I rush past them all and stop her. "Whoa, whoa—easy there. Who put you in charge?"

She gives me a piercing look, raises one eyebrow and says, "Let me guess, you thought barking orders is the same as having a plan."

"Would you prefer I whisper my commands instead? Maybe add a 'pretty please' just for you?" I growl back, as I come even closer to her.

She rolls her eyes at me and gestures with her hand for me to take the lead as she seethes. "You're insufferable."

Her breath catches when I lean to whisper in her ear, "Careful, Celestia. You keep poking and I might start enjoying it." She puts her hand on my chest and pushes me away.

Cerene comes rushing at us, "Oh my god, you guys need to stop whatever is going on here. We are all in this together. Let's figure out where these stairs lead. I'm beginning to suffocate just waiting around here for you to figure out who is in command." Cerene takes Celestia's hands and starts walking in front of me.

Gideon follows them and shrugs as he passes by me. My mother, on the other hand, has an amused look on her face. She chuckles as she brushes her hand on my face and says, "Hasn't life taught you anything? Women don't like to be told they can't lead, my son."

I look deep in her eyes. "I wasn't trying to. We don't know what's down there," I tell her, but she doesn't let it go.

"There are many tender ways to show your concern for her safety, or do I have to teach you how to woo a woman properly?"

I rake my hand across my face, anger lacing my voice. "Heavens, mother, that's not what this is, and it's for everyone's safety, not just hers."

She walks past me and follows the others down the steps. *Great. This is just great. I used to have only Cerene to worry about. Now I have three strong-headed women thinking I'm trying to prove my manhood. This is exactly the reason why I've never had a long-term relationship. The occasional one-night stand does it for me. Fun, casual, and no strings attached. We enjoy ourselves and then we go our separate ways.*

I'm startled out of my thoughts by Celestia and Cerene's loud screams coming from below, echoing around me. I rush down the stairs that seem to never end. All the worst possible scenarios play in my head, like them getting hurt or worse. I knew I should've gone down first to assess the place.

I stumble on the last steps as they come into view. They are all okay. They're standing and glaring at the pulsing, blue veins covering the black walls. "What the fuck was that scream?" My question comes out louder than usual and full of anger.

Cerene and Celestia giggle. "Proving a theory," Cerene answers me.

I clench my jaw. "Which is?"

Celestia answers this time. "That you care."

When I hear her teasing, sarcastic response, anger takes over me, and I charge towards her, pointing my finger at her. "Don't fucking test my limits..."

Before I can say anything else, Gideon steps in front of me. "Calm down, man. It was a simple joke. No harm done here. Take a damn breath."

I close my eyes and follow his instructions. When I feel calmer, I open my eyes to see Gideon still in my face. I shove him away and walk past all of them, deep in the tunnel, to see what lies ahead before I lose my mind and say things in anger that I'll regret later on.

I try to distract myself by looking all around me. The tunnel is carved from ancient black stone that shimmers in the glow of the pulsing blue vines that spiderweb its surface. No one has stepped here before. Dust lies thick and undisturbed on the floor, and the air is heavy, stale, like it hasn't been breathed in ages. This tunnel is alive with magic.

I don't think anyone knows about this place other than Silas. We don't have it in any of our city maps, so it makes sense it was just hidden. If Elder Edith knew, she'd harvest the whole place and consume its magic in a matter of hours. Everything looks strange, yet I don't see any clues. Magic or not, I still have to keep my guard up and make sure everyone makes it out of this place alive.

Chapter 44

Mia

I think our joke pushed Xavier over the edge. I definitely didn't think it'd make him that angry. He was shooting daggers from his eyes by the time he decided to take a walk deep in the tunnel ahead of us, leaving everyone behind. So much for caring for our safety. I don't ponder on his behavior too much and decide to give my attention to Hyda, who is observing these pulsing blue veins on the walls. I go to where she's standing.

"What are they?" I ask her curiously.

"I have no idea, my child. It looks like magic is flowing through these to illuminate the tunnel," she says in a serious tone.

I brush my hand against the vein, and I can feel it hum under my skin. It ignites warmth in my blood, as if it's connecting to my inner magic, recognizing who I am. I call for Cerene, "Come, put your hands on it. Can you feel anything?"

She places her hands on one of the veins closer to her, and her eyes widen. "Yes. What's that? It's so cold."

Interesting. While I feel warmth, she feels cold. "It's definitely amplifying the feel of our elements," I say out loud.

Hyda comes closer to where we're standing, takes my hand, then Cerene's. "Here goes nothing," she says as she places our hands on top of each other and puts them on one of the veins.

The veins hum and vibrate under our hands, and some new marks appear on the floor. Magnificent, ancient runes leading a path forward. Cerene and I pull our hands away and gasp.

Gideon, intrigued, "What in the bloody hell are these supposed to mean now? I wish I had a magic book guide to decipher their meaning."

"We don't have a choice but to follow and see where they lead," I point out.

Gideon laughs as he responds, "Oh, Xavier will love this plan. Just follow something we don't know blindly."

I know he's probably right, but I didn't come all this way to turn back now. "Your precious Xavier is not here and..." Before I can finish my sentence, Xavier's figure appears in front of us.

"I didn't go anywhere. You think I'm precious?" He winks at me. I don't dignify his snarky question with a response and move on further to inspect the trail of runes before anyone notices how my face flushes at Xavier's flirting.

Cerene and I walk ahead and bask in this enchanted trail. It beckons us forward as if we're pulled by an invisible string. The deeper we walk, the narrower the trail gets. Soon enough, we can only form a single file line. The trail doesn't just narrow, but the ceiling's clearance lowers, until we're crouching to pass through. I can feel the veins on the walls and ceiling press down on my skin from all directions, the friction making me feel uncomfortable. I hear Gideon and Xavier groan because their body mass is bigger than ours, and they are really squeezed in here.

"I don't know if this was such a good idea," I confess.

"I think we should head back," Cerene says behind me. I summon my flame to see if it's going to get better up ahead; the blue light is getting too faint. I'm feeling too cramped up, and my breathing is getting ragged from crouching and walking for the past hour or more. Time seems to cease in this tunnel. I try to extend my arm as far as I can.

"Guys, do you want the good news or the bad news?" I ask them.

Xavier curses from all the way back. "Fucking hell. What now?"

Gideon, on the other hand, says, "Good news, please."

"Okay, the good news is we are almost there. There is an open place ahead, and the ceiling is not low. The bad news is, the tunnel splits in two and both paths are dark. There are no veins or runes to light the way."

Hyda coughs before saying, "Let's get there, then decide where to go next."

I agree with her and continue forward, occasionally looking backwards to make sure Cerene is still following me. After what feels like forever, we finally emerge from that tight tunnel into a dark space. I catch my breath, stretch my limbs, then ignite my flame so everyone can see where they are standing.

Chapter 45

Xavier

I'm just relieved to finally stand with enough room to move. The last hour has been brutal, crammed in a tunnel too tight for my size. Celestia is standing tall and lighting up the place for us, but she's right—both tunnels ahead are pitch black. We have no other choice but to pick one and proceed to wherever it'll lead. We all take a moment to catch our breath, rest, and stretch before deciding what's next.

Celestia goes to the entrance of one of the tunnels and tries to see further with her fire, then does the same to the second as she says, "They are both identical as far as I can see, but there isn't anything visible to tell which way is the right way."

Cerene then tries to let some water go through both of them to listen if the path is descending further into the earth or it stops at some point, but no matter how hard we listen, the water sound eventually disappears, and we can't really tell anything from it.

"Let's split up and tackle both tunnels," says Gideon.

My mother agrees to that option, but Cerene and Celestia don't look so sure about that. Celestia is still holding her flame up and standing in the entrance of the right tunnel, so I decide to go in a bit further to try and see what's ahead. After I take a couple of steps in, a rumbling sound fills the air. Before I can make sense of it, the ground beneath me shakes violently. Rocks begin to rain down from the ceiling. Cerene screams as one stone strikes her head. The moment I steady myself, I grab Celestia away from the entrance and pull her to safety, just before it collapses completely. Darkness envelops us, and I feel Celestia's weight pressing down on me.

She scrambles away from me to reignite her flame. "What the hell just happened?" she asks me, as if I have an answer to that.

Cerene, Gideon, and my mother's voices come muffled from behind the rocks. I stand up slowly and pat away the dust from my pants as Celestia answers them from behind all the rubble, "We're both fine. Are you all okay?"

We can't really make out what they're saying. I unzip the pocket in my inner jacket and bring out the small Klinxer potion vial that I always keep with me for emergencies and hope to heavens Cerene or Gideon think of it too. As soon as I drink it, I hear Gideon's voice in my mind.

"So happy to hear your voice, man. Glad you had the potion with you," I tell him.

He chuckles and responds, "We are okay. I always have it with me. Are you two alright? And what just happened?"

"Yes, we are fine as well. I really don't know what happened. Maybe I triggered something when I walked further into the tunnel. Are you also trapped out there?"

"No, the other tunnel is open. Still dark though. I have some flashlights in my pocket, and Cerene has one, too. I hope they last till we figure out how to get you guys out of there," he explains.

Celestia watches me, curious at my silence, so before I respond to Gideon, I fill her in on the situation outside. "I think it's best for them to continue through that tunnel to see where it leads instead of trying to get us out. These rocks won't budge. We don't have the equipment nor the magic to remove them from the entrance. I think we should also do the same and continue walking this path and hope we get to meet at the end of it. Gideon and I have enough potion to keep us connected." She thinks about it, biting her lower lip before she nods in approval. With that, I tell Gideon the plan.

We walk in silence while Celestia stomps her feet as if she's angry. I glance at her every once in a while, trying to decipher what she's muttering to herself. "Wonderful. Trapped with you. This day just keeps getting better."

"No one told you to follow me into the tunnel," I say teasingly. She glares at me. "Do you want to take a break?" I ask her, but she continues to glare at me, and I swear I could see fire in her eyes. So I stop and lean on the wall, searching in my pockets for my flashlight. I light it and nod to her flame. "I meant a break from your magic. And you're welcome, by the way."

"Welcome? For what? For getting me trapped in this tunnel with you?" she seethes.

I lift one eyebrow and rub my chin. "I saved your life back there. If I didn't grab you at the last minute, you'd have been crushed under those stones."

She takes a couple of steps towards me. "Those stones didn't start coming down on us until you stepped inside the tunnel. Or did you think I didn't pay attention?"

I smirk and clap. "Smart girl. You do pay attention to details after all."

She unsheathes her dagger and comes at me. She pushes me against the wall, pressing her dagger at my neck. I fully surrender to her. I stay cool and collected, looking her up and down as she steps closer to me. Her eyes look deep into mine before she says, "Yes, I do. And if you think I haven't noticed the way you watch me, waiting for me to fail, for the other shoe to drop; you're wrong. I'm here. I'm staying. And I'll see this through, whether you believe in me or not. Hate me all you want."

I slowly lift one hand and tenderly touch her forehead to brush some loose strands of her hair away from her forehead. "You're bleeding. It looks like one of those stones got you there." She swallows hard under my touch and steps away from me, walking to the opposite side as she wipes her forehead with her hand and looks at the smear of blood coating her fingers, then wipes it on her cargo pants.

She sits down against the wall. Vulnerability lacing her words, "You might've had a rough life, and I can understand that. I had amazing parents, but that doesn't mean I didn't have a rough time, too. You don't know anything about me. I'm constantly feeling lost. Like something or someone is missing most of the time. Being in Eterna is the first time in my life where I have felt free, whole and more like myself. I can't explain it, but that's how I feel. I don't see why you hate me. I had nothing to do with how all our lives turned out. You can't keep on blaming me for the decisions of our parents twenty-one years ago."

I stay silent, watching her fidget with the laces of her shoes. I know I must look frigid, but my only answer to her is, "Let's move. Don't want the others to get to the end of the tunnel then worry about us not making it there." I conceal my features and try my best to not show any emotions of uncertainty about what I feel for her. If she only knew how my treacherous mind thought of her, how hard it's been to restrain myself from saying the words in my mind. The truth of her festering in my heart, thoughts of her consuming my mind and soul. I don't take rejection easily, and I don't know if she's going to stay in Eterna or if she feels the same way about me. I don't like to put myself in this position, so I choose to be an asshole instead and let her hate me even more. It's better this way. She'll fulfill the prophecy, go home, and forget I ever existed. I watch her get up from the ground without even sparing a glance my way. With her flame lit, she walks ahead, unaware, or perhaps simply uncaring, that my gaze lingers far longer than it should. I trail her like a shadow, not for protection, but to satisfy a selfish hunger within me. The way she moves, like an elegant gazelle confident in her beauty and power, lures me, and I have no choice but to follow.

Chapter 46

Mia

I feel like a fool. I just spilled my heart out to Xavier in hopes of making him see that I had no hand in all this. I loathe the feeling of him hating me. I know I shouldn't care, but I really do. I thought this mission would make him see that I'm one of them, and I had nothing to do with the past, but it seems like he hates me even more. He's always looking my way, but for what purpose, I'll never know.

We continue walking in an awkward, deafening silence, until we reach a dead end. Xavier mindlinks Gideon throughout the way, and it seems that they've reached a dead end too. I bring my flame closer to inspect the wall, looking for any clues that might let us know what to do next. I press my hand on the wall and feel a hum of magic. I turn to Xavier.

"Tell Cerene to touch the wall and report if she feels anything."

At her touch, the cold stone pulses with sapphire-blue light, veins of luminescence unfurling like ancient runes across its surface. Curiosity and astonishment flare through me. I place my hand upon it, my fingers tingling with fire, as the wall transforms into a glass-like wall. Finally, we see them.

Cerene gestures toward the corner of the wall on my side. Behind me, glowing wings, engraved deep into the black stone, appear that weren't visible before. I move towards it and press Silas's ring to it. A jagged crack splits the silence, like glass shattering all around us. We all close our eyes and shield ourselves the best we can to avoid the shards of glass, but when we open our eyes again, we realize nothing is broken, and the barrier between us is gone.

Relief washes over me to be able to embrace my sister again and be with her on the same side of the tunnel. A new feeling that I'm growing to love so much. Being with Xavier was nerve racking. I'm relieved to be back with everyone. Once we make sure we are all fine, we start to look for clues because it looks like we are stuck here without a way out. We can't turn back; there was nothing there either.

"Did we miss something along the way?" Cerene asks and I see Hyda thinking, the wheels turning in her head. Gideon is assessing our surroundings, looking all through the place with his flashlight close to the walls.

All of a sudden, Cerene and I freeze at the same time when we hear the Zarka speak to us in our minds. "I'm glad you made it this far. Your companions won't be able to enter the next cave. Only individuals who have magic in their bloodline may enter. The wall will reveal two doors. The one that is lit with pulsing blue light will lead your friends to safety, and they can wait for you there. The path marked by runes is the one that the prophecy children should take. A trial awaits you here, one that will test the depth of your abilities before the path forward reveals itself. Remain vigilant. We'll be watching over you."

The Zarka goes quiet after that, and Cerene tells our group what the Zarka said while Xavier and Gideon both protest, not wanting to leave us alone. Hyda speaks last, quieting the argument of both men.

"Calm down, everyone. We need to trust our ancient Zarka. If they said they will watch over them, then we have to believe them, and have faith in the abilities of Cerene and Mia."

Before anyone can say anything else, the floor shakes and rumbles as two doors appear, sliding down from the ceiling of the cave like elevators. They open to reveal the two paths the Zarka spoke of. Hyda rushes to give me and Cerene a tight hug, telling us that she believes in us and to stick together, no matter what happens inside that tunnel. Then Gideon and Xavier both hug Cerene and tell her to take care of herself. Xavier tucks the leftover potion in her pocket, telling her to use it if she needs them. Before they all step into the door meant for them, Gideon waves at me, but Xavier's eyes meet mine, just for a breath, and in them, something flickers. Something unfamiliar. Is it concern? Affection? Love? His gaze glows with a thousand unspoken words. *I also could be imagining things to make myself feel better about being an outsider again as I watched them say goodbye to my sister.*

Cerene and I step into the next door, the runes glowing brighter with every step we take. "Cerene, do you know what these mean?" I ask calmly.

"No. I wish I did. They look so beautiful."

We both stand in silent awe. The cave is no longer just lifeless black stone; it breathes with ancient purpose. Blue sigils spiral across the walls, glowing with a soft, otherworldly blue light, and etched between them are markings that resemble old writing, humming with magic. The air tingles with power. My nerves coil tight. Whatever trial lies ahead, whether to test our strength, our worth, or something deeper, it does not feel like a path I'm ready to take.

We hear a faint sound, some movement around us, and we look at each other in question. Before I know it, my worst nightmare comes to life—giant spiders are crawling all around us. We start running forward, but we are unable to lose them. We can't fight a million spiders with daggers. I try to think quickly, but my fear of spiders is consuming me. *Oh God, this is the way I'm going to die.*

Cerene grabs my arm as we run. "Mia, your fire! Shoot them with your fire." When I finally get a hold of myself enough to hear her clearly, I summon my fire and blast it behind us. We can hear the spiders shriek and retreat to wherever they came from.

Before we can catch our breaths, the ceiling starts to close in on us. The further we run, the closer the ceiling above us gets, looking like stone teeth ready to come crashing down on us.

Cerene summons her water and lets it flow under us, making us slide down the rest of the path, stopping in a puddle of water. Cerene's laughter echoes through the tunnel while I compose myself and stand to look at her.

"Did you just produce all that water?" I ask her, amusement in my voice. She nods as she stands up. "Thanks, I think you just saved us from being crushed," I tell her.

We walk further into the endless tunnel, wet and cold. The air around us becomes cooler, and we start to shiver. We reach a massive door made of white stone, a glowing blue arc full of engravings atop it, with wings in the center. On each side of the door, there is a scroll sealed with Silas's ring, floating in the air as if held by a silent force. We each step forward to one side of the door and reach out to grab the scroll, but before we do, the Zarka's voice rumbles in the tunnel this time and not in our minds. "By holding the scroll, you will have to surrender one of your core memories. It could be a bad one or a happy one. A significant memory. Choose wisely. It will become lost to time, and you'll never gain it back. Once you do, the wing on the top will glow, and the door will open. Each one of you will have to walk their path alone."

I watch Cerene reach out for the scroll, and within a second, the left wing on top of the door glows. I contemplate what memory to give away.

I try to dig deep in my mind, feeling the pressure. I decide to give away the memory of my first heartbreak. I surrender the memory and watch the right wing of the sign glow, accepting our offerings. The door in front of us opens slowly, revealing two parallel stone bridges, one path for each of us. Both end at the same place, where a Zarka waits.

Cerene and I look at each other and exchange a smile.

"See you on the other side," she says and winks at me as she takes her first steps onto the bridge. Something tells me that this is not just a bridge, so I hesitate, not in fear, but in caution.

I take small, calculated steps forward. Once on the bridge, I feel my body start to relax when nothing happens. I quickly realize I'm wrong and tense up as daggers start shooting from the sides of the bridge at me. I try to dodge them, but some of them manage to slash my bare arms before I realize they have a pattern. Three daggers shoot at the same time, then there is a pause, so I manage to take steps accordingly. Once the daggers stop, the floor starts to crack beneath my feet. I want to look and see what Cerene is facing, but if I lose my concentration, I'll fall to my death. I risk glancing at her anyway. She's shooting water balls at fire that's coming from her bridge. Distracted by the action on her side, my boot catches in a crack. The ground gives way beneath me, and I slip, plunging down through the opening. My hands scramble to find the edge just in time, bloody fingers clinging to the jagged stone. My arms tremble under the full weight of my body, every muscle straining, burning, and screaming as I pull myself up inch by inch. The stone bites into my palms as I haul myself upwards until I'm again on top of the bridge. I start skipping from one stone to the next as I assess which ones are still intact so I don't fall again. Glancing at Cerene was a mistake, but I wanted to make sure she was okay. With a final jump, I make it to stand next to the Zarka guarding the entrance. I catch my breath and feel at ease once Cerene makes her way to me. We both have some cuts here and there, but we are both safe.

Once we are both facing the Zarka, its wings covering the entrance, it bows down to us and flaps its wings. The entrance behind it turns from black stone into a ripple of silver, resembling a mirror, urging us to go through it. Cerene and I hold hands and step through it, and the world around us changes. We are standing into a vast cavern, so wide it seems impossible that it lays hidden beneath the earth. The air shimmers with enchantment, thick with the hum of ancient power. Every wall, floor, and soaring ceiling is veined with glowing blue patterns, pulsing like a heartbeat. The light isn't harsh, but soft and alive, casting long shadows that dance with every flicker. Massive stone columns, twisted with runes and carved vines, rise like giants around the edges of the space. Pools of crystal-clear water mirror the glowing lines across the floor, and above them, strange floating lights drift lazily like fireflies made of starlight. Magic lives here. It breathes in the walls, echoes in the silence, and coils around our skin like invisible thread. Neither of us say anything. Words feel too small for this place.

We go up a couple of steps to find a gigantic nest full of small, black eggs, with the same pulsing blue veins from the cave, guarded by many fully-transformed Zarkas, which makes me think this is their natural form. Some are resting; others are eating or bathing in silver pools. In the center of the nest, there is a throne woven of thick, emerald-green vines coiled and twisted with wild grace. Clusters of flowers bloom along its curves in deep violets and midnight blue blossoms that shimmer with dew, as if touched by starlight. The petals seem to stir ever so slightly, as if breathing. It isn't a seat of stone or power forged by men; it's nature's crown, alive and ancient, and somehow watching. We look on in awe and walk silently so as not to disturb their slumber while we figure out why we are here.

With every step we take, magic vibrates in our bodies, and the floor beneath our feet glows. Cerene and I both feel it as we look into each other's eyes. We are startled by the soft shaking of the ground. We look up to see the once empty throne now occupied by a magnificent, ancient Zarka, wings spread high above its head. This Zarka is bigger than the rest in size. Its wings are embedded with gold within the royal blue shades, and it looks majestic. It looks at us as if it's waiting for us to say something, holding its breath. Then the sweetest sound of a melody surrounds us, seeping into our bones, as if our magic is recognizing its tune, making us drop to our knees before this powerful bird, along with the rest of the birds, bowing their heads in respect to a superior being.

The Zarka on the throne has our full attention now. Cerene and I don't even seem to take a breath as its beautiful voice addresses us. "Welcome, Chosen Ones. I've been waiting centuries to finally meet you, my children. You may be confused. That's the way with humans, but I promise to explain everything that you need to fulfill your destiny. My name is Eternika." Cerene and I watch with wide eyes as Eternika continues to speak.

"I am the first and only Elder Zarka. I am made of eternal magic. I have existed before everyone. This was my land long before anyone was here. As you see, our kind is humble and peaceful. We fuel the land with our power so it can survive. It's not just magic; it's our hard labor that keeps this land thriving. We make these pulsing vines extend below the earth to keep magic flowing. We have forced our kind to be an insignificant, small bird to serve humans at a price. To transform us, humans feed us the magical Bazer, and in return, we take you where your heart desires. In reality, this was the only way to keep our eyes open, to observe and keep our land safe without being hunted in our natural form. As it happened generations ago, greed is growing potent, festering like a poison beneath the surface, and it needs to be purged before it consumes us all. Your ancestor, a great-grandmother to both of you, once was our savior who bravely battled the same greed and gave Eterna back to us. As gratitude for all her sacrifices, we blessed her with a prophecy and a lineage. A magic gift that will keep flowing into her bloodline and the bloodline of the person she chose to mate with.

"We predicted this would happen again when we granted her the prophecy. Your birth came when we knew we would need saving again. You were a security plan for the future of Eterna. Unlike your great-grand-mother, you have immense power and a vision of the future."

I'm baffled at everything I just heard. I take a deep breath and ask, "What are we battling exactly?"

Eternika's voice rattles the cave, showing her anger and grief. "The greed of individuals in power. They are consuming us and purging the land of its magic, and they must be gone by any means possible."

Understanding washes over me. "The Elders, the same people our parents fought."

Eternika's response comes quick and loud. "YES."

Cerene looks at me, then looks at Eternika before she speaks, "If I may ask, where can we find the prophecy? We have both been in the dark on that matter. We don't know what it consists of, or if our powers will be strong enough to take down the Elders."

Eternika responds kindly, "Finding the prophecy is part of your journey, as are the trials to prove your worth. As for your powers, they are greater than anyone has ever possessed, but I must warn you, sacrifices will be painful. Remember to be true to who you are. I know what lies inside your hearts. Trust in love and in each other, your power will grow stronger. The only thing I can bless you with is to tell you that the prophecy lies hidden under the main castle. Your great-grandmother was a trickster and hid it in plain sight where no one would think of looking. That's why no one ever found it, but you hold the key to everything."

Cerene and I wait for a couple of minutes before standing back up on our feet. Eternika's words seem final, and she doesn't add anything else, so I finally take the liberty of asking one final question that's weighing me down. "Saving Eterna will save everyone and everything... What if we fail?"

Eternika flaps her wings and starts to disappear into thin air as her voice vibrates around us. "Help us survive and nourish what's lost. Fail and we die. Eterna will perish, taking everything and everyone with it."

A tunnel appears behind Eternika's throne, Zarkas line up on both sides of it, bowing their heads to us as we walk through it, leading us to the exit, another portal door waiting for us. Once we step through, we find ourselves back in the blue-lit, black stone cave from before. Xavier is pacing while Hyda and Gideon are sitting on the ground, waiting for us.

Chapter 47

Xavier

Cerene and Celestia have been gone for more than two long, agonizing hours. Cerene didn't use the potion I gave her. I thought she'd keep us posted on what was going on with them. *What if something happens to them and I lose Cerene for good? I've never let her go on a mission alone, and if anything happens, that would break me without a doubt. I feel like the universe is testing me with all this, testing my feelings. Then the thought of Celestia comes to mind and how the last thing she'll remember is me being a heartless prick.* Those thoughts make my chest tighten with unease. I keep pacing back and forth, fidgeting with my necklace, trying to stop myself from feeling whatever this is—worry mixed with something else. I stop midstep, heart pounding, as a portal appears in front of us, then Cerene and Celestia step through it. I let out a loud breath and practically run to them to engulf them in a tight embrace, wanting to touch them and make sure they are really here. I've never shown this much affection before. Once I realize what I've done, I take a step back to clear my throat and school my features,

"Welcome back. Glad you guys made it through okay."

Taking a quick assessment, I notice scrapes, bruising, and what appears to be charred clothing on both of them. My mother asks them what happened as she embraces them. She tells them she's happy to see them again and how worried she was. *That makes two of us.*

"Can we please just get home? We'll fill you in later," Cerene says.

Celestia looks around and realizes there is another set of wings on the wall behind us. Without saying a word, she walks over and presses the ring to it, waiting for the walls around us to dissolve. We find ourselves standing in a dead land, yellow and dry, completely barren.

Celestia crumbles to the ground and clutches the dry grass in a fist. "We must stop this. The land can't die." Sadness laces her voice and I notice a single tear slide down her cheek.

I'm tempted to go and comfort her, but Cerene comes to stand next to her sister and clasps her shoulder, "We will make them pay for this."

Two Zarkas approach the twins, kneel down in front of them and say, "We are at your service. We are ready to take you home, Chosen Ones."

For the first time in my life, I hear the Zarka speak. The sound is low, clear, and ancient. I freeze. For a split second, I wonder if I imagined it. But when I glance around, Gideon and my mother are just as still. My mother's eyes are wide, her mouth slightly open. Gideon, who never flinches, looks shaken, his brows tight with disbelief. We don't move; we don't breathe until the twins gesture for us to mount the birds. With that, we climb up in silence, and they fly us back home.

Once we arrive home, the girls recount their journey then head to bed early. I can't sleep, so I sit in my room, trying to study a few maps of the Elders' Castle, though my mind is elsewhere. After a while, I abandon the effort and slip into the living room, hoping the couch might grant me the sleep I can't find, but sleep won't come, so I ascend to the rooftop, hoping the hush of the night and the sweep of stars might grant clarity to my restless thoughts.

To my surprise, I find the one person occupying my mind, *Celestia*. She lies splayed across the rooftop, gazing at the stars, taking my favorite place to watch the city below. I remain still for a moment, watching the gentle rise and fall of her chest before she senses my presence. There's a strange serenity about her; so peaceful, so achingly beautiful. She's dressed in her usual clean white tank top and black shorts, her hair fanned out around her like a dark halo against the sand-colored stone. The wounds on her arm look shallow now and not as deep, after being cleaned and cared for. My jaw tightens as my heartbeat quickens, my gaze unwilling—yet unable—to pull away from her.

I take a breath and it comes out louder than intended, so she turns her head around and her eyes lock with mine. "I know, I'm in your spot. I'll get out of your hair in a second," she says, sounding so defeated and tired.

"It's okay. Stay. There is enough space for both of us," I respond as I come closer and lean on the wall beside the entrance. I watch her eyes wander over my bare chest, lingering on the lightning tattoo that streaks from my neck down to my side, stopping just above the waistband of my pants. She swallows and turns away to look back at the stars.

"I don't hate you." I say the words casually in response to her question from the cave.

"Hmm... sure." She presses her lips tight. That's her only comeback, and it kills me to see her in this state. Restraining myself and failing, my legs carry me closer and closer. I kneel down next to her as she turns my way again and smiles. "Do you wear your daggers to sleep?"

It takes me a second to register that I have my twin daggers still strapped to my belt. "There you are," I say softly as I continue to lean forward and cage her head between my arms. I welcome the feeling of her not pushing me away. I scan her face as I brush the hair away from her eyes. "I don't hate you, Mia," I say again with emphasis.

Her eyes light up and twinkle at the sound of me saying her chosen name for the very first time. I linger atop of her, looking at her, memorizing every feature, my gaze lingering on her lips and then losing myself in her beautiful brown eyes, begging with mine for her approval, a testament that my feelings have changed. "I've spent time trying to hate you, but these eyes haunt me every night. One look and I'm undone. I'd walk through fire for you," I whisper.

The moment she blinks and gives me a slight smile, my control breaks. I crash my lips against hers, and she returns the kiss in kind. I get lost in the feel of her soft lips, her tongue grazing mine, and the feel of her hand gripping the back of my neck. The wind stirs, carrying with it the scent of coconut that fills my nostrils. I breathe it in, breathe her in, and for the first time, I know a feeling I've never known before. It's as if I'm being reborn.

Chapter 48

Mia

I'm lost in his touch, free falling, the stars above me blur, and all I see is Xavier's face. Heat rises in my body and everything seems to slow down as I get lost in his big, dark blue eyes.

"I've spent time trying to hate you, but these eyes haunt me every night. One look and I'm undone. I'd walk through fire for you." His breath fans my face as he says the words. I smile slightly and blink to make sure this is real and not a fabrication of my imagination, but his lips crash onto mine, and I close my eyes to savor the feeling. The world around me ceases to exist. I cradle his neck to deepen the kiss, feeling the press of his body atop mine, enjoying the comfortable weight of him. I'm comforted by his masculine scent—a fresh summer breeze with a lively mix of zesty bergamot, crisp mint, and the soft, grounding trace of cedarwood.

I'm transported to another place. Flashes of my previous dreams come to life in front of my eyes as Xavier continues to kiss me. The mystery man from my dreams is him. It has always been him. The realization fills me with joy as I pull him closer to me. More visions strike like lightning, rapid, chaotic, and impossible to stop. They are fragments of a war, faces, flames, blood shed, silence, and death... but no matter how hard I fight them, they keep coming. I push hard at Xavier's chest, putting an end to the kiss, and scramble from beneath him. "Sorry, I have to go." I run away from him, down the stairs, through the apartment, and straight to Cerene's room. I close the door and crumble to the floor, waking Cerene from her sleep as sobs escape me.

Cerene comes running at me, gathering me in her arms, letting me cry. "It's okay. Let it all out," she says as she makes circular motions, rubbing my back in hopes of comforting me. Once I'm all out of tears and finally able to catch my breath, she asks me, "Do you want to tell me what happened?" I nod yes, then shake my head no at the same time. She smiles and says with a chuckle, "I know that feeling, but trust me, I won't judge."

I lift my head and look her in the eyes, seeing the sincerity in them. I spill my heart out and tell her about all the dreams and nightmares I had when I was home, along with the new ones I just had as Xavier kissed me.

She swallows at the last part. and lifts her hand to stop me. "Xavier kissed you?"

I nod and bite my lower lip, feeling uneasy about telling her I kissed Xavier, but I won't keep the truth away from her. I continue with a soft voice, "It's complicated, I guess."

She responds, "Oh, trust me, everything about Xavier is complicated, but let's go back to all your dreams. If Hyda and the Zarka are correct, and you're a seer somehow, visions are sometimes warnings or predictions of possible futures."

I nod as she puts two and two together, and she realizes how scared I am. She squeezes my hand and says, "Mia, you have a gift people dream of having. Don't be scared of it. Embrace it. It is part of who you are. Once you do, it won't scare you anymore." Her words bring me comfort. I never thought of it that way,

"I need to accept who I am," I say to myself, she nods and pulls me off the floor and toward the bed.

"I know this is all new and hard, but please try to get some sleep," she says as she puts the blanket over me.

"Where are you going?" I ask her before I close my eyes.

"Don't worry, I have a brother to check on," she says as she closes the door behind her.

Chapter 49

Xavier

Celestia scrambles away from me, stealing the breath from my lungs as she goes, and I'm left on the rooftop on my back, looking at the same stars she was gazing at. She kissed me back. It isn't one of my fantasies. That kiss was everything. The moment her lips left mine, her eyes looked at me with uncertainty, and that look keeps playing in my mind. It wasn't rejection, not exactly, but there was something there, hesitation, a flicker of doubt, that snuffed out some of my joy. Did I make a mistake? I can't shake the feeling that I've stepped over some invisible line, and I don't know if she'll follow me across it.

I stand up as fast as I can and run down the stairs to follow her. I quickly realize that she went straight to Cerene's room. Not wanting to disturb either of them at this hour, I slump on the couch and decide to wait till morning. I can hear muffled sobs, then a hushed conversation between them. I can't make out what they are saying, but my heart plunges at the thought of making Celestia cry. I stay on the couch, lost in my thoughts. Suddenly, it's all so quiet, so I close my eyes, but then open them again at the sound of someone stepping out of their room. I lift my head to look and find Cerene standing at the edge of the couch, giving me a stern look.

She kicks my leg off the couch to sit next to me, biting down on her lips. She faces me and pokes a finger in my chest as she says in a hushed voice, "Damn you, Xavier, you had to kiss her and make things more complicated than they already are."

I raise my brow. "She told you?" I ask eagerly.

She eyes me and says, "Yes, along with many other things, but Xavier, this is not one of your one-night stands. I'll fucking kill you if you hurt her, I swear it..."

Before she can finish her sentence, I shush her so no one hears us arguing, "This is different." She raises one eyebrow at me, not believing my words. I sigh, taking her hand to put it over my heart so she can feel the words as I say them. "I've never lied to you in all our lives. You have been my sister and best friend. Listen to my heart, listen to it beating, and believe me when I say I'm as surprised about this as you are, but this is different. I ache for her. God knows how much effort I put into hating her, but it's all in vain." I let my voice drop and say the words I'd never utter to anyone other than Cerene. "For the first time in my life, I'm scared... scared of losing her and losing you in the process."

Her eyes soften at my vulnerability. "Damn it, Xavier." She swats my hand away from hers then leans in to give me a hug, whispering over my shoulder, "Be careful with this one. She's not easy." She stands up to go back to her room then says over her shoulder, "For what is worth, I'm happy for you. Just please don't be an idiot."

I laugh under my breath as she closes the door and leaves me on the couch feeling hopeful yet scared about what will come next. I lay back on the couch and close my eyes, sleep finally taking hold of me, and my worries retreat at least until morning.

When morning comes, new problems rise with the old. We wake to the earth trembling beneath us, the ground shaking us from sleep. I open my eyes, the chandelier above swaying left and right, its rhythm matched by the rising screams from the market outside. Cerene, Celestia, Gideon, and my mother run out of their rooms, leaning on the wall for support as the floor trembles beneath us. I try to get up but stumble back on the couch. Then the shaking stops.

"What was that?" Gideon asks.

"An earthquake," Celestia responds.

"A what?" Cerene repeats, looking at her sister.

"What you felt, that shaking, it's called an earthquake. The ground beneath us isn't as still as it seems. Deep down, massive layers of rock slowly press and push against each other. And when that pressure becomes too much, they shift all at once. That's when the earth trembles. It's not magic or a curse... just the world moving in ways we rarely see," Celestia explains as she puts her hand on her face. "Oh God, I sound like Google." She notices all of us staring at her and waves her hand. "Never mind." Her eyes lock with mine for a breath of a second before she rushes to the bathroom without saying anything else.

I look at my mother as she says, "I've heard of earthquakes back in Brookstone and witnessed one I barely felt, but nothing like this. This is something we never have in Eterna. Something doesn't feel right."

Cerene answers my mother as she picks up some of the things that fell from the kitchen cabinets. "Yes, Hyda, something is not right. Eterna is dying."

Chapter 50

Mia

*T*hey are staring at me. Did I just tell them I sound like Google? *What's wrong with me?* I lift my head and lock eyes with Xavier for just a second and then rush to the bathroom because I suddenly feel nauseous. I'm sure it's the earthquake's side effects or feeling too nervous about facing Xavier after the kiss last night. I close the bathroom door as fast as I can and rush to the bowl and heave, my stomach emptying itself. I continue heaving once, twice, and a third time before I can catch my breath. I slowly manage to get up to the sink and splash some water on my face and brush my teeth. I take a look at my reflection in the mirror and run my fingers gently across the dark color that has formed under my eyes from lack of sleep and the tears I shed last night. Those visions scared the hell out of me. I can't help but wonder what the kiss meant and what comes next with the weight of saving Eterna looming over me. I take a second look at myself and think, who is this person looking back at me? *Not so brave now, are you Mia?*

A knock on the door startles me. "Are you okay in there?" Cerene asks.

"Yes, I'll be out in a minute." I brush my hair the best I can, take a deep breath and leave the bathroom to face whatever the day has in store for me.

When I step back into the living room, there isn't anyone other than Hyda sitting on the couch. She lifts her head and looks at me. "Mia, something bad is looming over us. We have to be cautious."

I sit next to her and hold her hand. "Whatever awaits us, we'll meet it head on."

She taps my hand in a comforting way, "I always knew you had great power within you. From the moment I held you in my arms as a baby, you radiated magic. I watched you grow and I'm proud of the person you are. Your parents would be proud... both of them."

I smile and wipe my teary eyes. "Thank you, Hyda. Thank you for believing in me and for always being there and not leaving me alone, even when I didn't feel your presence." Hyda has become family to me. She has stuck by me through it all and left her own son to make sure I was safe. I continue, "Okay, old woman, I have to change my clothes and catch up with the others."

She looks at me in horror, "Don't call me that." I laugh as I get up and walk towards Cerene's room.

I find Cerene fully dressed and getting ready to leave. "What's the plan for the day?" I ask.

"Oh, no big plans for today, Xavier and Gideon went ahead to investigate what's going on outside after the shaking of the earth. You and I will do some light training, then come back here to meet everyone and set a plan to head to the Elders' Castle tomorrow to look for the prophecy. So, you're stuck with me. I hope you won't be missing a certain someone with, say... blue eyes and tanned muscles," she teases.

"Don't worry, I won't be missing anyone. We need to save Eterna and that is my focus." I get dressed fast and head out with Cerene.

The training room echoes with the hiss of steam and the crackle of flames. Fire meets water. Water dodges fire. And in the middle of it all, Cerene and I turn our daily dagger practice into a full blown elemental war.

"You singed my hair!" Cerene yells, hurling a wave of water so hard it knocks me flat on my back.

"You drowned me first!" I snap, sending a spinning ring of fire across the floor. It scorches the tiles and barely misses her boots. Steam curls around us like a battlefield of smoke. Puddles sizzle. The floor's a disaster, half flooded, half burned. The room gave up on staying intact a long time ago. *Xavier is definitely going to kill us for this.* Despite the chaos, or maybe because of it, we laugh, we fight, we curse, and we laugh again. Every strike, blast, and splash is a strange sort of love language only sisters understand, and for a while, it makes me forget everything waiting for us beyond these walls. Everything we have to do to save Eterna, and by the time we finally stop, we're soaked, blistered, and grinning like idiots.

"Truce?" Cerene says as she catches her breath from my last blast of fire.

"Truce. This was fun," I tell her. We try our best to clean up the mess and put things where they belong before heading back home.

We walk back to the apartment, despite our exhaustion, we're smiling. Cerene hands me my small dose of Klinxer Potion. She's been giving me a little since Natalie left just in case she tries to contact me.

"Mia, I've been wanting to talk to you about Xavier, I don't know if you want advice but, take it easy on him, will you? He doesn't show his feelings often." Cerene says as she nudges my shoulder with hers.

"I can tell, but I really don't want to talk or think about this right now. We have so much at stake. We don't know how everything is going to end." She doesn't say anything, but nods in understanding.

The smile leaves my face as thoughts of having to face him come to mind. We continue home in silence, observing everything around us and the damage the earthquake has done to the market. I'm relieved that no major harm is done, just a few carts tipped over and the produce still on the ground. The real damage is emotional. People are scared now.

With every step up to the apartment, I start dreading the fact that I don't know what to tell Xavier about my behavior last night. Leaving him on the roof abruptly after our kiss was not my finest moment, but I was really terrified of all the visions. They made the moment more overwhelming than it already was. I take a deep breath as Cerene opens the door to find Hyda, Xavier, and Gideon all gathered in the living room, talking and sipping tea. At the same moment, a rush of voices invades my mind and are all talking at the same time.

"Mom? Dad? Oh my God, Natalie."

Cerene turns around to look at me in confusion.. Then she mouths with wide eyes, "Oh, Natalie used the potion."

Xavier scrunches his brows at me in confusion. Ignoring him, I walk past them and go to Cerene's room to talk to Natalie and my parents. "My God, Natalie, took you long enough. Mom... Dad... are you guys still there?" They all reply yes at the same time, and I can hear the surprise in both of my parents' voices.

Natalie laughs one of her nervous laughs and says, "It wasn't as easy to convince them to understand and to take a sip of the potion, but I did tell them everything."

Then my mother's voice comes into my mind, full of love and worry. "Mia, honey, we miss you. Are you okay? When are you coming home and what did you find out?"

I smile. "Mom... I'm fine, I don't know yet when I'm coming back. There are a couple more things I need to take care of. I miss you, too."

I hear my father sigh before talking. "Are you sure you're doing well?"

"Yes, I'm good. Please don't worry. I'm safe and happy to discover more about who I am. I promise I'll find my way home once I know everything."

There is a small pause on their end, then my dad continues. "Natalie comes almost every weekend to have dinner, and we miss you every night. We even ordered your favorite pizza last night."

I smile as Natalie continues after him. "The apartment feels so empty without you, and I need to tell you something. You better get your butt over here before the art exhibition, because... I... don't hate me, I submitted all your paintings, and they loved every single one of them. You're all set for the gallery."

I'm shocked that Natalie did that. I wasn't going to submit those, but if they loved them, who am I to argue? So, instead of screaming at Natalie, I say, "Thank you. You really didn't have to do that."

She giggles. "What kind of friend would I be if I let your dream go to waste? You worked hard for this, and I thought those paintings were stunning."

"We will always be here for you and waiting for your return," my mother says as their voices start to come in and out.

"I can't hear you very well. Natalie, do you still have some potion left to contact me again?"

"Just—o—sp—" Natalie's voice is barely coherent, and the last thing I hear is them saying, 'We love you, Mia. Come home soon," as my mind clears out.

Talking to my parents and Natalie made me realize how much I've missed my normal life back home. I've longed to hear their voices. The thought of the gallery displaying my pieces makes me so happy. That would be a huge accomplishment to my career as an artist. Despite all that awaits me back home, Eterna is also where I'm needed. I'm not the same person I was when I first stepped through the portal. The voices arguing outside the room draw my attention, so I decide to go out and see what's going on.

Cerene and Xavier are at each other's throats, arguing and yelling at one another because Xavier finally realized that Cerene gave Natalie her potion. "You will need to learn how to be responsible at some point in life!" he tells her.

"I'm plenty responsible, dickhead!" she responds as Xavier clenches his fists and hits the table in front of him, rattling all the cups of tea atop it.

"Giving a magical potion to a person going to the other side of God knows where is not responsible! We were veiled away from others for a reason!" he shouts.

Gideon and Hyda seem to just let these two argue, but I won't stand for this nonsense. "Cerene gave Natalie the potion for my sake." I step in between them and look at Xavier, and his eyes soften when he sees me. "Cerene gave me the potion because I needed a way to communicate with my family back home. It might not have been responsible, but it was done with good intentions," I tell him calmly, trying to defuse the situation.

"I understand that, Celestia, but she should have checked with me first so we could decide what is best," he says.

I notice the use of my birth name again, and it makes me feel angry. "Not everything needs to be run by you. I think we have more important things to discuss, like the future of Eterna. It needs saving, by the way, and that responsibility doesn't fall on your shoulders, but on ours. So how about you take a breath and cut Cerene some slack for helping her only sister?"

I turn to leave, but he pulls me gently by the hand and says in an almost whisper, "Can we talk outside?"

I glare at him, not wanting to talk to him at this moment. "I said everything that needed to be said." I pull my hand from his grip and go to the room, dragging Cerene with me and slamming the door with all the force I can muster.

"Damn, girl, you're on fire. I'm more than capable of taking care of myself, especially when it comes to Xavier, but thanks for defending me. No one has done that before," Cerene says.

I turn to her and bite my lower lip before speaking. "I didn't mean to sound so harsh, but he really gets under my skin when he calls me that name."

She furrows her brows. "You mean Celestia?" I nod. "It's your real name, when you think about it. Why do you hate it so much?"

I let out a sigh. "I don't know... It just makes me feel like I'm not me. Like the life I lived wasn't truly mine. It's as if someone has stolen my identity, replaced it with something else, and is throwing my real name back in my face. It might seem like a small thing, but it hurts every single time I hear it." I close my eyes and take a deep breath to let the anger in me settle down.

"I'm sorry you feel this way but a name doesn't change who you are, Mia."

Chapter 51

Xavier

I couldn't sleep all night, and I didn't understand why Celestia was so angry at me. I wanted to take a minute and talk to her outside, but she didn't give me a chance. It pierces my heart to see her snatch her hand away from me and retreat to the room along with Cerene. I wait for a while for her and Cerene to come out so we can discuss the plan we put in place for tomorrow, but I eventually give up and ask Gideon to fill them in, then head up to the rooftop. I fall asleep beneath the same glittering stars I've watched all my life, praying to the heavens that we can save Eterna in time, before everything collapses.

I descend the old stairs, and as I walk into the apartment, I hear Cerene and Celestia's laughter before opening the door. They are teasing Gideon about something that makes him smirk with mischief. Once they see me come through the door, they stop and scramble to get ready to start the day. I walk to the bathroom, saying good morning to everyone as I go, but only Gideon responds. *Was yesterday's argument with Cerene that bad? I was just looking out for their safety. Why can't they see that?*

I take a quick shower and get to my room, finding my mother fully dressed and flipping through some old books on Eterna's history. She glances my way as I get ready for the long day ahead. When Gideon and I surveyed the land around us in the aftermath of the tremors, it wasn't good. There is more dead land, and the cracks appear to be spreading like veins across the earth. Farmers lost their crops, their cattle, their hope. If the magic continues to fade for even one more week, all of Eterna could die. Things are unraveling and fast. Today, we must find the prophecy by any means necessary so that Cerene and Celestia will be ready to face what's coming. I collect my gear and sheath my daggers on my belt, then tell my mother it's time to leave. Before we leave, she hands me the key they found in the Vega's house, in case we find something that matches it.

The Elders' Castle and its surrounding halls are vast and heavily guarded. This is one of the most important missions we've ever taken on. So, before we take separate paths, we each take a sip of the last Klinxer Potion we have on hand. We make sure to blend in with the townspeople seeking an audience with the Elders before we make our entrance. We go over the map of the castle one last time to confirm where each of us are supposed to go. My mother heads to the main halls. She'll investigate the walls and tapestries and see if there are any hints there. Gideon's responsibility is to plead his case with the Elders about the land dying. Cerene takes the west side of the dungeons, while Celestia and I take the east. *I'm glad she didn't protest the arrangement, I want to keep her close.*

Celestia and I start at the secret passageways that lead to the dungeons. The passage is narrow, lit only by flickering torches along damp stone walls. Our footsteps echo as we walk side by side. She keeps her eyes forward as I watch her assess every turn and wall we pass.

"So... we're just going to walk through secret tunnels like nothing happened?" I say, breaking the silence.

"Depends. Are we talking about the wrath you unleashed upon Cerene last night, or the fact that you need everyone to get permission from you for every action?"

I smirk. "Neither. I'm talking about the other night. The kiss under the stars."

She exhales and tightens her grip on the hilt at her waist. "Right. That. I had a rough day. People do strange things after knowing the world might be dying."

I quicken my steps to come closer to her. "Mmm. So it meant nothing?"

She turns her head my way. "I didn't say that."

"You didn't say anything. You just ran away, which is kind of the problem." I counter.

She laughs, sarcasm lacing her next words. "Sorry, I didn't know I owed you a post-kiss debrief."

"You don't. But I also didn't expect you to act like I imagined the whole thing," I say in a serious tone.

She shrugs, "You could've."

I chuckle, "Look, I kissed you because I wanted to. You kissed me back because you did, too."

She stops walking, finally meeting my eyes just for a moment. "I kissed you because I wasn't thinking."

I take another step closer to her. "Then let me ask, if you *were* thinking, would you do it again?"

She smiles as she turns away and says, "I think the real question is... what happens if I do?"

I watch her walk ahead, the torchlight catching the edge of her smirk as I follow her and smile. "I guess we'll have to find out once you stop running away from the question."

She scoffs. "Keep up, Xavier. You're the one dragging your feelings through the dungeon."

Our conversation is cut short by faint voices in the distance. We walk further in with caution and silence. The further we go, the worse the smell gets. Celestia covers her nose and mouth with her hand. Rot. Mold. Magic. Not the kind that shimmers with light and power, but something tainted.

The stone corridor stretches like a wide chasm, damp and narrow, lined with prison cells carved into the rock. Torchlights dance uneasily, as if reluctant to reveal what lay ahead. Iron bars stand crooked in their frames, rust clinging to them like dried blood. The walls weep moisture, streaking downward in thin trails. The cells lie in a long, unbroken row, like graves forgotten by time. Some have doors barely hanging on, while others are sealed with layers of ancient sigils still glowing with dull light. This isn't containment, it's an extraction of magic. The residue of magic hums faintly in the air like heat from a fire long dead.

Inside the cells, the chained prisoners barely look like people. Hunched figures, some wrapped in rags, others with skin so pale it looks gray under the torchlight, turn their hollow eyes toward us. They look as if they have lost all hope and are too tired to even flinch from the pain of the conditions they are forced to live in. One whispers something, voice cracked and raspy, but the words are too faint to be understood. Their magic is depleted. Whether completely drained or not differs from one individual to another.

I can feel the echo of it as if it's still being pulled from them without their consent.

Every few minutes, we feel a low hum in the air, as if the dungeon itself takes a breath. That's when the runes flicker and the prisoners jerk just slightly, enough to notice they are being tortured.

"Oh God," Celestia breathes, voice hollow.

"This isn't a prison," I say, my knuckles white on my twin daggers. "It's a siphon."

A figure in the far cell lets out a laugh. "You're too late," he rasps. "You'll see. She always takes what's brightest first."

I come closer to the cell. "Who is taking everyone's magic?"

The figure tries to come forward, chains dragging behind him. He's a hunched old man with hollow black eyes. He looks to be in better shape than the others. "Edith, she drains everyone. Most people wither and die, but the few of us who possess magic are not so lucky." he coughs and falls to the ground as another hum takes over. His restraints glow, draining more magic from him.

Chapter 52

Mia

My heart hurts at the monstrosity in front of me. Who on earth would do this? Realizing the severity of how much Eterna and its people have been hurting ignites anger in my chest.

I realize my hands are shaking, not in fear but in agonizing anger. "I'll make whoever is responsible for this pay for all your pain, I promise you," I tell the people in the cells. I can feel Xavier next to me sizzle with rage and sadness. We reluctantly continue forward. The deeper we get, the worse the condition of the people. I gag uncontrollably at the stench and quicken my steps, but this dungeon seems endless.

"How much longer, Xavier?"

"We should reach a turn in the next few minutes." His voice is stripped of the fire it had earlier. As we run, our footsteps echo in the silence of the dungeon. We both need to get out of this place.

Once we reach a turn at the end of the dungeon, the smell dissipates. We are faced with an iron door, though it doesn't look very old compared to the rest of the dungeon.

"This wasn't on the map," Xaviers says as I examine the door. It's strangely smooth, with a lock at its center, unlike any I've ever seen. It isn't a keyhole, not exactly, more like a disc of jagged, shifting, geometric patterns that retract or emerge like mechanical teeth whenever I get too close. Strange runes circle it, faintly glowing in pulses of dull red, like a heartbeat. It isn't clear if it needs a key, a spell, a blood offering, or something worse. There are no hinges on this side of the door. No handle either. Just the lock and the heavy silence with the occasional low hum that drains the magic from the prisoners.

I watch as Xavier holds the bridge of his nose, thinking about what to do, "Gideon is usually good at opening locks. Let me ask him."

I step closer to the lock while Xavier mindlinks Gideon. I brush my palm on the lock, and the runes glow, shifting into different patterns until one rune starts to glow brighter than the others. My breath hitches, "Xavier. Look!"

He comes closer to look at what I'm seeing. His eyebrows lift in surprise. "Is that a flame?"

"Yes. You see it too, right?"

He nods as I ignite my flame and ready myself to blast it, but Xavier stops me.

"Wait, Celestia. Let me try." He brushes his hand on the lock, and the runes shift again, but none glow as they did for me. Instead, an alarm blasts through the dungeons so loud it pierces through our ears. We look at each other in horror. Xavier quickly grabs my hand, and we run back the same way we entered.

We make it out of the dungeons and hide inside one of the secret passageways. Pressed into each other, my back flush against his chest, we try to steady ourselves. His warm exhale tickles my neck, our fingers still locked together. In the quiet, I whisper, "That was close." He chuckles softly, his chest rising faster against my back just before his other arm slips around my waist. His nose brushes gently against my neck, sending a shiver down my spine. *Oh God, I'm going to melt right here in his arms.*

Then comes his low murmur, teasing and a little breathless, "Why do you always smell so damn good?"

I quickly move away from him. "I think we are safe. Let's catch up to the others." Disappointment is visible on his face, but he doesn't say anything.

Cerene's voice comes into my mind. "Xavier. Mia. I found something. I went deep into the dungeons but didn't find anything other than an empty prison with a dead end. So I circled back. I'm in one of the main halls that leads up to the castle. I didn't see it at first. It's a small symbol from Silas's ring. I don't know what it opens."

I open my mouth to respond, but Xavier tells her we are coming her way.

We walk in silence, blending in with the waves of townspeople. We're in a sea of worn faces and fraying cloaks, walking with the steady pace of people who have nothing left to lose. Some carrying baskets, not with offerings, but with wilted herbs, dried roots, and broken tools. A few hold children close, shielding them from an invisible danger that has crept into the land like a sickness. Most walk in silence. Grief and hunger have long taken over their spirits, and now only the weight of hope or desperation keeps their legs moving. Despite their conditions, they still come to the castle; they don't cry out. They don't plead. They simply walk, filling the white stone halls in hope to see Elder Edith, who might grant them a solution. If they only knew she was behind their doom.

Just a few feet away, in the crowded hall, we spot Cerene leaning casually against the wall, waiting for us. We make our way over to her, avoiding the attention of the crowd. "Where is it?" I ask her in a hushed voice. She gestures to the hall behind her, and it's oddly empty compared to this one. While the guards are busy guiding the townspeople away, we slip into the hall to investigate. We start looking for clues. Looking at the wall near me, I notice the symbol of spread wings with a ruby in the middle. You'd miss it if you weren't looking closely, as it blended in with the wallpaper.

"How on earth were you able to see this?" I ask Cerene.

She smirks as she looks at Xavier. "I've been taught by the best to observe and pay very close attention to details."

I nod and smile as I further inspect the wall. It is lined with portraits framed in dusty gold frames, each one showing a solemn face from a time long past. Men in ceremonial armor, women in elaborate gowns, children with eyes too knowing for their age, all stare out at us as though they were watching us.

I look closer at one of the frames that's slightly askew, I push it further to the side and find the same drawn wings hidden behind the frame. I brush my hand against it and feel something like a small groove. "I found something, but I'll need help," I whisper to Xavier and Cerene while looking around to make sure no one notices us.

They both rush to my side, and Cerene asks Xavier to slightly remove the frame while she provides a lookout. "There is a small slot in the wall for the ring to go in," I say as I stretch my hand and squeeze it between the wall and the frame, pressing the ring in. We don't hear anything, but a small part of the wall starts to rotate slowly, like a secret door. We rush in before the door makes a full rotation and closes back the way it was, as if it was never disturbed. The room is pitch black, so I summon a small flame to give us a little light to see. The room is covered in dust and barely fits the three of us. I look around and find one key hole on the wall. Nothing else on the bare walls.

"Oh, crap. Hyda has the key. Maybe that's what it's meant to open," Cerene whispers.

"What do we do then?" I whisper back.

Xavier clears his throat, "We try the key."

I scrunch my eyebrows and turn to look at him as he puts his hand in his pocket and pulls the key out.

Cerene rolls her eyes, "Such a show off."

He extends his hand, places the key in the hole, and twists it a couple of times. We hear a *click* as a small box slides out of the wall like a drawer. Inside it lies an old scroll yellowed with age. My heart beats faster with excitement as Cerene reaches to grab it. We hear another *click* and the box slides back into the wall.

I bring my flame closer to her as she opens the scroll to read.

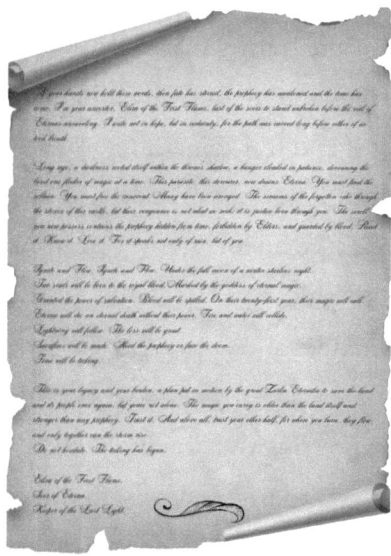

"If your hands now hold these words, then fate has stirred, the prophecy has awakened and the time has come. I'm your ancestor, Elira of the First Flame, last of the seers to stand unbroken before the veil of Eterna's unraveling. I write not in hope, but in certainty, for the path was carved long before either of us took breath.

Long ago, a darkness rooted itself within the throne's shadow, a hunger cloaked in patience, devouring the land one flicker of magic at a time. This parasite, this devourer, now drains Eterna. You must find the villain. You must free the innocent. Many have been wronged. The screams of the forgotten echo through the stones of this castle, but their vengeance is not what we seek; it is justice born through you. The scroll you now possess contains the prophecy hidden from time, forbidden by Elders, and guarded by blood. Read it. Know it. Live it. For it speaks not only of ruin, but of you.

Ignite and Flow, Ignite and Flow.
Under the full moon of a winter starless night.
Two souls will be born to the royal blood.
Marked by the goddess of eternal magic.
Granted the power of salvation.
Blood will be spilled.
On their twenty-first year, their magic will call.
Eterna will die an eternal death without their power.
Fire and water will collide. Lightning will follow.
The loss will be great.
Sacrifices will be made.
Heed the prophecy or face the doom.
Time will be ticking.

This is your legacy and your burden, a plan put in motion by the great Zarka Eternika to save the land and its people once again, but you're not alone. The magic you carry is older than the land itself and stronger than any prophecy. Trust it. And above all, trust your other half, for where you burn, they flow, and only together can the storm rise.

Do not hesitate. The ticking has begun.

Elira of the First Flame,
Seer of Eterna,
Keeper of the Last Light.

Cerene closes the scroll and looks up at me. "Our great-grandmother was like you, Mia. A seer and a carrier of the flame."

I let out a breath and nod. Words fail me at the realization that I've been a part of something bigger before I was even born. Cerene, realizing what I'm feeling, takes hold of my hand from one side while Xavier takes the other.

I lift my head to see both of them looking at me, as Xavier says, "I've got you, both of you. Whatever it takes, however far this goes, I'm with you. Even if it costs me everything, I'll give it all to see you safe. You'll never walk this path alone." Tears well up in my eyes and I smile at his vow to us. Two words fuel my soul. *Never alone.*

Chapter 53

Xavier

I meant every word I said to both Celestia and Cerene. As my words settle, their doubts fade. All that's left is resolve in their eyes.

I break the awkward silence. "Okay, we need to find a way to get out of here. And I'll also let my mother and Gideon know we found the prophecy."

Cerene and Celestia step back, searching for a way out of this cramped room.

Cerene tells Celestia, "Let's try to push the wall and see if it'll rotate again. There must be a way out." They try, but pushing against the door doesn't yield results. I start feeling around the wall with my palms to see if there is anything. My hand brushes against a very fine line that seems to be a bit higher than the rest of the wall. I push at it and the door begins to rotate again, revealing the same empty hall we were in before. Cerene looks out first to make sure no one is there, and, keeping our heads low, we slip out and disappear into the mass of townspeople unnoticed.

Gideon tells us through the mindlink. "There is nothing here other than one hateful person. Elder Edith is so cruel to everyone, dismissing everyone's concern. Something is off about her. I'm unable to stay longer. The whole atmosphere is not right... Guards are moving out of this hall after speaking to Edith. I'll meet you all in the main hall."

My mother hasn't responded to the mindlink since I informed her about finding the prophecy. I try to mindlink her but get nothing. There is no response. We start walking towards the exit of the castle halls, but Gideon's voice through the mindlink stops us, urgent and full of horror.

"Damn it. Xavier, can you hear me? They have Hyda. Edith has her. The guards are dragging her in as we speak. Hyda met my eye and gave a small shake of her head, silently telling me not to say a word."

My breath catches, and I take a minute to process what he's saying.

"Xavier, what do you want me to do?" I hear his voice again.

"Gideon, just get out of there." I take more time to process and continue telling him through the mindlink, "My mother is very skilled. If they have her, then she has a reason to let them capture her."

I lift my head, Cerene and Celestia looking at me with worry in their eyes, but I tell them, "Let's get out and regroup. She's not responding to our mindlink." Celestia steps in front of me, arms crossing over her chest. "We will not leave Hyda behind."

"We are not leaving her behind. We need to figure out what's going on and act accordingly. She'll not be happy if we all get captured. Especially now that we hold the prophecy," I explain.

Before she can speak, the crowd begins to stir. Uneasy murmurs ripple through the hall, quickly swelling into panicked screams echoing from deep within the castle. Gideon bursts into view, sprinting toward us, his voice raw and frantic. "Everyone, evacuate!" he bellows.

Behind him, chaos floods the corridor. A wave of people surge forward, some with blood streaking down their faces, others deathly pale with vines pulsing beneath the surface of their skin. Their eyes are vacant and inky black, as if their soul has been drained away. They don't scream. They don't blink. They just run like they are being controlled by some force.

We stand aside, letting people through the exit as we wait for the pale-ones to arrive, ready to defend ourselves from whatever this is. Gideon finally makes it to our side, catching his breath. "I noticed something was not right up there but didn't see these people coming... What are they?"

Cerene answers him with a trembling voice. "They look possessed."

Our horror intensifies as we watch the pale figures drain the life from the townspeople with a simple touch. Wisps of light like silver smoke rise from the victims' bodies, pulled through their skin and into the hands of their attackers. The air shimmers with it, glowing threads unraveling from mouths and eyes, twisting upward like dying breaths. The drained collapse without a sound, their eyes vacant, their bodies limp as if their very essences have been stolen.

Cerene and Celestia both start shooting their magic, trying to help people escape this horrifying fate, while Gideon and I guide people with children to the exit.

"We are outnumbered here." I tell Cerene, Celestia, and Gideon.

As always, Celestia has something to say. "You think?"

Cerene smirks at her sister's remark and adds, "I'm calling a Zarka to take us out of here."

A few minutes later, two Zarkas land behind us, ready to fly us off. "Let's go. We can't save everyone," I say loud enough for them to hear me through the chaos. Both girls hesitate, so I move toward them and pull them by the arm.

We all mount the Zarkas, and within seconds, we are above the chaos. We finally see Elder Edith emerge from the main hall, cackling, hands raised high, abusing her Elder magical gift, consuming all the power from the people with an invisible force, devouring all the fallen souls. Her eyes land on the Zarkas carrying us, and her face twists with disdain.

She stands like a shadow given form, draped in black silks that shimmer with stolen power. Her eyes are a piercing, unnatural violet, glowing faintly with the magic of dozens, maybe hundreds, of drained souls. Where her gaze falls, the air grows heavy, as if the very world itself fears her attention. Her beauty is sharp and cold, the kind that wounds if you dare look too long. High cheekbones, lips curved in an evil smile, and hair the color of midnight cascading like liquid around her. But beneath it all, there's hunger, an endless, devouring hunger. Magic clings to her like armor, flickering and twisting across her skin in faint tendrils. None of it is hers. All of it is stolen. I can feel it, the presence of magic that was never meant to coexist inside a single person. The more she consumes, the more twisted her aura becomes, like something once divine is now rotted by greed. And the worst part of it: she has Silas, my mother, and who I assume is Freya in shackles behind her.

Chapter 54

Freya

Silas walked into our cell with a wound on his forehead and a strange look in his eyes. When he said he'd met our girls, I started sensing them more. I feel them stronger every day, closer with each passing hour. Their magic is distinctive, unmistakable, and powerful. I've been wanting to meet them and hold them in my arms. I'll do whatever it takes to get out of here, even if I have to give myself up to Edith. Silas has been trying to advise me otherwise, but I've made up my mind. When the guard comes today to take Silas, I'll join him and tell her I can give her what she wants in order to just be out of here. I sense my children are so close today.

I dig my fingers a million times into the dirt to feel the flow of magic beneath the cell, and I know in my heart that they are here in the castle. Worry overwhelms me. "What would the twins be doing here in the castle?" I ask Silas.

His eyes widen. "What do you mean here in the castle?"

I stand up and wipe my hands on my dress, not caring about the dirt staining my only clean dress. "I'm telling you they are here."

We both stop talking as we hear one of the guards approaching, keys clinking as he tries to open the cell door. I move to stand in front of the door along with Silas, and the guard looks at me with questioning eyes. Silas gives me one final pleading look to change my mind, but I stand my ground "I'm surrendering myself to Elder Edith."

The guard's eyebrows shoot up in surprise, then clears his throat, "She'll be delighted."

We start the walk to the main hall of the castle, and I can't help feeling the excitement blooming in my chest and stomach. With every step I take out of this place, I feel my girls closer to me, as if we are attached by a thread. These prison halls are narrow, barely wide enough for two people to walk side by side. Silas's hand brushes my back guiding me forward as we follow the guard. The stench of dried blood and rot clings to the walls, making the air stale and humid. I'm grateful Edith didn't put us in the dungeons, but I can't help the dread that fills me for the others she has locked down there.

At last, the tunnel opens into a wide corridor lined with dark wood and polished stone. Rich tapestries hang from the walls. The hum of life returns, echoes of conversation, the clink of cutlery, the faint chords of music drifting from somewhere high above. And there, at the corridor's end, stands the great oak doors, tall and imposing, carved with ancient sigils and edged in gold. Beyond them lies the main hall, bright and warm, a world completely removed from the cell I've known for the past twenty-one years. I close my eyes and remember a time when I was welcome here, when Otto stood in these same halls, arms open, embracing me with his love.

The moment the door opens, Edith's gaze falls on me, a smirk playing on her lips. She wears an extravagant black silk dress that shimmers with magic I know she didn't possess before. Her eyes are an unnatural violet color, glowing with power and something far darker—an evil force I've never felt until now. Her onyx hair flows behind her, moving as if it has a life of its own. I freeze, clutching Silas's arm in a silent signal, telling him something is wrong. Deeply wrong. Sinister, unnatural, and dark.

The Zarka hovers above the chaotic scene in the castle. I watch in horror as Silas, Hyda, and another woman stand behind Elder Edith while she drains the life out of the rest of the townspeople who didn't manage to escape in time. She has created an army of drained people, controlling them like puppets. The land surrounding the castle, once full of colorful bloom and life, is now wilting and dying. She isn't just consuming souls, she's consuming life itself from everything—people and land. Cerene and I shudder as we watch miles and miles of land drying out and cattle dropping to the ground.

I ask Cerene, my voice strained and angry, "What is she going to do with Hyda and Silas? Is that woman with them our biological mother?"

Cerene's voice mirrors my own as she answers, "I don't know. I'd like to think she's not going to harm them since she's still after the prophecy."

I turn my face to look at the other Zarka flying next to us and watch Xavier look below. His face is strained, unwilling to leave his mother behind. My heart aches for him. From above, a group of guards catch my attention. They are heading out of the castle, taking a path through the dead land towards a rocky area in the distance.

"Hey, Gideon. Look at those guards. Where are they heading?" I ask. It seems I got everyone's attention and not just Gideon's because now we are all tracking the guards.

"Let's land a safe distance away from the castle, reassess, then investigate further. We have seen enough for the day, and we lost my mother," Xavier says, and we all nod in agreement.

The Zarka lands gracefully on the only green land left in Eterna, right beside a flowing stream. The giant bird lowers its wings, and we dismount in silence. Without a word, we let it rise into the sky again. I move toward the water, drawn by the sound of it, soft, steady, and clean. Kneeling at the edge, I splash handfuls onto my face, letting it cool my anger. I drink deeply, the chill running down my throat, as if I can wash away the horror we just witnessed. I settle beside the stream, the grass cool beneath me. The air is different here, lighter, scented faintly with wildflowers and damp earth. I glance down, and for the first time in what feels like days, something stirs in my chest that isn't fear or grief. The water is crystal clear, so pure I can see the fish darting between rocks, bright scales flashing as they swim in a lazy, peaceful motion. Their world is untouched, unaware of the ruin spreading across the rest of Eterna.

The sky above begins to shift, turning gold and amber, with streaks of rose stretching across the clouds. It's almost sunset. The light glows warm on the grass, turning the greens into something beautiful. For a heartbeat, everything is still. For the first time in a long while, I allow myself to breathe. I glance up. Cerene, Gideon, and Xavier all wear somber expressions. No one speaks. The silence between us is heavy. Each of us is wrapped in our own thoughts, carrying pieces of what happened today but unable to put into words how we feel. Xavier stands with his hands still clenched, eyes on the horizon. Cerene and Gideon are dipping their fingers into the stream, as if trying to ground themselves in the moment. "We will save them," I say, breaking the silence.

Xavier looks at me and responds, "Let's rest here tonight and then continue in the morning." Gideon and Cerene nod, so I agree as well. We are all tired and need to be prepared to face what comes next. *I sure could use Hyda's words of encouragement and comfort right now.*

As we settle for the night near the stream, Xavier takes the first watch. Sleep evades me once again, so I turn to watch Xavier lean against a massive tree, stargazing as usual. He must be feeling awful for not being able to get his mother out of the castle and away from Edith. I quietly get up and walk to him, but the moment I'm up, his head turns my way. *This man has impeccable hearing.*

I continue walking the short distance towards him, "Never got the chance to ask, are you okay?"

He brushes the question away. "I'll survive."

I take a deep breath and sit next to him. "You know, Hyda means a lot to me, too. It's because of her that I finally got some answers. It pains me to know that she put her life on the line." I swallow and continue, "I feel it in my gut, she'll be fine. She's a survivor and a great warrior." I lift my head to look at him and find him staring at me.

My focus goes to his lips as he says, "Thank you." His hand is resting on the grass, grounding him, so I reach out, giving it a gentle squeeze. He looks at my hand atop his. "Celestia, is this pity? Because if it is, I want none of it."

I shake my head and think for a minute before saying my next words. *I'm trying to extend an olive branch, but he's making it hard for me.* "Okay, let's be honest with each other. I'd never pity you. And can you please call me Mia?" He glances my way and scans my face, so I continue talking. "After everything at the castle today, I started thinking. This prophecy is no joke. The way those people just dropped... and Edith, taking all their power, their souls, feeding on them..." I pause, the memory flashing behind my eyes. "It terrifies me. I don't know what tomorrow will bring. I'm scared of losing the chance to meet my biological parents... to really know them. I'm scared of losing Cerene, Gideon, Hyda..." He gently brushes away the tear trailing down my cheek. and I breathe in shakily. "But more than anything," I whisper, confessing, "I'm scared of losing you—and whatever this thing is between us."

His expression shifts, softening with something unreadable. His voice is barely above a breath. "What are you saying?"

I smile, just a little. "I'm saying I want more of us. More time to get to know you. More kisses... like the one on the roof."

His face lights up with a smile as he comes closer to me. "Hmmm... more kisses like this?" He brushes his lips softly on the tip of my nose.

I smile as he pulls slightly away. "Yes, under two conditions," I say.

He lifts one eyebrow and smirks. "Which are?"

I bite my lower lip, his eyes zeroing in on the movement, enticing him further before I say, "Call me Mia from now on, and stop being a controlling prick."

He laughs a hearty laugh and whispers in my ear, lighting up my body with goosebumps and heat. "As you wish, Mia." Then he lifts my chin to look at him. "Whatever tomorrow brings, we'll face it together. But right now, you're here, with me. Let the world wait." With that, he engulfs me in his arms, tucking me away from the world, kissing me into oblivion. We stay tangled up next to the tree, drowning in one another, and for these moments, there is no Eterna dying, no prophecy, just us underneath the stars.

I open my eyes with the first light of the sun, my head still nestled against Xavier's chest as a shadow towers over us. Cerene is looking down with a bright smile and eyes that have so many unspoken words. "Rise and shine, lovebirds," she says as she starts to walk away.

Xavier stirs and his arms tighten around me as I feel him plant a kiss on the crown of my head. I savor the moment, dreading the day ahead, "Good morning. It's time to move." I start to get up and I hear a growl escape him in protest.

"Xavierrrrrrrr," Cerene teases from the side of the stream. I smile as I approach her.

"You're in a good mood," I tell her as I wash my face in the cool water.

"Of course. What could be better than waking up for the last watch and finding you and Xavier fast asleep, tangled together beneath the tree?" She smirks as she twirls a ball of water in her hands before throwing it at Xavier.

"Damn it, Cerene, I'm up," he responds. Gideon chuckles, and for a moment, we just stand there, looking at each other savoring the moment, knowing that we'll have a hard day ahead .

Once we are all ready, we start walking the same trail the guards took yesterday. Gideon and Xavier lead the way as Cerene and I follow. Cerene keeps teasing me with her questions, summoning tiny droplets of water and flicking them my way. "Come on, Mia, give me something."

I laugh under my breath. "What do you want to know? We came to a truce. If we survive, there may be an us."

She bumps my shoulder with hers. "Eeeek! I'm so happy for you! Truly, both of you. He could use someone like you in his life." Her words make me smile and I nod in acknowledgment.

Xavier and Gideon come to a halt once we reach the rocky area. They motion for us to be quiet. We huddle close and Xavier tells us, "It looks like another cave. Keep your eyes open. Be prepared for anything. I didn't know this place existed. And if there are any of those pale people, do not let them touch you." We nod as we all make sure our weapons are ready. Before we approach the entrance of the cave, Xavier pulls me by the arm, slowing me down as Gideon and Cerene go forward. "Mia, stay alive. Blast your fire at anything, and don't slow yourself with your dagger."

I lift my eyebrow and whisper, "Careful, if someone hears you, they would think you're afraid to lose me."

He pulls me in by the back of my neck and kisses me on the lips. "I mean it, Mia," he says as he starts walking toward the entrance, then glances back at me one last time. "And for the record, I am afraid of losing you."

The moment we step through the entrance, the cave pulses with unnatural energy. Shadows stretch across its jagged walls, lit faintly by a single glowing blue crystal embedded in the rock in the middle of the cave. A hooded man is hunched next to it, fingers deep in the earth, a luminescent blue flowing from the earth like mist as he absorbs it through his fingers. The moment he notices us, he vanishes into thin air leaving remnants of magic. Around us stalactites hang like stone fangs from the ceiling, dripping into dark pools on the ground. Bones litter the cave like the aftermath of a massacre. We move slow and steady together. Cerene summons her water at the tip of her fingers, and I summon my flame to give us a better view of what lies ahead.

The pale ones emerge with bony faces, eyes drowned in black, and skin laced with dark, pulsing veins. Their movements are jerky, inhuman. Behind them, standing atop a natural ledge of stone, is Elder Edith, wrapped in a cloak of living shadow. Her violet eyes glow, reflecting the twisted magic she commands.

"How on earth did they all get here without us seeing them?" I whisper to my companions. I step forward, the light from my flames reflecting off the damp cave walls. "Now or never," I mutter. Fire blooms in my palms, casting gold and orange arcs across the darkness. I thrust both hands forward and send a roaring column of flame into the front ranks of the pale ones. Some ignite instantly, but they do not stop. Even burning, they charge forward.

Cerene raises her arms, and the still pools of water at her feet swirl to life. She draws them up into ribbons, sharp as blades, and sends them lashing through the undead swarm. Each strike slices deep, but it takes more than wounds to stop them. The cave is full of noise, fire roaring, water crashing, footsteps slapping wet stone, and the metallic ring of blades. Xavier darts through the chaos, his twin daggers gleaming. He ducks low, drives a blade into one creature's gut, and spins away, dodging another one before its fingers can graze him, but one manages to catch his shoulder. Black veins bloom instantly, crawling across his skin like roots.

"Xavier!" My heart sinks as Gideon throws a knife into the creature's throat and grabs Xavier, dragging him back.

Cerene rushes to them, forming a sphere of glowing water around them. As the veins start moving down from his shoulder to his arm, he grits his teeth, trying to resist the pain, but then his body starts trembling. From where I stand, panic claws at my chest, but Cerene holds Xavier's arm, and for some unknown reason, the veins stop growing. "Don't let them touch you again," she growls.

More pale ones pour from hidden cracks in the stone, summoned by Edith's raised hand. Her voice echoes across the cave, laced with something evil. "Chosen Ones, I was wondering when you'd show your faces. Your parents did an amazing job hiding you from me." Her voice echoes in the cave as she continues. "Souls are meant to be used," she says. "Why waste them on the weak?"

I snarl, launching a wall of fire up the slope toward her. The flame crashes harmlessly against a dome of shadow she conjures with a flick of her wrist. "She's feeding off the pale ones and draining them like a parasite," Gideon says, panting.

"Then we cut her off," Xavier replies, eyes narrowing. Xavier and Gideon move together, taking the left side, dodging falling rocks and weaving through the chaos. Their blades flash in the low light, fast and precise. They aim for knees, joints, eyes, anything to slow the creatures down.

Cerene and I push forward through the center. Fire and water surge through the cave, steam rising in great clouds, fogging the battlefield. I burn a path to the ledge while Cerene uses her magnificent water spheres to shield us from any attack that comes too close. The stone shakes and cracks beneath Edith's feet as her power intensifies. Souls swirl visibly around her, drawn from the fallen, glowing like wisps. Her onyx hair lifts on wind that doesn't exist.

I leap onto the ledge, flames rising high in my hands. "That power doesn't belong to you."

Edith smiles. "It does now."

I hurl fire while Cerene sends a wave crashing up behind me, and below us, Xavier and Gideon fight with bloodied blades and grit.

Surrounded by echoes, darkness, and the scent of smoke and stone, the battle rages on until the waves of pale ones finally begin to recede. Edith's power starts to falter. There are no more souls left for her to consume. Just before Cerene and I strike her with a final blow of fire and water combined, she cackles and flicks her hand. In a burst of violet light, Silas, Hyda, and another woman appear. Both women are in heavy shackles, but Silas is free from them, his arms are around the other woman in a protective way. I gasp as realization hits me, that woman is Freya. Our biological mother. My attention is brought back to Edith as she continues to speak.

"Prophecy children, are you willing to sacrifice your loved ones to save Eterna?" She surges forward to grab Cerene, but Silas intervenes. He throws himself between them and takes the hit meant for my sister. The dark magic slams into him like a tidal wave, lifting him off his feet. He crashes to the ground, but instead of staying down, he rises. Staggering and bleeding. He fights.

He swings at her, wild and precise all at once, the way only a seasoned warrior can. He knocks her back, just enough for us to move.

"Help him!" Cerene yells, and we do.

Water surges from her palms, wrapping around Silas's body in a protective veil. I throw fire, not to burn, but to counter the dark energy choking him, trying to push it back.

"Hold on!" I scream, throwing everything I have at Edith's magic. "Silas, hold on!"

He grits his teeth and pushes through the agony. Black veins race up his arms, but he doesn't falter. He drives a punch into Edith's gut. A growl tears from his throat as he tries to rip her hand away from him. His knees buckle, but he plants one foot forward. He's still moving. Still fighting, but the magic is eating him alive.

Cerene stumbles to his side, trying to shield him with more water, shouting his name, her voice ragged with panic. I blast fire at Edith again, desperate to break her focus, to stop whatever curse she's weaving into his skin, but it's not enough. The black veins spread up his neck, crawling over his face. His body convulses, and even then, his hands don't stop. He's still clawing at her grip. Still trying to stand between her and Cerene. His gaze finds mine. Something flickers there. Pain. Pride. Love. And acceptance.

"Silas!" I cry, reaching toward him

"You two were my greatest hope... even from afar." He says, looking to me then to Cerene.

With that, he falls. The sound of his body hitting stone is final. A horrible, hollow thud.

Cerene screams, dropping to her knees beside him. Her hands are trembling as she touches his face. "No, no, Silas, please..."

I follow, fire flickering uselessly in my palms, unable to stop what's already done. He's gone. He fought and died to protect us. Silas is gone. Edith lowers her hand. Her smile is slow, cruel.

Freya moves with shaking limbs towards Silas's body. Her sobs and wails echoing in the cave make everyone stand still. My heart slams against my ribcage. Sorrow consumes me, and tears start spilling down my face. I look toward Cerene to see tears there too, for the loss of a father we'll never get to know.

Rage surges through me, radiating through my flames and magic, seeping from my skin as I charge at Edith with full force, shooting flames with one hand and planting my dagger deep in her throat with the other. My hand shakes when I pull my dagger out of her flesh. Her warm blood coats my fingers, and the resistance makes my stomach turn. Her violet eyes stay locked on mine as she sinks to the ground with a smirk.

"You think it'll be over once you kill me?" She laughs, choking on her own blood. Her magic spills from her like a soul torn loose, bright and writhing, desperate to escape. We all look at the magic moving away from us towards the hooded person once again standing next to the entrance of the cave by the blue glowing crystal, one hand digging in the dirt and the other high above him snatching the magic that Edith lost. I glance at Xavier and Gideon, and they give me a signal that they will hold him back till we can free Hyda and Freya.

Cerene takes quick steps to free them, while I watch the man peel his hood off. His eyes are inky black, but his face and hands are pale, pulsing with blue and black veins. His voice is rough and sinister. "No one will save you now." As he speaks, the blue crystal pulses brighter, as if he's fueling himself from it. I walk towards the man, but Hyda's grip on my shoulder stops me.

I turn to look at her. She has frantic eyes as she speaks. "No... this can't be... Oh God, no." I hold her, unsure what is going on in her mind and glance back to see if it's Xavier she's looking at, but she continues in a louder voice. "Mateo?" The hooded man stands still for a breath, and I take the chance to move next to Xavier and Gideon. Mateo's eyes flash between black and deep green, looking at Hyda as if some part of him recognizes her.

Hyda scrambles away and runs towards him while mumbling, "What have you done?" her voice trembling.

"Hyda? Is that you, my love? Eterna took you and our son away from me." Mateo's eyes shift back to black. He lifts both of his arms, summoning power from the crystal, letting it surge throughout his body. Hyda tries to talk to him from a safe distance, and his eyes shift green. He looks like he's trying to resist the power taking over him, his neck is straining as he talks to her. "I thought all of you were dead after the rebellion that day. I needed closure, needed to destroy the Elders, Eterna, and everything with it for the despair I lived in after knowing I was the only survivor, or so I thought. I consumed all its magic... I'm long gone. Forgive me, my love."

Hyda sobs as she extends her hand towards him, wanting to touch him, but his eyes shift to black one more time, and he loses control as he hurls a strong wave of power towards us. Before I can ignite my flame, Hyda steps between us and Mateo, taking the hit and struggling with her pain. She resists the magic, battling him with all her might and strength. I throw another fire blazing towards him to help Hyda, but she falls to the ground. Xavier runs to his mother's side in haste. I try to shield him with my flame as he checks on her. His eyes brimmed with tears, his jaw clenched tight with the kind of anger that only grief can ignite. He falls to his knees beside his mother's body, hands trembling as he reaches for her, like maybe, somehow, he can still pull her back. I take a breath, my voice low but steady.

"Gideon. Go guard Freya and send Cerene here." He nods.

I start taking calculated steps towards Mateo, all the while keeping my flame blazing at him. He falls to his knees and digs his fingers into the dirt, consuming more magic, unaffected by my flames.

His eyes shift for a second, just enough to say, "Oh my precious Hyda! What have I done?" Only for them to shift back to the inky black ones as evil consumes him once again.

I'm close enough to see Hyda drawing her last breaths, clutching her son's arms. "I love you, Son. Forgive me for not being there with you. You have done so well. I'm proud of you. I give you my legacy. Protect the twins at all costs. Save Eterna, our home." I start to tremble hearing her last words, emotions consuming my mind. Xavier leans to hug his mother's body, whispering something in her ear, one last private moment for the both of them, and his tears fall down his face. Xavier's anguish fuels him as he charges, daggers clenched tight. He gets close, close enough to plunge one into Mateo's thigh. Mateo snarls, then swats him aside with a surge of magic, sending him crashing to the ground.

Cerene and I scream in unison watching Xavier fall. Our pain and grief consume everything around us, rattling the cave with our powers. Fire and water collide as one, and stone starts to fall down from the ceiling. Our voices are united, blasting a magical force throughout Eterna, and the blue crystal in the ground explodes, causing part of the ceiling to crack and fall.

Cerene surrounds us with a sphere, and everything moves in slow motion as I watch the cave crack all around us. Thunder booms outside the cave. Cerene and I watch as every fallen pale one burns to ashes. Everything quiets down slowly, and Cerene and I drop down to our knees together. Once Cerene sees there is no more danger around us, she lowers her sphere. I'm choked up, and tears fall uncontrollably down my face seeing everyone around us on the ground, unsure who is still alive. The cave is unrecognizable; the walls are cracked, and the smell of dust, blood, and fire lingers in the air. It seems to be raining outside the cave, as if all of Eterna is mourning with us for the lost lives. I manage to stand up on wobbly legs, shaking and moving towards the place Hyda and Xavier fell. I brace myself for the crack in my heart. I kneel down next to Hyda's half-scorched body. Her face is bloody and her eyes are half open. Her left arm is extended towards Xavier's body a few feet away from her, as if he's the last person her eyes saw. I close her eyes with my hand. As I whisper my last words of goodbye. "Hyda, you were a great mentor and a guardian. You died defending everyone and everything you love. I'll miss you dearly. You found a way to stay nestled in my heart."

I look at Xavier and my legs don't want to move. I refuse to say goodbye to him, too. I refuse to not see those big deep blue eyes look at me again. I refuse to let go of our moments together. Cerene comes behind me and helps me stand, and we both go and sit next to him. Cerene holds one of his hands and cries without saying a word.

I stand there looking at her. "NO! NO! ETERNIKAAA!" I scream with all my might, until the cave shakes, and Eternika materializes with her massive wings shimmering more than before.

"Chosen Ones, thank you. Your blood line saved us and Eterna once again."

I cut her off. "I don't want your thanks. Look around you. Everyone we love has fallen to fulfill your prophecy," I scream at her, grief lacing every word.

Eternika looks around the crumbling cave. "The prophecy foretold sacrifice, and the blood spilled, but it also foretold the great power you hold. You both can restore the order." I furrow my brows, sick of the riddles of this prophecy. Eternika starts flapping her wings, rattling all the rubble around us, and disappears. I turn to Cerene, who is still crying over Xavier, and notice the ground beneath her and around her turning green. I move towards her as I see Xavier's hand twitch.

Not believing my eyes, "Cerene, what is happening?"

She looks at me. Her face is wet with tears, dried blood, and dirt. She wipes her face with her arm as she looks around. The earth around my sister starts to bloom. I rush to Xavier, lean down, and put my ear on his chest. I gasp. "He's alive, Cerene. He's alive." My voice cracks as hope blooms in me.

I hold my sister's hand as she places it on the green grass sprouting next to her. The Zarka's voice comes into our minds once again. "Where you burn, Celestia, Cerene flows. Water gives life to everything, and with her touch, Eterna will bloom again."

I chuckle. "Of course, and you couldn't tell us that before."

Somewhere in the cave, I hear Gideon's voice. "Hello? Is anyone still here? If you can hear me, we are trapped behind rocks."

Chapter 56

Freya

*S*ilas is dead... Silas is gone... I can't hear anything around me. I lose myself to the loss of him, sacrificing himself to save the lives of our daughters. I wail and scream, unable to control my sorrow. Someone comes to unshackle me, but in my haze, I don't know who it is. Time seems to slow down around me. I don't know how long I stay like this. I'm snapped back to reality when a massive surge of magic hits from all around me, and I hear a man's voice tell me to take cover as he lunges his body atop mine. The cave shakes beneath our feet and rocks start to fall all around us. Then suddenly, everything quiets down. It's too dark in here. I cough as dust fills my lungs, and the man shifts away to tell me, "We are trapped on this side of the cave with no way out."

I cough again. "Who are you?"

"I'm Gideon, a friend of Cerene, Xavier, and Mia's."

I feel confused. "Mia?"

He also coughs, then turns on a flashlight. "I mean Celestia."

I nod in acknowledgment while trying to stand up. "Hello? Is anyone still here? If you can hear me, we are trapped behind rocks," Gideon calls out.

It takes a while for others to come find us, but once the rocks start to clear, I lay my eyes on my girls. They stand side by side in the stillness after the storm. One has blood trailing down her temple, soaking into her shirt. Her eyes betray the weight she carries, eyes that have seen too much in too little time. The other grips her side, fingers stained red, her breathing shallow. Strands of hair, once tamed, now hang in tangled waves across her dirt-smeared face. Neither speaks. They just stand there, as if holding the grief in place by sheer will alone.

I move forward, opening my arms wide, and they step into my embrace. I close my eyes and breathe, my heart is full, despite the loss of Silas. As a mother, I feel complete to finally hold my girls in my arms. They are safe, and they fulfilled their destiny. Looking around the cave, Hyda, Mateo, and many more are on the ground. Our loss is great, but Eterna will prosper.

Over the next few days, we take the time to bring the wounded to the Healers Hall, bury our loved ones, and free the prisoners from the dungeons. As Eterna returns to its usual bloom, I take the time to listen to how my girls grew up, and in return, they hear me tell them how everything started, from their birth and our time in prison, to Hyda and Mateo's story.

Mia asks me for portal keys. She needs to go back to where she grew up with her adoptive parents. I walk the girls to one last place Silas had hidden from the world. His personal treasure of emergency supplies. In the main hall of the castle, under what used to be Otto's favorite seat, lies a small ruby embedded with the designs of the golden chair. One click and a whole wall behind the chair shifts open to reveal weapons lined against the wall and rows and rows of portal keys. Both girls' eyes light up.

"I don't think there was anyone as cunning as your father."

Chapter 57

Mia

Two days later in the Elders' Castle

I take a final look at myself in the mirror, assessing all the bruising and injuries before heading to the Healing Hall to check on Xavier. The healer says he might wake today. Outside, on the patio, Cerene and Freya sit together, catching up on lost time, and it makes my heart swell with joy that Cerene finally gets to feel the love of a mother. It still feels strange to be in this castle and to see Eterna in full bloom. I peek through the window and tell them, "I'm going to check on Xavier." Cerene nods as I give her a smile and leave.

Morning in the castle is quiet, the kind of stillness that comes after too much grief. Sunlight filters through the tall windows, warm but distant. My footsteps echo softly through the halls as I pass them, and my heart skips a beat at the thought of finding Xavier awake. The past couple of days, Cerene and I haven't left his side, but he didn't wake up. I want to be here when he wakes. I stand in front of the Healing Hall door for a minute, taking a deep breath and slowly pushing it open.

Xavier is still in bed, white sheets covering his body, looking comfortable and healthy. If only he'd open his gorgeous blue eyes. I move the chair in the corner and sit next to him. I need him to wake up. I never got the chance to tell him exactly how I feel about him. In the midst of the action and the events to save Eterna, the first kiss on the roof, then the night before the battle, I didn't want to be vulnerable, but my feelings changed. At first, I was conflicted about how he felt about me, about him hating me and blaming me for Hyda choosing to stay with me, that I didn't see him actually care for me. I never got the chance to respond to his last words before battle. *"I'm afraid of losing you."* A sob escapes me as I reach to hold his hand and whisper, "Xavier, please wake up. I don't want to see you like this. I miss you... Wake up... and pester me like you always do... Look at me and steal my breath away." I rest my head on the bed, and suddenly, the bed slightly moves. I lift my head to look at him, a faint "hmm" escapes him as his body shifts, breath catching like he's rising from a deep dream. I abruptly stand up. "Xavier, can you hear me? Oh my God, you're finally awake."

His eyes flutter open, and happiness blooms in my chest at the sight of them, those eyes I thought I might never see again. He blinks a few times, gaze drifting around the room, until something shifts in his expression. His eyes dim with sadness as he clutches his necklace and remembers losing his mother. I squeeze his hand and shake my head. "I'm sorry." My voice is choked up and somber.

He turns his face away as tears roll out the corner of his eyes, "Who did we lose besides my mother?"

"We lost Silas and Mateo among many innocent lives."

He nods as I promise to continue informing him of everything Freya told us after he's fully recovered.

I help Xavier get ready to leave the Healers Hall after the healer checks on him one last time. Once he's ready, I move to stand next to him. "Xavier, I have something for you." He looks at me but doesn't say anything. I unsheathe the dagger from my belt and press it gently into his hand. "Hyda gave it to me," I say, my voice low, "but I think she'd want you to have it now."

He swallows, and I watch his Adam's apple rise and fall like the weight of her memory is lodged in his throat. His fingers close slowly around the hilt, as if holding her one last time. He closes the distance between us, embracing me tightly as I hear him smell my hair and mumble a low, "Thank you, Mia."

Epilogue
Mia

Brookstone

I smooth my knee-length, strapless black dress in front of the mirror, slightly moving sideways to glance at my shoulder, my beautiful blue wing birthmark visible, a reminder of my connection to my twin and the Zarka. It's so strange to be back home in my apartment with Natalie. I miss Eterna so much, even though it's only been a week. Freya was appointed as Master Elder of Eterna. Cerene, Gideon, and Xavier each took a role to help her manage everything in order to keep the peace and justice among everyone. I, on the other hand, am going back and forth because I have work and family in both places.

"Are you ready?" Natalie asks from the doorway to my room. "You don't want to be late for your own art event."

I smile and move to give her a hug. "I'm ready. It's happening thanks to you."

She smiles back at me. "I'm glad to have you back home. Let's go." We head out of the apartment together, smiling and chatting along the way.

We step into the gallery and a wave of sound meets me, soft conversations, clinking glasses, and the low hum of admiration. The space is alive and warm with people and light. I spot familiar faces and unfamiliar ones too, all drifting from piece to piece, their eyes lingering on the work I created in silence, sadness, and joy. Spotlights spill from overhead, casting a soft glow across the polished floors and highlighting the frames that cradle pieces of my soul. My breath catches when I see one of the portraits across the room, one that will forever have a piece of my heart. It hangs quiet and proud, and suddenly, the crowd feels far away as I smile at the memory of Hyda and wish she were here with me tonight. I stand still for a moment, watching strangers react to pieces that once belonged only to me. Now, they belong to everyone. My parents call my name from nearby, excited. I move toward them, and they both embrace and congratulate me on the beauty of my pieces.

"I'm just happy they agreed to showcase them along with all these amazing artists. It's truly an honor."

I spend the next half hour talking to people about what inspired all my work. Natalie texts me, *Mia, come to the entrance, I have a surprise for you.* I excuse myself and make my way to the front of the gallery only to gasp as my eyes land on both my parents and Natalie standing with Freya, Cerene, Gideon, and Xavier.

I rush to hug them, not believing they are here. "How on earth did you all make it here?"

Freya squeezes my shoulder gently, tears of joy filling her eyes. "I wouldn't miss your accomplishment for the world. Also, I wanted to meet the amazing people who raised you."

Cerene adds, "We are all so very proud of you, Mia. Besides, this one wouldn't stop talking about how much he misses you." She swats Xavier on the chest. I laugh, overjoyed with emotions. I let them wander around the gallery and enjoy themselves, getting to know each other.

I take in the sight of Xavier in a black suit and tie. *God, he's so handsome.* I lean into him. "I never imagined there'd be a day I'd see you without your daggers."

He raises his eyebrows and smirks as he moves closer, moving the side of his jacket to expose the twin daggers tucked into his belt.

I laugh. "Of course you'd bring them with you."

He leans forward and kisses me on the forehead. "Can I take my beautiful woman on a walk?"

I nod as he laces his fingers with mine and leads me outside into the night. I breathe in the cool breeze. "I'm sorry we can't see the stars like in Eterna," I say with a shrug.

He turns to face me and tugs me closer to him, "Why would I look at the stars when the only one I want is standing right in front of me?"

I look at him and realize how much I missed looking into those eyes. "Hmmm, tell me more," I whisper.

He closes the distance and brushes a soft kiss on my lips, then says as he breaks the kiss, "Show me your world, and I'll show you the stars later tonight."

I smile and walk with him through the night, showing him my favorite places around town, then take him to the Auracle, Hyda's store. We stop in front of it. "So... I think this is yours now." He gives me a confused look. "This is where it all started. This is your mother's store. I have a key. Would you like to go inside?"

He nods and I lead him in, showing him around the space. He smiles as he looks around, "The place is so like her."

I nod then move to the chair at the back of the store where Hyda always left his baby blanket draped. I lift it gently, handing it to him. "This was yours when you were a baby. Hyda always kept it close. It was my first clue that she was connected to me because I have one just like it."

I watch his eyes fill with tears, and I feel the weight of it in my chest too. I sit with it for a moment, his silence, the grief between us. Then I speak softly, not to move on, but to keep us anchored.

"What do you think you'll do with the place?"

He seems to think for a minute before answering, "The possibilities are endless. It can be a place for me when I come here... a place for us."

I move closer to him. "Us?"

He nods and looks deep into my eyes. "Eterna is not the same without you in it. I don't want to be away from you anymore. We can decide where we want to be. We can have a home for us in both places."

I smile. "I like the sound of that."

He pulls me into his chest. "I thought you'd need more convincing. I had a whole speech prepared." He kisses me one more time.

"What I need is for you to show me the stars." I kiss him and close my eyes. Flashes and visions take over me again, taking me to another place and time, seeing a future that doesn't scare me or make me pull away, and I lose myself in him because this is where I want to be. I found myself and my home in him and Eterna.

Some answers come looking for you. Some places never let you go. And some destinies are written long before you're ready to claim them.

The End.

In Memory of

Hyda Protector and General of Eterna

Acknowledgment

Writing *Visions of Eterna* **has been a long journey and a labor of love.** It truly takes a village. I've been blessed with wonderful people who have supported me and cheered me on throughout this journey. I want to take the time to shine a spotlight on them because they have earned it.

Thank you to my amazing street team and ARC team, you have all been so good to me. My Alphas, **Renée** you were a superstar. My Betas, **Daniel** you were the sweetest. you guys made the journey more enjoyable with all the comments and feedback, I can't thank you enough for the help you have given me.

To **DeAnna**, who has been my rock—you guided me through the dark and into the light when things got rough. Thank you for always being there when I needed it the most. Your friendship means the world to me.

Asha, I will forever be grateful for your support. You stepped in and picked me up when I was lost and helped me push through. With your help, guidance, advice, and teaching moments this book is shining. You have been a true sister.

Thank you to all my author friends who were so happy for me and told me to keep going and not give up, no matter how hard the journey got.

Thank you to **Nate** for the beautiful art and cover design, you truly brought my vision to life. Thank you to **Allison**, who has been my writing companion and saw the early drafts. I can't wait for you to publish your own book.

To my sisters, who have been my personal cheerleaders—especially **Safa** and **Shahad**—you two have been my backbone. Thank you for the multiple re-reads and sleepless nights spent making sure the story was intact, even when my brain was stuck on "mind linking is awesome." I love you girls to the moon and back.

To my best friends, who had a twinkle in their eyes and tears of joy when they knew I had finished writing my book.

Farah, thank you for always believing in me. Your emotional support has been impeccable.

A special thank you to my parents for always being there, I love you both very much.

Last but definitely not least, thank you to **my husband**, for always letting me pursue what I want. Thank you for supporting my impulses, no matter how crazy they may have sounded, until I finally found my calling.

To **Lara** and **Leo**, I know that some days I was too busy to do many things in order to finish this book. But this book is for you both—to show you that there isn't anything in the world you can't accomplish. With a will of iron, you can reach for the highest and brightest star. Don't ever let anyone tell you otherwise. Your mama is seeing her dream come to life.

Thank you all for everything. I love you.

A big thank you to all the readers who have taken a chance on *Eterna,* your support and love are what made this book possible.

About the Author

S amara Kalz is an Arab American author of romance and fantasy, currently residing in Texas with her husband and two children. A lifelong lover of books, Samara holds a B.A. in English Literature and has been passionate about storytelling for as long as she can remember.

When she's not immersed in writing or getting lost in a good book, Samara enjoys spending quality time with her family and creating hand-made crafts for her home and loved ones. As the eldest of a large family, she developed a strong sense of responsibility and a deep-rooted love for caring for others—qualities that often find their way into the heart of her stories.

www.ingramcontent.com/pod-product-compliance
Lightning Source LLC
Chambersburg PA
CBHW030352120726
47901CB00007B/1990